A COMMON PERSON
and Other Stories

THE RICHARD SULLIVAN PRIZE IN SHORT FICTION

Editors
William O'Rourke and Valerie Sayers

1996   *Acid,* Edward Falco

1998   *In the House of Blue Lights,* Susan Neville

2000   *Revenge of Underwater Man and Other Stories,*
        Jarda Cervenka

2002   *Do Not Forsake Me, Oh My Darling,* Maura Stanton

2004   *Solitude and Other Stories,* Arturo Vivante

2006   *The Irish Martyr,* Russell Working

2008   *Dinner with Osama,* Marilyn Krysl

2010   *In Envy Country,* Joan Frank

2012   *The Incurables,* Mark Brazaitis

2014   *What I Found Out About Her: Stories of Dreaming
        Americans,* Peter LaSalle

2017   *God, the Moon, and Other Megafauna,* Kellie Wells

2018   *Down Along the Piney: Ozarks Stories,* John Mort

2021   *A Common Person and Other Stories,* R. M. Kinder

A Common Person

and Other Stories

R. M. KINDER

University of Notre Dame Press

Notre Dame, Indiana

University of Notre Dame Press
Notre Dame, Indiana 46556
undpress.nd.edu

Published in the United States of America

Library of Congress Control Number: 2020950364

ISBN: 978-0-268-20005-3 (Hardback)
ISBN: 978-0-268-20006-0 (Paperback)
ISBN: 978-0-268-20007-7 (WebPDF)
ISBN: 978-0-268-20004-6 (Epub)

To Baird Allan Brock, my everyday hero.

CONTENTS

Acknowledgments   ix

A Common Person   1

Everyday Sky   20

Tradition   31

Little Garden   47

Signs   60

Alvie and the Rapist   74

Brute   81

A Fragile Life   102

The Bully's Snake   113

The Dancer's Son   118

Dating in America   133

Small Courtesies   138

Recovering Integrity   157

A Rising Silence   165

Mother Post   174

Bay at the Moon   181

The Stuff of Ballads   188

ACKNOWLEDGMENTS

Grateful acknowledgment is made to the publications in which the following stories, sometimes in earlier versions, first appeared:

"Alvie and the Rapist," *Literal Latte* 4, no. 3 (1998): 19–20.

"Bay at the Moon," *Big Muddy* 6, no. 2 (2006): 85–91.

"Brute," *Zone 3* 21, no. 1 (2006): 35–54 (*Zone 3* 2006 Fiction Award).

"The Bully's Snake" (as "Bully Snake"), *Daily Star Journal* (Warrensburg, MO), September 30, 2017, B2.

"A Common Person," *Arts & Letters* 37 (Fall 2018): 7–25 (*Arts & Letters* 2018 Fiction Prize).

"The Dancer's Son," *descant* 59 (Fall 2020): 43–51.

"Dating in America," *Passages North* 24, no. 1 (2003): 37–41.

"A Fragile Life," *Confrontation* 108 (Fall 2010): 212–21.

"Little Garden," *descant* 106 (Ontario) (Fall 1999): 49–60.

"Recovering Integrity," *Chariton Review* 28, no. 2 (Fall 2002): 35–40.

"A Rising Silence," *Hawai'i Pacific Review* 24 (2010): 77–84.

"Signs," *Notre Dame Review* 24 (Summer/Fall 2007): 206–17.

"Small Courtesies," *Notre Dame Review* 10 (Summer 2000): 10–24; and *Notre Dame Review: The First Ten Years* (University of Notre Dame Press, 2009): 370–84.

"Tradition," *Other Voices* 30 (Spring/Summer 1999): 109–21.

A Common Person and Other Stories came into being through the encouragement and support of so many people that I can't name them all, and to name only a few is risky. Among them are friends and colleagues in the Blackwater Literary Society and Mid-Mo Writers, respectively, Chuck Hocter, Jim Taylor, Chanda Zimmerman; and Debra Brenegan, Phong Nguyen, and Trudy Lewis. Others who aided me in different ways, and certainly enriched my community, are Tom Averill, Bob Stewart, Ben Furnish, Mary Troy, Michael Czyzniejewski, G. B. Crump, Cate Browder, Sam Ligon, Mary Frances Wagner, and Mary-Beth Kamberg.

My thanks also go to the editors and editorial staff of the literary journals listed above, some now closed. The editors' close readings and careful suggestions led to the tightening of each piece and the gradual expansion and unity of the collection. A few names include Jim Barnes, Jenine Bockman, Barry Kitterman, Karen Mulhallen, Laura Newbern, Gina Frangello, Susan Swarthout, Joanna G. Semeiks, and Jack Ventimiglia. Some rejection letters were a gift, too, one in particular, from Betty Scott.

To my family, brother Michael Hobbs, sister Wilma Lee Kincy, and aunt Virginia Goff Hopkins, I am indebted for confidence and comfort, a timeless, unwavering support. They have also refueled my familiarity with the language of my upbringing, which I once tried to overcome. My daughter Kristine Lowe-Martin has all along been my best critic, literary companion, and friend. Her standards are high, but she's softhearted.

Finally, I'm grateful to the Department of English at the University of Notre Dame, to all those individuals in the Creative Writing Program who publish the *Notre Dame Review*. Early on, at a time when I had little faith in my writing, the journal's editors accepted two of my stories. For that welcome encouragement, I thank Valerie Sayers, Steve Tomasula, Kathleen J. Canavan, William O'Rourke, and John Matthias. Now, as recipient of the Richard Sullivan Prize in Short Fiction, I'm also indebted to the University of Notre Dame Press, especially to Stephen Little, Kathryn Pitts, Matthew Dowd, Stephanie Hoffman, and Katie Lehman. They have been professional, gracious, enthusiastic, and warm to boot. Working with them has been more than a pleasure. It's an honor to be associated with the University of Notre Dame Press and to have my work included among its publications.

A COMMON PERSON

and Other Stories

A Common Person

"Maybe someone will shoot him before he takes office." Maggie posted that statement to her Facebook page. She did so early on a Monday morning, with her first cup of coffee already downed. As she fixed the second cup, she rethought the post. It was the kind a person could pay for in many ways, now and later.

In her tiny study, she returned to Facebook and saw five likes already. She hovered over the number and the responders' names appeared. Friends. She didn't want to be cowardly. She preferred boldness in most areas. Still, she opened the drop-down edit box and clicked *delete*.

Are you sure?

Maggie clicked *Yes*.

Then she turned to real work, house and yard tasks. She was seventy-six years old, retired, but highly energetic and fascinated by many activities and subjects. She could get sidetracked on Google and study something for hours, dark matter, seahorses, vocalizations of nonprimates, Victorian dress styles, the smallest dog. She avoided the computer except to check her Facebook page, ensuring that the post was gone. Even though it was obviously deleted, she scrolled down the feed page, too. Someone might have shared it a split second before the delete. It existed somewhere, she had no doubt.

Nothing ever put into cyberspace could be completely destroyed. It was like a thought wave that traveled throughout the universe.

In the afternoon, as she was refilling bird feeders, her cell phone chimed. The message was *update completed*. She checked the app icons. There were so many she wouldn't recognize a change. She wished she still had her old phone, a flip one that could be snapped shut. This one required a most sophisticated silencing. From the kitchen, she watched the birds descend, then startle, then descend again, wave down, wave up. They perched in the plum trees, quick, not too hungry, flitting and living their lives. Maybe she had been a bird once, she loved them so. Maybe she would be one. At 3:00 p.m. she answered her ringing home phone and, in seconds, heard the click that usually meant a computer call. A couple hours later, that happened again. Her cell phone was updated again, too. Someone was checking on her.

She felt a little quickening of her breathing and heart. She needed not to blow this all up into a threatening situation. It was how she thought—always to the extreme. She was hypervigilant by birth, not by choice.

They came for her after seven, in the midst of a televised update on the president elect's last outrageous tweet. She heard the car pulling into the driveway, heard two doors shut. She turned off the television and stood back from the front door. A horizontal, oblong window allowed her to see them approaching. They wore suits. How ridiculous to be so obvious, but then, that was a kind of honesty. Suddenly, she wanted to text her daughter in California, saying, "I posted a joke about guns and I'm afraid I'm in trouble." She didn't have time to text anything. They were knocking.

The men were courteous and upfront, simply responding to a concern raised by a Facebook post.

In a short time, she was in the back of their car, one of them beside her. They had her cell phone, her purse, and the medication she had been allowed to gather up. They had also her two revolvers, the scant ammunition, and a fishing knife she had been given long ago and kept in the nightstand drawer. "I'm not a well woman," she said to the man next to her. He was blond, and very lean, with a sharp nose. "I have to stay calm."

"You're not in any danger," he said. "This is a process and will be over soon. You just need to answer some questions and give people time to check your answers."

"It's a scary process from my end of it, and unnecessary. I can answer questions from my house." She had already explained three times that the post meant nothing, was a kind of joke, and she had deleted it because she realized it wasn't funny and could leave the wrong impression. "I want to phone my daughter."

"Later."

"I protest," she said, and focused on the terrain, on small points, as she might have done if she suffered from motion sickness.

"We have a facility in Kansas City," the man in the front seat said. "It's very comfortable. You'll have dinner, bed, whatever you need."

That meant she was staying, no telling how long.

"What about my dog and my cats? I have two cats who are probably home now."

"They'll be taken care of."

The need to cry and run swelled in her chest so she gulped for air but didn't turn her head away from the window. They passed deep fields, twilight softening the shapes into shadows. Fireflies flickered. She saw a mare and colt, saw cattle. Cars passed them, headlights cut the night ahead. The flat land turned to gentle hills. Her fear became more a pulse and she could think in the dips. In at least a day or two, her daughter would begin to worry and would take steps to locate her mother. She wasn't really alone or at the mercy of strangers. This was America, her country. She had done nothing. She was just an old woman who owned guns and made a foolish statement. She would be inconvenienced. As would her companions.

"Is someone going to feed my animals tonight?" she asked. "They're accustomed to dinner at six."

"That's being handled," from the blond one.

"How do you know?"

"It's pretty standard procedure."

From the other one: "Please don't worry, ma'am. We follow a procedure. We report where we are, what the situation is, and we request any need be met. If there are kids or animals involved, they're taken care of."

"You wouldn't have known about my cats if I hadn't told you. And what about the birds? I feed them twice a day, sometimes three."

The man beside her held a tablet up, the screen lighted and showing her Facebook page, a past post of her two cats lying on her desk. He scrolled down to another post. The bird feeder with a burst of bird flight like an umbrella.

"The birds can actually feed themselves," he said, leaning back.

She didn't respond. The exchange and the screen had involved her in the mystery of the day's occurrences and of her future. She believed the men that she wouldn't be harmed, not by them. But terrible consequences could ensue that the men might not consider harm. She might be housed and fed and medicated for the rest of her life. She might never see her home again, or her animals, or her daughter. Might never be free again, not physically.

They bypassed the city proper where she might recognize streets or stores and came to a stretched-out industrial park, seemingly deserted. The building they parked near was five or six stories, austere, with black, glass windows. The ostensible lobby was empty except for a clerk behind the counter. A small woman eventually came from a hall, her heels clipping on the tiled floor, and introduced herself as Rita Quitano. She was cheerful and chatty and showed Maggie to her room for the evening, explained its features—bath, shower, pajamas, extra pillows and blankets, no television.

"I don't want to be here," Maggie said. "I want to call my daughter, and I want to go home."

"It's a standard procedure, hon. You'll probably be home tomorrow."

"I'm not at ease. I'm very frightened but I'm trying to cooperate. I want it noted that I have asked to call someone and to go home."

"All right. Noted."

A younger woman, slim, with red hair so curly it could have been rolled in corkscrews, brought a cart with dinner tray. The food was some of Maggie's favorites. "Anything about me they don't know?" Maggie asked.

When they left, taking the untouched food with them, Maggie waited a few moments and tried the doorknob. It didn't give. She didn't try the phone but if she needed to, she would try. Any minute. She prepared for bed in the glare of the tiny bathroom. Only once did she think of being locked in as a fact, no windows, no escape hatch, no large vent, no hope, and that moment her body flooded with intense heat and she had to relax, relax all over, let it pass, let it pass. She was so weak then that she trembled as she walked to the bed. She sat down, stared at her feet, thought about relaxing from toes upward, and then about changing the colors of a tree she remembered. That brought the birds and her yard and the babes, her dog and cats. She sat very still, head bowed. Slow, Maggie. Slow.

She didn't truly sleep, but she slipped into dreams and came out to feel the room was dream, too. She left a light on and was grateful they hadn't timed it to go off, plunging her into darkness and a personal kind of terror.

The meeting room was two halls, L-shaped to the left, from where she slept. It was small, windowless, but with a built-in screen in the center of one wall. Three well padded, upholstered chairs with low arms were positioned at a round, low table. A coffee service, three cups, and a platter of individually wrapped cinnamon rolls were on the table. Maggie sat down in one of the aligned chairs, though she assumed the more separated one was hers. She poured coffee into a plastic cup and opened one of the roll containers. She preferred a different sweetener than they provided, which was comforting. They didn't arrive for an hour, or so she timed it. A man, blond and bulkish, but sweet looking, much like her Uncle Carl as a young man. And the young woman who brought last night's dinner, now in blue slacks and heels—no stockings—and a pale yellow blouse. Her hair was in a large, unruly bun. She looked like a bouquet, which, Maggie, thought, she was. "You're very pretty," Maggie said. "I like the color combination."

"Thanks," with a terse little clip nod, charming despite her intent.

The man was Bruce, the girl Sally. He laid a folder on the table, opened a roll, and as he unwrapped it, began their exchange.

"Your post about shooting someone was reported, as I'm sure you know. We're meeting because you have been associated with violence and with violent people for a long time. Given that, and some of your personal tendencies, you pose a possible threat that has to be evaluated and, if necessary, contained or deflected."

"I'm not a violent person at all," Maggie said. "I can't bear violence."

"Yet you said maybe someone would shoot the candidate before he was elected. You want that to happen, it seems."

"If it would be best for our country, then I wouldn't mind if it happened. But I don't *want* it, and I wouldn't *do* it."

"You'd support someone else doing it."

Maggie entertained that thought, weighed it. "In principle, probably. I wouldn't actively support it."

"What do you mean by *actively?*"

"Join a group dedicated to that or give them money. I would accept the necessity, but leave it up to someone else, and especially to God. Maybe we've earned this president in His opinion."

"What faith are you?"

"None. More hope than faith. Could we stay with guns? Or could I go home? May I demand to go? I need to be there. My creatures are accustomed to me and I am to them. They're my small responsibility. I wasn't suggesting someone shoot a person. I was conjecturing what might happen. My history, which you must know, surely indicates I've never been violent in any way, never even went hunting. Most of my life I've attempted just to stay calm. It's a battle."

Now he seemed amused. He had cocked his head as she spoke, and raised a blond, bushy eyebrow. It might have been an appealing look in another situation.

"You're describing what the file shows," he said. "You haven't been in therapy for years. That can be a red flag, especially if you begin talking about violent acts, against yourself or someone else—thus, our reaction to your post. Even your leisurely activities show you're drawn to violence. You like suspense and survivor movies and books."

"I read history too, explorations, research, anything about animals."

"Yes. But you *favor* violent, dangerous activity."

"It keeps up with my body."

"What?"

"Sometimes reading what you can't do dissipates tension."

"Like feeding a hunger."

She had considered that herself. "Possibly. Probably that, too. But here, mentally," she touched her temple, "I favor history and the natural sciences—for the layperson, of course. I'm a commoner."

"What does that mean to you? Commoner. Do you see society divided into commoners and royalty?"

"Of course I see society that way, but that's not what I meant. I meant I'm a common person, not an intellect, not a scientist. I'm not even a mathematician. Admittedly, I know our country is severely divided between the wealthy and the not wealthy. We're losing a middle class. But I'm not taking up arms in that fight, which has, as anyone knows, always been with us. It will right itself."

"How?"

"Resistance to the old always rises. The new asserts itself and a new paradigm rules."

"You're talking rebellion."

"Could we go back to my guns or my violent history? The conversation is leading to my execution."

The girl gave a small snicker, not ugly, and Maggie frowned a bit, just to indicate it wasn't an appropriate response, though it might have had a positive effect on the male interrogator. It lightened the moment.

The man smiled. "All right. Let's get back to what I know instead of where you're leading me."

"I'm the follower."

"As you see it, for now. According to this file, you have owned four pistols which were not registered and were used in violent acts by someone else. One pistol was used in an armed robbery, one in a shooting, one in an attempted rape, and one in a barricade situation involving numerous employees at a hotel." He stopped. "Well, what do you say to that?"

"I knew about the last one, the barricade. But the others, no. One pistol was stolen from my house in the Southwest. Someone pried open a window and took the pistol and a television. I hadn't paid for the television. And the deductible was more than it was worth, so I kept paying for something I didn't have." That still seemed so wrong, but it was a minor aggravation, nagging when she recalled it. "Another pistol was probably taken by a coworker. She called me to help her. She was Papago, and had been so sorely beaten. So battered. I picked her up and brought her to my house and let her sleep. Only after she was settled with an attorney and another friend did I discover my pistol was gone. I had kept it in a drawer in my bedroom. Did she shoot her husband? Was the shooting by a woman?"

"You know the answer to that."

"No. I told you what I did and what I believe. I don't know any more about that gun. It was small. Pretty. I liked it." She remembered, suddenly, that she had owned another pretty one after that, with pearl handles. It, too, had been taken from her bedroom. She knew the thief. A visiting friend, a tiny nurse who had fallen in love with a visiting Arab student half her age and was heartbroken that once he returned home, he didn't contact her again. She had cried and cried. She was a woman who painted her toenails pink or red but kept her fingernails short and fiercely clean. A good nurse. Dead now, though younger than Maggie. "I may know who attempted a rape. I dated a trucker in my fifties, so long ago," she looked at the girl. "He asked if he could borrow it for one run. He was afraid of hijackers, he said. He was going to bring it back. He told me the police confiscated it when he got in a fight with another trucker. Maybe he lied. He liked women and was too rough. He was married, too. Did the police confiscate that one?"

"I don't know."

"I wonder how you know about these guns if they weren't registered."

"It's obvious. Your name appears in police reports as the source of the guns."

"If the police have them, can I get them back?"

"What?"

"If they were stolen from me or even loaned, as in the one case, then they were mine and I'm innocent of any violence. Can't I claim them?

"Do you have any evidence you owned them?"

"I have photos of them, and serial numbers. I'm meticulous with records though I don't have the best memory."

"You could file a claim, I suppose, and ask for the return. I doubt you'd be successful."

"I doubt it, too, but it's comforting to know I have some rights."

Though there was no window and the light was artificial, it was a white light, and it seemed to brighten gently as if the room itself took a small breath.

"Of course, you have rights. Many of them." He looked to the girl, back to Maggie. "We're going to take a break here. You want someone to stay with you or would you rather be alone?"

"I'll be okay alone. I'd rather have my pets."

"They wouldn't be comfortable here."

Why should she alienate him by saying she knew that better than he did?

"I could stay with you," the girl said.

"No. You go with him. I'll rest."

The girl gathered up the empty papers and napkins, swept crumbs into an empty cup. She had delicate hands and graceful ways. Slim ankles. Maggie had always been tall and didn't know the world from a small woman's perspective, or a dainty one's, though she wasn't huge or heavy and was graceful enough. She closed her eyes before they closed the door. She couldn't hear the snap of a bolt, but she assumed the door automatically locked behind them. If she didn't know for sure, it could be open. And without raising her eyelids, she could assume the room had brightened even more. She took deep, slow breaths, and though one quickened and she gasped, she came back to slowness.

As preparation, she began tracing her gun history. It went back further than she had realized. A sheriff had shot a dog beneath their house. The house was on stilts, and he wouldn't crawl under there until the dog was dead. She was how old? She didn't know. She remembered squatting to see under the house, and remembered her knees were bare. They were white, which she now knew was from skin being drawn tight over the bone. She was very small. After a tremendous noise that hurt her ears and heart, the sheriff had crawled under and dragged out the dog. It, too, was blond, or light brown, gold, long-haired. Limp.

Her father had kept a pistol in a drawer under white shirts all of which her mother had ironed and folded. He came home one night to get the pistol and hurry back to shoot a man named Walter. He didn't leave. Her mother stopped him. But he had hit Walter with a wine bottle a week or so later. No jail time. It was a small town.

Maggie had married a sweet man who was a farmer by nature and tried to work for his dad. She had ambled out to the farm pond during her early marriage and had used a .22 rifle with a peep sight to shoot insulators from the high lines, to shoot birds—always missed—and to shoot, shamefully acknowledged now, frogs. Poor frogs. Poor everything. She *had* been violent. The farmer became a policeman. He misfired his gun into the carpet in their Southwest home. It scooted a ridge in the carpet, like the mountain range of a tiny country. Another time, he shot out a plate glass window of their living room, again by accident. Once he knocked her, with his fist, against a cabinet. They were married twenty years. He talked about rape and murder cases and he often worked nights. She was afraid of the dark, but she slept in an unlighted room so their daughter would not copy her fear.

She wondered if she were under surveillance. She opened her eyes. The room was sterile and quiet, no window. She got up, difficult from the low chair, and went to the door. Her reflection, as she passed the wall screen, was elongated and warped. The doorknob was silver and had no turnlock in the center. She looked for push-turn space behind it, and there was none. It should open easily. She touched it with one fingertip and let that satisfy her need to try. By her chair again, she stretched her arms out and up over her head and down to her sides, repeated the series three times. "I'm ready to begin when you are," she said, for the camera, wherever it was.

They knew so many things about her, which alarmed her at first though it didn't surprise her. She had always believed everything a person expressed in any way could be known by everyone. If a person couldn't keep a secret to herself, why believe anyone else could? She confided discreetly, judiciously, even to a counselor. Even to God. If He knew, He knew. Knowing was one of his properties. She did visualize—not fantasize about—shooting someone, in a particular spot, just below the pectoral muscle, or left breast, at a slightly upward slant. It's where she believed the heart was positioned. When she disliked someone intensely, an unbidden image of the shot—not the victim, just the aiming and the trajectory and the specific impact point—rose. She identified that image as only that, an image, like a fleeting thought. She would never do it and she would never allow the image permanent berth in her mind.

"Why would you take a Citizen's Academy course in another county?"

"Our sheriff's department didn't offer one."

"Another reason?"

"I wanted to know the legal processes. We talk about systems without knowing how they work. Some television shows make everything seem so simple."

"They taught you about stun guns, how to handle a variety of guns, including a sniper rifle."

"We only fired pistols on the range. The sniper rifle was unloaded and was on a table in the classroom." She hadn't been able to hold it properly because her neck was too stiff to position hand on the trigger and eye on the sight. If she had been able to lie on the ground, on her stomach, in the right manner for that kind of weapon, she might have been able to hold it properly. She wasn't going to tell him the age and condition of her body precluded her from using that weapon as it had been set up. "It was a Glock on the range. I was afraid of a shotgun. Was that in the report?"

"Actually, yes."

The red-haired girl tucked her head down. Laughing?

"Are you allowed to ask questions," Maggie asked the girl. "Or are you here because he's male and I'm female?"

"I'm training."

"That doesn't answer either question."

In a second, the girl said, "I know."

Maggie nodded her head.

Excerpts of her life were in a folder and in a tablet he occasionally consulted. A trip across country alone, letters to editors, a protest about a halfway house, four different counselors over the years, testimony in two friends' divorce trials, a name change, studying Spanish, then German, owning French, Russian, Serbian, and Chinese dictionaries. "Why all the dictionaries?"

"I like words and learning. And I don't sleep much. I have a globe, too, and an atlas and a Bible." She remembered a bow and arrow set. "You know I don't pose any threat to anyone."

"I don't *know* that." He pushed his chair back. "But I believe it's true. We could continue for hours, but I think we're done. You'll spend the night, and we'll get you home tomorrow."

"Why not now home?"

"We have to type up notes and submit them."

"Put in your notes," Maggie said, "that I request to go home now." She looked at the girl who looked away. Training.

Dinner, breakfast, and then lunch were brought to her room. She ate a little each time. She thought of all the people who were left in worse conditions for days, weeks, months, nearly drowned, beaten, hung up by elbows, shocked, buried in a box, shut in a box. She had a bed, a bath, air conditioning, blankets.

At 2:00 p.m., wearing the same clothing she had arrived in, Maggie followed a chatty Rita Quitano through the empty hall. Rita was glad Maggie was on her way home. She hoped Maggie had been comfortable. These safeguards were necessary but unfortunate. People had to play their part in the security system.

No one was in the lobby. Just outside the front door waited the sharp-nosed guard, who spoke to Rita and then ushered Maggie toward his car.

The sun was startlingly bright, and too near.

He held the back door open for her, though no one was in the vehicle's passenger seat.

"I hope I'm truly being taken home," she said.

"Yes. That's the plan."

"Why the back seat?"

"It's safer."

"In case of what?"

"Standard accidents."

She felt bruised, though no one had struck her. She was weak. The urge to thank him for taking her home almost gagged her, but she wouldn't utter it. Honor required her not to beg.

Outside their vehicle, other cars held people, and people walked here and there, waited at a bus stop. Geese were on a green bank by a channel. Clouds were flat bottomed, billow-topped, fantastical structures. And the moon, that transparent gray gauze was visible in daytime. Not possible. A universe with billions of galaxies, an earth with billions of fossils from billions of years, monsters and miracles. It was a dream world. She had never lived at all, scurrying from nightmare to nightmare, an eternity of ignorant coming into being. A swarm of such beings.

She expected him to eventually take a little side road, where she would be ended completely with a quick blow. But he competently drove along the route she would have taken, and when he took the ramp up past the cemetery in her town, past the old trees and white sculptures and gray stones, she ducked her head so he wouldn't see in the rearview mirror, her hope attained. He drove directly to her house, into her driveway, was out of the car slowly and coming around and opening the door for her which she allowed.

He held up a small dark bag. "Your belongings," he said. "Let me take you inside, check things out for you."

She took the bag, "If I have a choice, No." She headed for the house, just a step or two ahead of him. Her legs betrayed her. They buckled and he grabbed her upper arm quickly. She pulled away. He followed her as she knew he would.

The door wasn't locked. She heard the yipping before she stepped inside.

She crooned to them. She couldn't help it. No matter how proud and noble she wanted to be. The terrier was a whirl of blond curls, whiskery face, hairy ears, short yaps and little clicks of not biting. She buried her nose in his furry neck, carried him to the kitchen. She pulled out a kitchen chair and sank down. The black cat, Dinky, was stroking her shin back and forth with the length of his body. The calico had come to the doorway and sat silently, with wide circle eyes incredulous and accusing.

"You go on," she called, in case the guard was still in the front room. "Just go on. Go."

None of it was real. None of it was settling into place. The sun shone through the windows—the curtains were pulled open. The cooing of a dove came soft and haunting. Traffic hummed not far away. Yet.

Maggie put the terrier down, went onto the deck. Shadows were the same. The flowers along the fence still bloomed. She didn't recall her trees being so very tall, thickly leaved. The bird feeder was half full, and the little creatures were drifting down as if they had swept away just seconds before and could now lower in place. But it wasn't right. She needed to run away somewhere. She had to stay put.

Inside again, she opened every door, beginning with the refrigerator and the cupboards. Then she pulled out every drawer. With lights on in each room, she sat on her bed to open the blue bag. Her purse was inside, her medications, her cell phone. She looked through the purse, at her IDs, credit cards. Everything as it had been, including the angel coin given to her by her daughter. She gripped it tightly in her palm, kissed it, and dropped it back. Her eyes were tearing up. She didn't want to start that. Twelve messages on the phone. She was afraid to read even one.

She called her daughter and spent an hour talking and listening and reassuring. Her girl threatened with lawsuit and newspaper contacts. "I even called the police."

"What did they say?"

"They went by the house and decided you were just away for a while. The animals weren't there. They said they'd keep an eye on the place and I should contact your friends if I was concerned."

Maggie resisted all the suggestions. She downplayed the invasion. Her eyes searched the crown molding of the room, studied shadows, frames, lamps and bases. "I think it happens all the time," she said. "I hadn't done anything, so I had nothing to worry about except the creatures. And they're all right."

"You could have had a heart attack, Momma."

"I could have, and it would have served them right. But I didn't. And I'm the stronger for it."

"No you're not."

"Yes I am, truly."

Her daughter called three more times, and Maggie understood why and was grateful. It established their nearness, the smallness of the earth, a connection that could be next door, connection of heart and mind and family and love. Maggie asked her not to call back tonight. "I'm going to bed soon, and I plan to turn my phone in tomorrow and get a different one. I need an upgrade."

She slept on the sofa, with the calico lying on her chest, occasionally purring, occasionally kneading so the claws were little pains in Maggie's skin, but familiar and light and welcome. The terrier slept at her feet, and the black cat in his spot on the sofa back. The lamps were on, the doors locked. Maggie roused now and then, knowing soon where she was, and comforted that night settled around like a soft blanket and the moon cast pale slivers like ghosts. She wasn't locked in anywhere except on the planet and in her particular dream.

When she woke with that sharp quickness that meant sleep was done, she fed her babes, showered, dressed in jeans and sandals and an old white shirt. She clipped her hair back and up, casually. She had a message from her daughter on the phone. "Call me." Maggie texted a reply. "I'm up. Much to do. Talk later."

She had breakfast with the television on but muted. The food was tasteless, but she ate it, and took her medication and her vitamins. She tapped remote buttons, scanning the activities and news and interests. She turned the set off and looked out the window. She couldn't reconcile the two worlds—three, really, counting her mind and heart. Maybe billions of worlds, one or more for each human being, or even each creature.

They had her guns. She remembered a time when the big one was new to her, the .357, given to her. It was on New Year's Eve. She was only in her forties, but alone, and dressed up rarely, for a party. She had to drive to a private residence outside town, in a wooded area with strange roads, so she had loaded the gun and had it lying in the passenger seat. It was so comforting to know it was there, and loaded, and if by chance she was stranded and had to walk up to a stranger's house or along a dirt road, she had protection in her own hands. She had been excited and too quick and had unfortunately made a left turn before the left-hand arrow—there was no traffic, but there was a policeman. He had pulled her over. Trained by all the warnings to citizens on how to behave at such a stop, she had announced as he walked up, "Officer, I have a gun on the front seat."

He was at the window right then, saying "Get out of the car." He retrieved her gun, then led her into the headlights of his vehicle while he questioned her and phoned someone. All the while cars zoomed by on the holiday evening. She was dressed in a long pale gown, her hair loose. She had until then felt beautiful. "Okay," he said finally, completing his call, and guided her brusquely back to her car. When she was seated, he handed her the gun and then the bullets, dropping them into her palm like coins. "Have someone load it for you," he said. Her husband—ex-husband—was still a policeman at that time. They all knew each other. Citizens of law.

She liked that gun and the little .25 revolver. She had owned them. Bought them. They were as dear to her in some ways as the creatures gathered around her. They were part of her world. They had a history and a place. But people who were to protect her could come in and take everything, anything they wanted, and leave her bereft.

"I don't want to fight," she protested to the walls of her kitchen.

She sat at the computer and drew up the folder with photos of her few precious items. The photos of the revolvers were taken from different angles, on a white cloth, with a description as a jpg in the same file. She printed copies of each. She assumed those photos were now in files elsewhere, as perhaps were all of her photos, her documents, the entire contents of her hard drive, of her phone.

The computer was no longer hers. Nor the phone. Possibly the house wasn't either, but she and her three companions had lived here fairly comfortably and might still be able to. It was possibly as good a place as any.

Maggie didn't like pawn shops because they had an atmosphere of desperation, but she appreciated their function and she knew where they were, always some at the best entries into and exits from a town. She found one that bought gold items, though she wasn't selling anything. The guns were in glass cases, on glass shelves. She didn't like Glocks. They were big and blocky, and she liked round, smooth guns, all black or with pearl insets for the little ones. She didn't like brown and black together. That was raspy and rough.

She chose a small pearl-handled .22 revolver, an all-black Ruger .357. Rifles were fastened to the wall. She hadn't held one since the farm years, that old time, and didn't know anything about them except how that one had felt in her arms. Without asking questions, she bought a Savage Mark II .22 rifle, and a Glenfield Model .25 rifle with a wooden stock that had been knife scrolled by someone with an artist's touch. The clerk filled out the form for her and ran the check. She waited for his face to register a denial based on something that had happened yesterday, but she was clear.

"You need ammunition?" he asked.

"Yes."

"Gun case? For the Glenfield? The Savage comes with one."

"Yes."

He showed her the case he thought best suited the Glenfield, which was a really nice rifle, and the case was light and durable. "Easy to tote."

When she had paid and had the receipt, she asked, "Do you keep a list of people who train for permit to carry?"

He did. He was obviously very pleased to give it to her though he didn't say anything but "You bet."

At home, despite the activity, she was so morose she was unable to breathe easily. The skin of her hands was so old it looked like waxed parchment with small brown stains, the color of weak coffee. Her hands shook when she held the camera, but she took photos of the new guns and the accompanying paperwork. She had a bit of lunch so she could take her noon medication. She put one rifle in the back of the coat closet and one in her bedroom closet. She loaded the pistols, put one in her nightstand and one in the bottom of the wardrobe.

She meant only to nap, but she slept the afternoon and into the evening. She vaguely heard purring but it was like clouds whisking by and she was in a hurry right then, chasing something, and was so tired. When she woke, it was in the dark, dark time, and no lights on in the house. She would see moonlight like a floating universe in the upper part of the room and she wondered if dying might be like this. The terrier must have felt her movements and crawled from her feet onto her chest, smelling earthy and solid and sweet as dogs do, and licking her face. He brought her back. Perhaps he would wake her in another world some day or night. She got up, went about readying herself as though dawn had arrived. She dressed anew and pulled her hair to the nape of her neck and remembered the red-haired girl. That beautiful thing who had a whole life to make choices, right and wrong, and in a strange profession.

When her charges had been taken care of, she texted her daughter, "All's well." At 8:30 a.m., she was at the sheriff's department. She had with her the photos of her old .357 and .25 revolvers. The clerk at the window was a young woman, a little plump, with heavy black eyebrows but a pretty mouth. "I need assistance," Maggie said. "I haven't ever been arrested for anything, and yet the police have confiscated two guns that belonged to me. I need instruction on how to retrieve my property."

It was beyond the girl, obviously. Her dark eyes showed fear. "I don't know anything about that. I'll have to get someone else."

She disappeared, though it was Maggie's understanding about police protocol that the girl shouldn't have left Maggie alone in the front. She should have used the intercom.

A deputy appeared, not too big, boyish, with a cocky stance. "You want to come with me. We have a room where we can talk."

Maggie followed him. Another one came to a doorway. This was a maze she was entering, like an underground. From here, the outer sun must be extremely high, and probably smallish, and didn't cast warm light. That wasn't reality but it was what she felt. She was old, tired, timid—afraid of fear itself—and armed with only a thin file of photos and records. But she had to claim her property, so the right to own it would remain hers.

Everyday Sky

Coming home from school along his normal route, Milosh was surprised to see a dog at the bottom of a sloping yard, chained to a pale wood doghouse, a new structure. The dog, however, was familiar. Fairly big, long skinny legs, long ears, dark-red, short-hair coat. It had belonged to the people in that house for at least two years. Milosh had seen glimpses of it as one of the owners occasionally walked it or tied it in the front or side yard. Now, standing at the length of the chain, the animal protested, one sharp bark after the other, like shots.

"Hey you," Milosh called back, congenially, advising. "Dog Buddy. Sssssh. No barking, huh?"

He walked down the slope a few yards and a frenzied barking ensued, like an affectionate and impatient invitation, accompanied by a stiff body and then, suddenly, a fiercely wagging tail and a whine. The dog sat down, which Milosh interpreted as *Please*. "What did you do?" Milosh asked.

Three short barks in return.

"Yeah. Well I know how it goes."

He wanted to pet the creature, but he wasn't all that sure how it would react. He fished in his pockets for something the dog might want to eat. A piece of gum was the only likely item. Milosh glanced

20

around on the ground, because if a walnut was handy, he'd crack it open and get the meat out for the dog. Some of them liked nuts.

He heard someone call to him and realized a woman in another yard was wanting him to either leave or stop the animal's yelping. "Sorry," he said to the animal, and bolted up the hill, running along the edge of the narrow residential street until he turned onto his block, then shifting to the uneven sidewalk and walking the last few yards.

His mother had fixed stuffed cabbage and fried potatoes, one of his favorite dinners. From his second serving, he saved into a folded napkin one of the smaller cabbage rolls and a piece of bread spread thick with cimać. He had intended to save his last three slices of potato, but he weakened and ate them. When he scraped his plate into the trash can by the refrigerator, he tucked the napkin into an empty can. It was his job to carry out the trash. He and his brother helped clear the dishes, then he tugged up the garbage bag, tied the red strip, leaving an opening big enough for later retrieval of the scraps. He carried it out the back door, straining a little to hold it above the steps. Once the bottom of a bag had ripped, probably snagged on a splinter, and the contents had sort of gurgled out. He had picked it all up without complaining. The lesson was learned. Take care.

Milosh aligned the three trashcans, looked down the narrow alley. The city crew often cut back trees and bushes, so it was a clear but winding path connecting all the neighborhood. The stars above spread over all of them, equally, like beauty was there for everyone. But here, life was daily and not great. Little pleasures, his dad and mom said, were man's lot. Simple things, like a good night's sleep, enough food, a roof over your head, and a job well done.

From further down the alley, faintly, came a high-pitched sound of anguish. Milosh knew for certain it was the dog. It probably wasn't starving, but it had specifically spoken to him and he planned to feed it tonight. He couldn't tell his brother, though he wanted to. Pravi was the favorite, partly because he would tell the truth about anything, wise or not, and partly because he cried easily. He couldn't be trusted. Pravi was still in the kitchen now, staying near their mother. But their dad was coming outside, as if Milosh's secret desires had flown straight into the man's thoughts. He was a big man, but light-footed and soft-voiced. His presence made everything else bow down. So Milosh thought. Maybe even grass.

"You headed somewhere, Milosh?"

"No, sir. Just garbage duty like every day."

"A little quicker than every day."

His heart was beating faster. That was the answer. His dad could hear the drum drum of Milosh's planned wrongdoing.

He sat with his dad while the man smoked a cigarette, then the two went inside. At eight, the grandfather came to pick up Pravi, who was afraid of the dark and had diet problems. The grandparents had more time to watch over him. The boys' father was a little too strict for Pravi's nature. Everyone agreed. Even Milosh.

On the way to and from school for the rest of the weekdays, he checked on the hound. Always it had water, and the bowl, though empty, bore signs of fresh food. The animal unleashed its passionate voice to Milosh each visit until Friday, when it suddenly responded to "Ssssshhh," by sitting, its long, skinny tail sweeping side to side in the dust.

"Hey boy." Milosh made a clucking sound, as if calling a horse, but it sufficed. He came up to the now squirming creature, who nuzzled him wildly and roughly, licking, whining, and standing with paws on Milosh's feet, so that the boy fell backward, into a sitting position. Then the hound wanted to be closer and managed to lie across Milosh's legs, pinioning him, but not painfully. "Good dog," Milosh said. "That's a boy. That's it. You're okay. I got you." He had bought a single strip of jerky. He tore at the wrapping with his teeth, pulled the strip free and bit off the tip for himself. He gave the rest to the hound, who at first dropped it in the dirt in favor of sitting on Milosh, then did eat it. "Savage beast." Milosh rubbed the neck fondly and slid his hand under the collar all the way around a couple of times.

He soon saw there was another dog in the house, rather, one that lived in the house, but came outside to do its business. There was no fence. The back door was open, and the dog scurried down the steps, looked around while it squatted, and in seconds ran back in. That one was obedient. Cute, too, Milosh guessed. It was a Scottie, with long black coat clear to the ground so the feet weren't visible, just the curtain of hair. Purebred, Milosh thought. Worth money, probably.

Down the hill was the hound, quivering though standing still, eyes riveted on that little shiny rival.

Milosh couldn't stand it. He didn't hate the Scottie. He hated the owners. Who could chain one animal at the base of the yard, day in and day out, and parade in front of him the favored one? He bet the dogs had different diets. The little one got that Caesar's this or King's that or Special or Champion. He even briefly felt bad that he had brought cabbage rolls and bread. Peasant food. That's what his dad called some meals, but lovingly, being crazy about his wife's cooking. So was Milosh. Pravi, too, who preferred to eat supper with his own family, and spend the rest of the time with the grandparents.

The chain holding the dog had only a push-open hook at each end. Milosh could walk away with the dog, if it wanted to come along. Or he could just set it free. He thought it would only rush up the hill to the back door and beg to be let in, would yelp and whine and further anger the owners.

"For now," he said, roughing up the dog's ears and snout, "you got to stay where you are. Your turn will come. Everybody gets what's due them."

He went on to school and football practice. He had wanted to play last year, mostly to please his dad, which made failure a silent partner of his desire. He'd been so much bigger than the kids his age, the coaches couldn't let him on the team. If he wanted to play in his age bracket, he had to lose weight. His mom and dad had helped him. They put his portions on the plate. If he wanted extra, he could have it. The serving dishes were right on the table as always. Sometimes he did take an extra piece of chicken or slice of pie. But he made a habit of only eating half of anything above the allotment. It was a compromise with hunger. An extra bite or two and the satisfaction of willpower.

His father believed in overindulging on special days, saints' days, or at dances, or at funerals. Wherever eating was part of the community of man, a person should eat appropriately. For most of man's activities, moderation was the best choice. For children, what they were told to do was the only choice.

At football practice, during the first runs around the field, with the sun low and rather gold in the west and his hope so feverish about outlasting everybody, being the fastest and the strongest, Milosh fainted. He didn't know that's what had happened. He woke on his back, with the gray-blue sky sort of streaked with black, with the coaches kneeling by him and a cold cloth on his head.

"Did you eat today?" he heard.

"Yes sir?"

"How do you feel?"

"Fine." He was confused and sat up. The other boys were watching, little groups of interest, maybe not laughing. He knew some of them. He tried to rise but a hand held him down, not harshly.

"You stay put for a minute. We're calling your dad."

"Don't," he said. "I'm okay." He leaned away from the man attempting to keep him still, rolling first onto his knees, then pushing himself upward. "I want to play." All turned black.

He woke this time to his father's voice. "Hey, son. You're okay. Nothing broken."

Milosh looked back at the other boys starting a single line run. When he came back, this would still be his first day, always his first day, and a year too late even then.

One coach walked them part of the way to the car. "We got room for him as soon as you know he's ready to play."

"I'm ready now," Milosh said to the pavement three times before they reached the car. His dad started to open the passenger door. "I got it," Milosh said, and slid in. He slapped his thigh, didn't say any ugly word though he knew a couple. Slapped the dash.

"Who you slapping?" his father asked.

He felt humiliated and weak. A gorge came up in his chest. If he thought of the hound the misery worsened, like it was one misery, growing outsize.

"You know that red hound dog on Jefferson street? They used to walk him by here."

His dad did know, after a minute.

"They leave him chained outside all the time now," Milosh said. "They don't play with him or walk him. They just feed him."

"And how do you know this?"

"I check on him. I saw him chained up, so I go by there and see how he's doing."

"Maybe he's not clean enough for inside."

"They got another one in the house. It's got long hair. It's a show dog, I think. They're ashamed of the big one so they stuck him down the hill. He can't even see the street, nobody walking by. He's got nothing."

"Got you."

Milosh felt a little eased by that, almost tearful. He nodded. "Got me."

On Sunday afternoons, his family often went to a big hall where they helped cook and serve food and lead dances and listen to music. When they got home this Sunday, it was already dusk, and kind of lonesome, since when that many people had been around and were suddenly gone, the world seemed mostly him alone, and quiet, so quiet that the songs he'd heard seemed to be bottled inside him and coming out into the world in weak strains, trying to be full-bodied and real music. His dad went out back for a smoke. His mother lay down on the sofa with the television on very low. Pravi had ridden home with the grandparents.

Milosh went out to the front porch. Linden trees were on either side of their front walk, right at the end, before it met the official sidewalk. They looked like portals to the coming night. They made him anxious, made him want to run and accomplish something that would put the world right, fill it up with the people who would behave well to one another.

He struck out walking without knowing at first that he was headed anywhere special. But when he was striding up Jefferson, he knew, and he tried to focus on exactly what he must do. He thought perhaps he had to steal the dog or shoo it away or just crawl into its shelter and take up residence with the ignored creature. He went to the house's front door instead. At his knock, he heard inside a yipping that he found annoying, high and kind of fading.

A man opened the door. He was a normal kind of guy, about the size of Milosh's dad, only with a round belly, and balding, with a mustache that was partly gray. "Hello," the man said. "I've been expecting you. I heard you'd been coming around. I guess you're wanting to get that dog from me."

Milosh was startled. "I can't have a dog," he said. It hadn't occurred to him to ask, to challenge a rule established long ago. "My mom and dad say no animals in the house. We haven't got a fence."

"Neither do we. So if that's not what you wanted, what is it?"

Milosh looked at the little yapper that, though not barking, wasn't happy, sort of drawn back, ready to take offense and give injury.

"I wanted to tell you that you shouldn't leave the other dog, the big one, out there by himself. He wants to be up here. He wants to live in the house the way he used to."

"He can't. He tore up an entire door. He chewed through it and ripped up over five square feet of carpet on the other side of the door."

"You could play with him or take him for walks. Or," he thought rapidly, "get a muzzle for him. Or. There's a pen that goes in the house or the garage."

The man was getting irritated, though Milosh didn't feel threatened exactly. Just that he had overstepped a boundary, which he knew anyhow. "The dog can't understand. I see him looking up the hill at your back door. It breaks my heart," he said, using his mother's words and now his words, too, though he wouldn't have chosen them.

"I see. Do your parents know you're over here?"

"No."

"What's your name?"

"Milosh Lukovich."

"Your folks in the phone book?"

"Yes."

"I'm going to call your parents. Just a minute. You stay here."

He didn't wait. He ran around the side of the house and toward the slope, but the sheer pain of that animal down there, driven to some kind of crazy behavior that drove its beloved owners away was more than he could endure right now. He couldn't help it. Much as he wanted to, he couldn't. He ran home instead.

The dog's owner had called.

"The animal's not happy," Milosh's father said. "Maybe true. But its life could be worse. The owner says he doesn't hunt anymore, and he doesn't want to put the dog in the pound. Sometimes he takes it to a friend's property and lets it run. The animal gets special time. Okay? Everything evens out. Maybe you should offer to take the dog for walks."

"I could do that. I want to."

"Okay. Good. Now think of this. If you start it, you have to keep it up. You can't have that dog looking for you every day and you not come. Instead of looking at the back door, it would look for Milosh. It would wonder where is that boy? Why can't I go home with him? Why can't I sleep with him? How come I get only this little bit of time? Shouldn't he feed me, too? Shouldn't I eat under his table? You see? You start something big, something less is not enough."

Milosh's mother was standing by her husband now, hand on his shoulder. She was small and slender and, to Milosh, extraordinarily beautiful. He didn't know another mother who had the grace and charm of his, had that soft voice and the touch that could quiet night fears and ease illnesses.

"I'll walk him," he said. "I won't fail him."

Every day, either before or after supper, he walked the hound. When rain flooded the streets and gushed down the alley ruts, Milosh went for the animal, slipping and sliding down the hill, struggling back up. In lightning once, the sky crackling around them. His mother had protested but his father had said, "Let him go. It's his job now." Milosh asked the owner to get some straw and the man did. Milosh spread it around the little house, put some inside, and there spread towel rags his mother gave him. He begged for another hay bale and Milosh's dad bought two. They tugged them down the hill and made a wind break for the creature.

"You've gone crazy," his dad said. "You understand how it works, doing the job right, so maybe skip a day. The dog may need a rest."

A rare cold spell came, with ice, and the owner answered the door, easing Milosh's worry. "We've got him in the garage. It's too cold for him and too cold for you. I think I should find him a home. It's a hardship on you, doing this. I think you should stop it now. We actually regret letting you walk him. I admire you, but, it's too much for the situation."

"It's no hardship." Milosh wanted to go inside the garage, see if the hound was really there. He thought he could hear a high keen, real faint. "You didn't give him away, did you?"

"No. I wouldn't do that without telling you."

He sounded sincere, but Milosh doubted him. Things happened.

Milosh loved the musky smell of the hound, the rough smoothness and comfort of that coat, of the heavy chest and the solidly beating heart. He thought how lonesome he would be one day if the hound died, because dogs didn't live as long as humans, but that was a long way off. Now it was his dog, his companion, just on short jaunts. He had always in his pocket a bit of something to share. He could put his cheek next to the hound's muzzle and feel what he thought was love.

What his mother and father felt for him. And for Pravi. And what the grandparents felt for him and Pravi. And what he felt for his brother. He didn't know what Pravi felt for him. He hoped it was this. Akin to it, at least, maybe not as much.

He gained weight that winter, and height, and breadth, too. He might be as big as his dad. "Maybe bigger than your father," his mother said. He was sitting down then, and she patted his shoulder and kissed the top of his head. "Already so." She left the room and he wondered at what she said.

One Friday, in spring, he found the doghouse gone. The ground was bare. Food dish and water dish gone. Hay raked up and away back from the cleared spot. Off the face of the earth. Some adult's words. Now his.

He ran up the hill, to the front door, knocked. He heard the high yap of that Scottish traitor. He knew they were in there, at least the woman of the house. He wanted to kick the door, put dirt through the mail slot. "Where is he?" he yelled, and hit the door once, his hand stinging. They'd given the hound to a hunter, or to a shelter. They were tired of his, Milosh's, encroaching on their territory, of enforcing their own rules. He was caretaking the animal as they wanted. Everyday duty, done with love, with care. Not neglected. Not that animal. All he was allowed to give, he gave. He would have walked him twice a day. He would have slept with him at times. He was a dumb creature and couldn't ask for all he needed, just bark and stare and quiver and hope the signs and sounds were understood.

At home, Milosh stepped into the house quietly, breathing a little hard. He smelled one of his favorite dishes, lamb and noodles. He didn't want it. There had to be something momentous he could do. Write the hound's name in the stars.

"Is that you, Milosh?" his mother said. "Wash your hands. Come set the table." The kitchen was rich with light and smells. A stack of plates was on the table, loose silverware nearby. Six settings.

"The dog's gone," he said. "I went to walk him, and he's gone."

"Maybe to the veterinarian?" she said, half turning, a quizzical expression, then back to her cooking.

"The doghouse is gone, too. They've given him away. Sold him."

"Your father will be home soon. He'll know what to do." She pointed at the plates. "Wash your hands, set the table. Your grandparents are coming."

He obeyed her, placing the china plates so the cluster of painted blue flowers was at the bottom, and the slender blue fronds around the sides and touching at the top. It's how she had taught him. The knife pointed directly at the water glass. The napkin could be pulled by one corner down and over the lap.

Milosh's chest was too full, ached from restraint. He could not cry or hit anything. Even the dog's house was gone. At least, the hound would have something familiar. His dish, too. But the spot of earth nearby was now forever changed. Grass might not grow. Leaves would shun it. Milosh would go always a different route. He had to grieve. He had to get the dog back. He turned to look at his mother's presence as if she were strange. How could she hum so, and go about her daily work? "I think I hear them," she said. "Have you finished? Go help them."

Something was odd here. Through the kitchen window he had glimpsed a point of wood near the alley. There was a smell, too, he almost recognized. It was tantalizing and yet he was afraid to seek it, to give in to what it might be in case it wasn't. He had a budding hope that made his steps to the door so precious. He heard the vehicles rounding the corner down the street, heading this way, slowing down, the blend of voices. The house was going to swell with family and pleasure and small grievances. And something else. He was for a brief moment filled with dread. A hard lesson could be coming, one that prepared him for the rest of his life. It's what had to happen. But he could feel the sound of joy. Oh, the goodness of it, that shiver of the world as his family approached up the front walk, the rest of his own family, including that bounding hound, that musky, squirming, leaning, licking, loving hound.

Tradition

I wake up and don't know it's not a good day. The sun's shining venetian-slat shadows over my bedspread. I lift the blinds, and there, right outside my window, a bluebird is sitting in the vee of redbud branches. Color galore. Spring bursting out all over, as my mother might say. The thought of her sobers me, though she's not a somber person. She's not a normal person in any way, actually. You can't pin her down to being any set thing. You think maybe she's going to blow her stack over something you tell her, and boom, she's understanding. Openminded. You think you'll touch her heartstrings with another story, and boom, she wants somebody executed. She believes in capital punishment for child molesters and brutal rapists. A common rapist just gets a prison term. She's got categories of good and evil. She read C. S. Lewis when my sister and I did, and she listened to my sister's sincere but sappy desires to save a world. My sister, Mary (wouldn't you know she'd have a name with a legacy), said, "all the great battles have been fought." Yep.

The bluebird flies away. And the redbud isn't going to make it, anyhow. This is desert country. The landlady came from the Midwest and thinks she can make a redbud thrive wherever she wants. My family's from the Midwest, too.

I have to have an abortion and I have to tell my mother about it. I could just schedule the damned thing, clutch my sin to my heart, so to speak, and live it out alone, but something in me—probably my mother—says I have to confess.

I'm twenty in years and far older than my sister, though she has two years on me. She was born first, but she's cautious. I came out and zoomed by her. I'm bigger than she is, too. She's about five foot six, and I'm five foot eight. She's got bones like a bird or an angel—delicate and long—and a face that looks like unspoiled, unegotistic virtue. She was born good. She's never tempted by anything ugly or less than ideal. If Plato's forms are real, she got a chance to memorize them before she appeared on this earth.

My mother, by the way, is five foot eleven, earthy by nature and spiritual by desire. She's had a rough time reconciling the two. I think I take after her, but with my father's pragmatism. She's bright; he's a hard worker. They've been divorced for three years, about fifteen years too late. I recall my childhood and their marriage. Painful.

It's the first day of my weekend—Wednesdays and Thursdays—but I shower quickly and dress in jeans and a sloppy shirt that billows over my waist and stomach. I'm not showing yet, of course, but maybe I choose the shirt because it symbolizes what I could be—getting ready for what's not going to happen. And I'm going over to Mark's and he doesn't like sloppy clothing. Maybe I want to defy him. He likes tight bodies, too. He'll pinch an extra inch and say, "you better get back to the gym."

I've tried pressing and curling this baby away, but it hasn't worked. I'm healthy and it's stuck. Justice, perhaps.

I can't stay away from Mark. He doesn't want to live together. He lives with his mother, though he's thirty-two, but he has real good reasons. She's sixty. His father died years ago. She's never worked. She's afraid to be alone. And he's Italian and "family comes first." They have traditions, you know, roots in the Old Country and all that. Holidays at his place means hordes of relatives, food all day, lots of joking and hugging. I'm not too demonstrative but he doesn't lavish that much attention on me, anyway. It's reserved for family.

His mother opens the door. She seems real fond of me and is always pushing food on me. She has to know Mark and I sleep together, even though it's at my place, but she never gives a sign.

"Leslie," she says, and ushers me into the kitchen. She's in a housedress, her black and silver hair pulled up tight. She has fine, dark skin with few lines. She's slim, too. Petite. A little Italian mama who dotes on her only son. "Mark's in the shower, honey. He's got a job interview this morning."

"I know. I thought we'd have a cup of coffee together." She always announces what he's doing as if I'm a virgin brain and couldn't possibly know. That keeps him belonging to her, I suppose.

"Don't you work today?" she asks.

"My day off. Or night, actually. I work nights, you know."

"That's right. I just forget. I guess it seems unnatural for a woman. I'm fixing an omelet for Mark. You want one?"

"No. Just coffee."

"You're so thin, Leslie. You need meat on those bones."

"Mark likes skinny women."

She laughs. What can she say? I'm right. And *she's* skinny.

Mark comes out and I'm shy and ugly immediately, sitting in his kitchen with my crummy pale skin, big bones, and shoddy clothes. And pregnant. When his mother turns to the skillet, I nod a big yes to him, meaning no mistake, a bambino is on the way.

"You're out early," he says.

"Wanted coffee with my fellow." I've got light and easy ways when I have to have. He likes that.

I guess I came hoping to read some hesitation in his dark features. After all, he is Italian, and they do love family. I'm certainly family, or breeding one. But he's the same Mark. No bluebird in his redbud tree.

"If I get this job," he says, "there's a chance I'll be assigned to Hawaii. They need a district manager."

"Hawaii!" his mother says.

"Great!" I say, matching her enthusiasm for enthusiasm. I don't like islands. All that ocean. They could be wiped out with one swallow of the sea. "You'd love it, Mark. Vacation land."

"Living costs are high."

So what does that mean? You, Leslie, couldn't afford it? I wait for that little crumb sign that means we'd go together if he goes at all. But he's putting more butter on his roll, cutting up his eggs like an energetic, handsome man who's on his way somewhere alone any minute.

"You coming by after the interview?" I say. "I'm going to visit my mom today and want to work out."

"You go ahead," he says. "I told Louie I'd go up on the mountain with him today. He's got business up there."

I know Louie's business. I don't remind Mark it's my day off. He knows that. He knows I'll want to talk about all this, the baby, my mom, Hawaii. Sometimes he avoids my emotional lapses. He thinks I should work out my aggressive moments in the gym.

"Tonight?" I say, knowing I'm debasing myself. I'm a fool in love.

"I guess. Yeah. We'll be back. May be late, though."

Oh the appetite of a healthy, complacent man. I hate his guts.

"See you later, then." I stand up and lightly hug his little mother. "Thanks for the coffee."

She pats my hand like I'm dear to her. "You don't have to rush off, Leslie. Just because Mark's going, you don't have to."

"I've got things to do, too. My mom wants to hear from me."

"Well, you call her. I know you two don't get along, but children should . . . ."

She keeps her motherly spiel going all the way through my exit. I don't think she really likes me at all.

He's a bastard, you see. My Mark love. He's smarter than my father and less effusive than my mother. He's all the world to me.

I rage in the car, and I cry hard enough I have to pull over for a while. Then I drive to a Circle K and call my mother.

Talking with my mother requires ungodly patience. She was raised in a family of interrupters—so many people that learning where to edge in a word was a matter of survival—and while I'm supposed to have a good mind (the highest IQ in the family, if that means anything to anybody), I'm not quick with spoken words. Mother says I monitor all the time. Maybe. I do look for the right moment.

"Oh, Leslie," she says. "You are so thin. Why do you do that, honey?" She hugs me fiercely, like she'd scrunch me inside herself if she could. There's no doubt that you're loved around my mother. "You're meant to be plump. That Irish face, curly hair. Oh baby." She kisses my nose and is sad for me while she pours coffee, lights herself a cigarette, and opens a window so the smoke won't make me sneeze or give me a headache. If she knew a baby was in me, she'd be all over herself with guilt, but she wouldn't quit smoking. She'd stand on the porch and talk with me through the screen door.

"You need someone who loves you the way you are," she says, and rips open a package of Girl Scout cookies—the peanut butter ones. My favorites.

I take three. That will slow her down. "You have girl scouts in this neighborhood?"

"No," she says. "I ordered them from the department secretary. Her daughter's a scout. She's a single mother and I knew she'd buy them herself. I don't like her much, but . . ."

"How many boxes?"

"Why does that matter?"

I bite into one and talk while chewing, which she never minds. Mark does. "I bet you bought six," I say.

"Just about."

So she bought more than six. She's in school herself, graduate school, and lives on a teaching assistant's salary. She doesn't have much money. "Maybe you bought twelve."

"Ten. Okay? Okay? I bought ten boxes."

"All peanut butter?"

"Five peanut butter for you and five mints for Mary."

The desert sun honeys up her living room. It's got pine floors which she waxes regularly—the varnish wore off decades ago—a little red adobe fireplace, a deep blue sofa of sags, a rocker, and a dirty white overstuffed chair broad enough to curl up in. I'm in the chair. Outside the front window, a desert willow tree waves fronds.

The window is many-paned, and mother has meticulously painted the narrow wood strips white. It's a lovely window. It opens in, but she'd have to move the sofa and it's heavy. She likes that window, too. She's chattering about Mary's frugal ways, how Mary ate just green beans for three weeks because she found them on sale. Mary's in school, too, finishing her B. A. I dropped out after my first year. I'm a waitress, training for bartending as soon as I hit twenty-one. And I make more than my mother does.

"Mary likes green beans," I say. "It wasn't a hardship for her. It would be for you."

"I like green beans."

"That's not what I mean."

"What's wrong, Leslie? You're not acting okay. What's up?"

"Does something have to be up for me to visit my mom?"

"Yes. I usually have to track you down just to hear your voice, and now you're over here in the daytime, before noon, and on your day off, too."

"Nothing's wrong. Ease up, Mom."

"What's he done? Is it another woman again? Honey, why do you put up . . ."

I raise my hand, give her my that's-enough look. "He's been fine. He's got a job interview and may be going to Hawaii."

"Good. Get him out of the country."

I don't say anything, but she stops herself. We've come to some understanding about Mark. If she bad-mouths him, I'm out of here. She's a better person than he is, but that's not the point.

"But something's wrong, right?" she says. "Talk to me, Leslie. Don't make me fish. Is everything okay? Your job? What?"

"If you'll slow down, I'll tell you."

She waits and so do I. Now I've made it all harder, you know? I've set a stage for something spectacular when I should have been trying to get onto the courtyard stage, less expectations, less tension, a quick, little half-assed show and out.

"It's not all that much," I say. "I want to tell you something, but I don't want any lectures or advice. No big blowout of emotion. I just want to talk."

"You always do that, Leslie. You cut out the other person's right to be human. You want me to listen how that bastard uses you, and never say one word of recrimination."

I stand up and she shuts up. I sit back down. We're silent for a few minutes, and I'm pretty sure she can hold onto it. She's real stubborn.

"Now I'll tell you," I say. "And please don't make me feel bad." She's a little angry, and that's good. Anger is better than concern. I look squarely at her, because it'll only take a minute and I'll last that long. "I'm going to have an abortion. I've made up my mind, it's scheduled, but I didn't want to do it without telling you."

Her whole face changes without her moving at all. She is stricken. No other word describes it. Stricken. And that makes me feel heartsick myself. She always could do that.

"Does Mark know?" Her voice is hoarse, too. One wonders how the human body does all that in one second. Changes all the outward signs of self.

"Yeah."

"And he would let you do this? The big family-loving man? The lousy . . ."

"Watch it, Mom."

She lights up another cigarette. She walks to the front door, seems to be looking at the street; comes back, kisses me on top of the head, and then takes her coffee cup into the kitchen.

When she returns, she says, "I want it, Leslie. I'll raise it for you."

"Not a chance. I didn't tell you so you'd help. I told you for some reason I don't know. I didn't want to do it without telling you. And now I'm going to go."

"Please don't. Not yet. Let me talk it out."

"Not if it hurts me."

"I won't. I won't say anything."

Then we sit there in silence again, only I'm all choked up, and if I cry she'll think I'm wavering. I eat the damned cookies. I even get three more. They are dry. Dry.

"Have you told your father?"

"No. And I'm not going to. And don't you tell him, either."

She nods. Then she gets up and comes to sit by me. She puts her arm around my shoulders and leans her head against me and sort of rocks. "Oh, I would love that baby," she says. So I turn a little, kiss her right on the lips, lightly, a mother-daughter kiss, and I stand up. "Well, I told you. I'm leaving now. I'm supposed to meet Mark." She doesn't believe in untruths, but I know what peace such lies keep in the world and I'm smarter than her in some ways.

"Don't go."

"I have to."

"I want to talk about it some more."

"I don't. And it's mine to talk about."

"You knew I'd try to talk you out of it."

"I hoped you wouldn't."

"You knew I would. It's like 'Night, Mother. You want to be talked out of it."

"No, it's not. It's not like anything you've read or seen, Mother. It's me. Blunt and simple." We're at the door, her right behind me, tugging at me just with feelings, no touches. "I'm pregnant and I'm having an abortion. Bye, bye."

"Leslie. Honey. Stay here."

I'm on the porch, on the walk.

"Leslie. Please."

At the gate. By my car. "Bye Mom."

"I love you."

"Yep. Love you, too."

And then, of course, I wind up crying again. It's all those hormones. And it's my mother. She brings out sentimental crap just by believing in it.

I should have anticipated the strength of her code. She tells everyone, or everyone who shouldn't have been told: her mother, my father, his mother, and Mary. Mary the angel. And every one of them wants to take the baby. I stop answering my phone. Saturday morning, Mother shows up on my porch, but I won't let her in the house.

"You betrayed me, Mom. I trusted you."

"It's like killing you," she says. "It's like asking me to let you die. The baby's part of you. It may look like you." She's pacing and crying, this tall, skinny, wild-haired, chain-smoking mother. She was beautiful once and now she's still good-looking, but she's aged quickly. She has a sister, too, and her sister isn't aging. Some patterns are repeated in families. I've got my mother's skin and many of her ways. I'll be walking and crying on a porch someday. So I open the door and have her sit down and I get a saucer that'll serve as an ashtray.

I don't want to kill the baby. I *have* to. But I can't tell her that.

"Calm down, Mom. It's okay. Maybe I knew you'd tell everyone."

"I was just looking for a way to stop you."

"There isn't one. I've made up my mind."

"Why kill a child when people are ready to take it? It's needless. Have you seen pictures of aborted . . ."

"I've seen them. Everybody in the world has seen them. I'm not going to think about them."

"How can you . . ."

"Drop it. Listen, Mom. Say I let someone else take the baby. Then all my life I have to live knowing that someone else took my responsibility. Maybe I'll feel guilty. Maybe I'll try to take the baby when I don't really want it. Or, say I don't take the baby. All its life, it'll wonder why its mother didn't care and doesn't care. I'll be saddling myself with my lack of responsibility. This way, I'm shouldering everything. I take all the responsibility, all the guilt. I can handle it."

"No, you can't. You always think you can handle the world. You're a fragile woman, Leslie. You're not nearly as hard as you pretend. You think you have to hide how you feel, but it comes back to get you, I tell you. You can't sluff away what comes natural."

"I'm not a natural mother. You are. Mary may be. I'm not. I'm a pleasure seeker."

"Stop talking like that. Listen to your voice. Honey, you're scared to death."

"Of course I'm scared. But I'm more afraid of having it."

"What if it looks like you? What if it looks like your dad? You're crazy about your dad, Leslie. What if it's the spitting image of him?"

"And what if it's not? What about that, O mama mine? What if it's the spitting image of Mark? What if it's just like him? Would you want it then?"

"You bet. You bet. Because it's yours, too."

"And what if it doesn't look like either of us? What if it doesn't have a nose? Or is missing an arm? Or a brain? What if it's a dumb, ugly little kid? Huh? You had pretty kids, Mom. Maybe I won't. Maybe mine will be ugly, sniveling little monsters. You want to keep it then?"

"Yes," she said. "Yes I do. Ugly as sin and I'll take it."

"You won't take it, because I'm not changing my mind."

She tries for a little while longer, but I shut her out and she knows it. I can feel the smile she doesn't like playing on my lips and when I look directly at her, I keep my eyes as empty as possible. I just hold them more open than usual and look between her eyebrows. It maddens her. It shames me, sometimes, to lie with my face like that, but it's been effective with customers, Mark, my father, and especially with my mother. She spins herself out trying to crack through. She leaves.

But she calls later: "Do you have the money you need?" "When is it scheduled?" "Will you let me go with you?" "I can't let you do this by yourself, honey. I couldn't live with it."

I tell my mother she can take me to the clinic. It's set for a Friday morning and she doesn't have a class until eleven. "Mark will pick me up, though," I say. "He wants to."

He hasn't said he wants to, but he has agreed to pay for the abortion. I'm going to make him be the one who brings me home. Maybe I won't. Maybe I'll just take a cab.

Maybe I'll die before then. Mom's always planning her own demise. I take after her. People do die from abortions. Would Mark grieve? Not as much as I grieve thinking about it.

The bluebird is in the redbud again, but it doesn't mean squat.

My mother picks me up at eight. She comes in, remains standing while I find a book to take along. She looks haggard, but she's dressed differently. She wears jeans a lot but not today. She has on a long cotton skirt, a white blouse with a high, prim collar, and she's pulled her hair back to the nape of her neck. She's wearing stockings and wedgie shoes her own mother might wear. "You look nice," I say. "Thanks for taking me."

"You know I want to. You know everything I want."

She stops with that. Outside, she opens the car door for me as if I'm truly an invalid, or as if I'm suddenly the old woman among us.

She makes the wrong turn at the first intersection, so I know she's not okay. Then she stops at a green light.

"You're going to get us killed," I say. "You want me to drive?"

"No. I'm going to drive. I'm okay."

"Sure you are."

"You can change your mind any minute."

"I'm not going to."

She nods, looks straight ahead. "How long will you be there?"

"About six hours total. I'll be sleeping part of the time."

"When's Mark coming?"

"Before I'm ready to leave. Don't worry about it."

"I'm not going to leave you there alone."

"Yes, you are. That was the deal."

"Deals."

I am scared. It's just a clinic on the east side. Clean, professional. Pleasant clerk. Another woman waiting. I fill out the forms, and my mother stands right by my side.

"You can go," I say. "I'll be all right."

She doesn't respond, but she doesn't leave.

We sit down. Her face and neck are flushed. She tries to smile but she can't. When she's like this, she looks really old, her face all down-lines. "Look Mom," I say, "you've handled this well. But I'd be more comfortable if you'd go ahead and leave. I don't want to worry about you, too."

"I'm making it worse?"

I nod. It's not actually true, but it'll get her out of here.

"I don't want to go. I feel like I haven't done enough. I can't bear it."

Now she's got me near crying and she sees it.

"I'm sorry," she says. She pats my hand and stands up. "I'll go. I'll do whatever you want."

I get up with her and walk her to the door. I'm chilled, suddenly. She is, too. I hug her. "I'll be okay. I'll call you later."

"I don't want to leave you here."

"But you will, right?"

She sighs and nods. She goes out the door. I watch her drive away. She'll kill herself at some intersection.

I try reading, but my mind churns away. Mark got the job and he doesn't want me to go. He hasn't said so, but he hasn't invited me. He doesn't speak of "we." I've listened very closely and he hasn't left a chink of wanting me. He's having a celebration party. Tonight. He's not leaving for three weeks. Why does the party have to be tonight? He says it's just a few family members. Louie will be there. The favored cousin. The dope dealer. Mark's secret source.

When they usher me in, it's like I'm watching another person, a cool, tall, big-boned, hardhearted gal. Her voice is clipped. She does everything they tell her matter-of-factly. She clutches her book like she plans to read through the procedure. I do dream, sort of, a twilight memory of the night Mary, Mother, and I went to the theater to see 'Night, Mother. Those two bawled so loudly, so wetly, so long, that we were still in our seats when the theater was empty. I've always envied their depth of feeling, though I don't want to feel such pain, not even if it's my own.

When I wake up, I think they'll tell me my mother came creeping back into the lobby and was out there the whole time. But they don't. I finally ask.

"No," the nurse says. "If she was there, I didn't see her. Want me to ask the receptionist?"

"No." I'd rather believe she was there. See? What a hypocrite I am.

I call Mark and he comes right away. He treats me well, gingerly, like I might fall down. He has one arm around my waist and holds my arm with his other hand. He's wearing black slacks, a white shirt, and his skin is so rich brown it makes my throat hurt.

"How was it?" he says. "You look okay. A little pale, maybe."

"I'm fine. I feel a little nauseated."

"You want to go straight home? You need to eat something first?"

"Home."

His car radio is on, and the rest of the world is happy music and his fingers drumming on the steering wheel. He's been on the phone a lot today, checking out rents in Hawaii. He's going to fly there next weekend to find a place.

"Want me to go with you?"

"Can you afford the plane fare?"

Oh, desert sky. Country mothers and Italian lovers. And me bleeding so ugly.

"No," I say. My voice is crystal clear and sounds happy enough. He's content. He takes my hand and squeezes my fingers.

At my apartment, I decide I can't bear for him to be at a farewell party while I, part of the farewell, am not present. It's like making lonely double-fold, with me in the center.

"Are you sure you feel like being there?" he says. "It'll be loud. Probably last till midnight or after."

"If I get tired, you can take me home."

I take a change of clothes with me and put the clinic's care package in a big satchel. His mother will think it's makeup.

I spend the rest of the afternoon lying in their guest bedroom while he and his mother—and Louie—prepare food and fill ice chests. Mark checks on me from time to time. The bedroom is almost as big as my mother's house. Not a book in sight. Heavy furniture, all polished, with gold handles.

I have to dispose of certain items, and I wrap them carefully and tuck them in the satchel. I feel dirty and full of questionable and shameful intentions. His mother thinks I'm getting the flu and brings me juice.

"You should probably be in bed, Leslie. You sure you want to stay for the party?"

"Yes. It's our party in a way." I am a pathetic person, with none of my mother's and sister's strength of character.

Louie knows. I see it in his sloe eyes and his smirk. I dress in a black sheath, with a gold chain around my neck. My shoes have spike heels. I'm tall and commanding. Mark's girl. The bleeding little virgin. Louie sells coke and other good-mood stuff. Mark cuts deals and makes much money from this sideline mothers don't know about. He had me try some a few times and then got indignant because I used it too much.

"You're turning into a cokehead," he once said.

"You sell the damned stuff."

"But I got enough sense not to get hooked. That's all I need, a jealous, whining, clinging cokehead."

So I know that he and Louie, and maybe some of the younger cousins, are partying higher than most of the guests. I stay in one corner of the sofa and sip juice. I'm not going to use the stuff anymore, not ever. Not in my whole life. Surely I can be just that strong. Mark comes over twice and says, "How you doing?" with that half-glance way. He has to be moving all the time. He really is beautiful. And sophisticated. He likes upbeat worlds.

Someone calls my name and I see Mark's mother waving the phone receiver at me.

My mother is on the line. She has an unbelievably soft voice, and she wonders what in heaven's name I am doing at a party. She's sick. She doesn't know what to do. She wants to come get me immediately. He's a bastard. He doesn't have a human bone in his body. On and on, righteous mother. "I'm fine," I say. "If I weren't, I'd go home and go to bed. Stop worrying about me." She says she can't. She's eaten up with guilt for leaving me alone at that clinic. Can't she come and get me? Please. Please.

"No. Just leave me alone, Mom. If I need you, I'll call."

"Promise."

"I promise."

But how do you know when you need a mother?

She comes anyhow, of course. She rings the doorbell, and someone brings her into the living room. She's still in her cotton skirt outfit, but her hair is down and streetwalker wild. She tries to smile at everyone, avoids looking at Mark, and says something about my sister being sick. She wants me to come with her. "Mary needs you," she says as plain as day. So I get my satchel full of leftover sin and I kiss Mark in front of everyone, and I follow my mother out the door.

Mary really is there. She's in the car. And I suppose she's sick, as much as my mother. She sounds hurt. "You okay, sis?" she says. "I wish you'd let me go, too."

"I didn't even want Mom to go."

"I know. She told me."

Mary's driving, and she goes toward my mother's neighborhood. I don't argue. Not even a C. S. Lewis villain could take on the two of them. They ask if I need anything they should pick up on the way and I tell them no. They talk about traffic and snowbirds, people who move to the West and don't follow the rules. Neither says anything about Mark. "He's just celebrating his new job," I say, so they won't feel like they're choking on what they can't speak. "But I think he could've treated me a little better." My mother makes some sound, like clearing her throat. Mary honks the horn at someone. She never does anything like that. I've screwed up everyone's perfect nature. My mother's house is a tiny adobe with that one lone tree in front. We go inside and mother brings out one of her nightgowns. It's white. Wouldn't you know.

"I'd better not. I don't want to stain it."

"I want you to wear it. Stains come out."

Mary heats soup in the microwave and mother fixes tea. She hates tea, but she has this idea that women should drink it in times of crisis. They make me lie on the sofa, and Mary carries a tray in, hot tea, hot soup, crackers, peanut butter cookies and mint cookies. Mother lights a cigarette but sits by the fireplace as if the smoke will exit that way. It doesn't, and we all know it, but what does it matter?

They don't mention the baby, little have-no-name. I don't mention it either. I don't tell them their Leslie has been into drugs that could damage a spirit just shaping, that she'd rather kill something outright than have it creep through life with less than a full chance. They're protecting me in their way, and I'm protecting them in mine.

And each of us is protecting self. It's so hard to know when you're acting right. Here we are. Our own family, tight frazzled circle.

"What kind of tree is that out front?" Mary says. She's in the rocker, her legs drawn up. She's blonde and, right now, peaked, not as lovely as usual.

"Desert willow," mother says.

"Was it here when you bought the house?"

"Yes, but scraggly. I've been watering it like the dickens."

I tell them about my landlady's redbud. "She thinks she can make it grow here," I say. "More fool, her."

"Don't underestimate her," my mother says.

"I don't. I'm rooting for the damned thing."

For a reason I know, but can't express, that makes my mother get up, come over, and kiss me on the forehead. Mary cries a little, stifles it like the brave heart she is, and I sit up and drink tea with the two of them. I don't like tea, either, but I drain the cup. We all do. I guess it's a tradition in my family. "I'm not going to Hawaii," I say, and they both nod. They leave it alone, though. We talk about crazy things, continents and islands, cities and country, jobs and school. Momma tries to make me take her bed, but I refuse. She's only got one bedroom; the other is a study. She brings me pillow and blankets, protesting all the time. She and Mary scoot the sofa out so the window can be opened. They know I like fresh air. I fall asleep with their voices droning pleasantly. When I wake, they're still talking, only the sound is muted, not in the room. I remember yesterday and last night, and my stomach knots up, maybe from shame and a kind of loneliness there's no answer for. Mark is a bastard and I'm not a good woman. Morning sunshine and spring can't change that. From the front porch comes the sound of splattering water—not rain—and I know Momma and Mary are hosing down the dusty desert, watering everything in sight. Mary says something about me. I hear "Leslie" in Mary's gentle voice. My mother says, "A strong name, isn't it?" They talk a little about women going to gyms, that maybe it's not a bad idea. Mary thinks she herself got the weakest body in the family. Momma tells her it isn't so. I get up and make my way carefully to the bathroom. I'll clean up, dress, and go out there and argue with both of them.

Little Garden

On the ground floor of the old house, Jonathan Pierce sat at the piano, playing scales absentmindedly. He played beautifully but heavily, and his beer can, on top of the piano, slid in its own water ring. Behind him, double windows gave to a summer morning. Thick vines meshed along the outside casing. The scent of honeysuckle and rose filled the room. His roommate Carl came down the stairs, dressed only in white briefs, grunted "Morning," and pushed open the swinging doors into the kitchen. Jonathan scooted back the bench, ran upstairs, and was back at the piano before Carl emerged from the kitchen with a cup of coffee. Carl was oldest of the three students sharing the house, his chest covered with curling black and white hair, his muscles deep from weight-lifting, but soft when he was at rest, as now. He sat down on one of the sofas. "You're up to something," he said. "What is it?"

"Me?"

"You. Where's David?"

"In his room, I imagine, choosing the best attire for his first class."

"Why do you pick on the kid?"

"I like him. I want him to cut the crap, get with the game."

"He's not gay. I'd bet on it."

Jonathan played triplets on the high key. "Oh my, how do you know?"

"Something about his eyes. He meets you head on."

"Good choice of words."

"Let it up, Jonathan. Whatever he is, he doesn't hurt anybody."

In the upstairs bathroom, David stepped from the shower. He was a striking young man, slender, fine boned, with broad shoulders and lean muscles. He dried and glanced twice at the sink, as if it troubled him. Something was out of place, a reflection of black in the white porcelain. The bathroom window was open, screenless. A magnolia tree blossomed lavender and opulent right in the window. Something could have slithered in. He wanted to inch backward, toward the door, but he couldn't. That's what always happened in these situations. He was as solid on the floor as a column of marble. Around him the steam gradually dissipated. The blue-flowered wallpaper took on sharper tones. All time had stopped.

The door opened and his roommate Jonathan ambled in, not quite naturally. He grinned, reached toward the sink, screeched, "Snake!" and simultaneously flung something upward. A black curve arced up, then hit the glass door of the shower, and fell languidly, falsely, at David's feet. It was rubber.

"Gotcha, buddy. That makes five times this semester. Step back from that." When David still didn't move, Jonathan tossed a towel on the rubber snake, then gripped David's shoulders, turned him around, and pushed him toward the hall. "Kept waiting for the scream," he said. "Decided you were never going to see it, so I had to help get things started."

"I saw it."

"You know, if you'd scream, you probably wouldn't be so afraid."

"I'm not afraid. I'm frozen."

"Same thing."

"I don't think so."

"You'll never make it camping." Jonathan went back in the bathroom, retrieved the snake. He waved it toward David as he passed.

"Maybe you should stay home and let me take that girl you found. What was her name? Becky. Sweet Becky."

"I like camping."

Downstairs, Carl looked at the rubber snake, said, "You asshole," and returned to the newspaper. Jonathan put the snake in a plastic bag in the closet, sat back down at the piano. He ripped into "Up on Cripple Creek," then "Rag, Momma, Rag." He stopped for a drink. "Good thing we're not at war," he said, "That kid'd do us no good at all."

"Not all wars are in jungle terrain."

"They have been lately."

When David came down, Carl was out running and Jonathan was still at the piano.

"You know I'm trying to help you, don't you?" Jonathan said.

David turned toward the kitchen. "Yeah. I know."

Jonathan started another tune, muttered, "You gotta get over this, my man." When he stopped playing, he saw the water ring left by the beer can, wiped it with his shirttail, and drained the beer. Then he went to see what David was doing.

The group of young couples, in two cars, drove south from St. Louis the next morning. Much of the highway had been carved through hills and occasionally tan cliffs edged them in. The sun sluiced down, burned the very air they breathed. In the front vehicle, without Jonathan and David, they talked openly about getting David over this "snake thing." Only Carl expressed reservations. "The kid never complains. You never know how he feels about anything." The bag of rubber snakes was in their trunk, crunched behind sleeping bags and coolers. "If it happens enough, it'll get old," Jonathan had told them all. "Trust me."

In the trailing car, Jonathan and his girlfriend were in the front seat, David and his friend in the back. Jonathan grumbled, "Eating dust," though only heat waves rose from the road.

"Pass them," David said.

"I told Carl I'd follow, and I'll follow. Man of my word." He drove in silence for a mile or so then suddenly belted a few lines as if the song just burst out on its own. "Give me young women, wild whiskey, and fresh horses."

David's companion rolled her doe eyes. "I'm hot," she said.

"Oh, honey! Let me stop this car." Jonathan swerved as if to pull over but caught David's gaze in the rearview mirror. "Just kidding, buddy. Just kidding. She's all yours."

This girl was an art student who was failing her English requirements and had come to the house once a week for tutoring by David. Her name was Rebecca. She was lithe and brown. Jonathan had invited her. He had just straddled a chair at the kitchen table where they were studying, said, "Why don't you join David this weekend? We're headed into the wilds." She didn't know, she had told David, if she was a camper, but she'd like to go along.

Now she sighed and lifted her hair from her shoulders. "I hope this is fun," she said.

"Do that again," from Jonathan.

"Do what?"

"Lift your arms and say, 'I hope this is fun.'"

Jonathan's girlfriend slugged him in the right ribcage. "Damn you." Her ponytail swung back over the seat.

"If it isn't fun," David said, "just tell me. We can go back anytime."

"In whose car, buddy?"

"We can always flag down a bus. No one's trapped in this country."

"Then you better get out now. Once we're off the main road, you're a happy camper, like it or not."

"I'll like it," David murmured and watched the landscape drifting by. Surreptitiously he studied Rebecca's profile. She was the same sandy tone as the rock cliffs they passed.

They followed the front car onto a dirt road that looped narrowly up into the side hills, then down again. A river churned at the bottom. "Blue water, blue skies, beer." Jonathan shifted into low gear. The cars rocked on down.

"And bathroom," his girlfriend added.

"Not a chance."

They parked on the edge of a wide, deep clearing. The water lapped pleasantly at the dirt shore. Small rocks lined the bottom.

"See?" Jonathan said. "Clean enough to swim in, too. Regular little garden of Eden."

The six people in the other car spilled out, healthy and whooping. One girl in a blue halter top ran to a large flat rock near the bank, clambered up and held her arms out. "Mine," she said. "Perfect tanning spot. Sun and no dirt."

Rebecca was trying to fasten up her hair. The skin at her elbows was darker than elsewhere. Her neck was absolutely smooth, the same perfect texture all the way to the tops of her breasts. Beyond her the hills rose up lush and dense green.

"I want a Coke or something," she said, as if David should attend immediately to her need. She lowered her voice. "And what's wrong with your friend?"

"Nothing. He's always that way. He's a musician. A good one, actually. Works his way through school by playing at different bars."

"Is he mad at you?"

"No."

"I'd hate to know how he'd behave if he were."

"He doesn't think about what he says. He thinks in lyrics and rhythms. He can't pass up the next line."

"And you think in silence," she said.

"I guess."

"Have you decided what I do?"

"You have a scale model of your future in your head. You plan to redraw the world."

"What do you mean by that?"

He shrugged. "I imagine you know better than I can explain."

They drank beer, changed into suits. Everyone swam. David was the last in the water. They watched him wade in slowly, his eyes darting over the surface. Once he stopped, peered down at his feet.

"Stick," Jonathan called. He was standing behind his girlfriend, had both hands on her midriff.

"Yes," David said. " 'Tis."

David found the first rubber snake when he tried to leave the water. Someone had placed it just at the edge, where it glistened and rolled from the lapping waves. Everyone fell quiet. Jonathan, making a campfire of stones, turned at the silence, sat down, and watched. From deep water near the other shoreline, Carl saw them standing still and began swimming back.

"What is it?" Rebecca said, and looked at David's back. "What's wrong?"

Someone shushed her. She, too, became quiet. Then the girl in the blue halter said, "Oh Jesus Christ," and pushed herself forward in the shallows. "It's rubber, David. Can't you see that?"

When she had tossed it yards onto the shore, he said, "Yes, I see that," and waded out toward camp.

Jonathan slapped him on the back. "You would have stood on that shoreline forever, wouldn't you?"

"Probably. Evolution could pass me by and I wouldn't be able to do anything about it."

"What are you going to do when you have to piss? Can you walk into the woods?"

"Sure."

"Just don't piss in the water."

"I think I'm through swimming."

"You gonna quit life, too?"

Carl loomed beside them, toweling off. "I think we should just have fun on this trip, okay? Everybody leave everybody alone. Fun. Fun. Got that?" He put his thick hand on Jonathan's shoulder.

Jonathan pushed the hand off. "I think David knows what I'm doing and appreciates it. Right?"

"I know." David turned his gaze up to Carl. His eyes were deep blue, almost black, and sad. "It's okay. Really."

The girls whispered among themselves, explaining to Rebecca what was about.

"A snake bit his father under the eye. David was just a kid."

"And his father died?"

"No. Well, yeah, but much later, not from the bite."

"He's terrified of snakes, though. Jonathan thinks he can get David over it."

"He did walk past it to shore," Rebecca said. "Maybe Jonathan knows what he's doing."

"I thought you were David's girlfriend."

"No. I'm just along for the weekend."

The halter girl thought it was a cruel game. "I'm going to find every one of those damned rubber snakes."

The girls found only thirteen. They enjoyed the hunt. Jonathan drained a beer and clued them with "cold, cold, warmer, warmer." But he wearied of it, yelled, "Hey, Dave, let's hit the river," and plunged into the sun-heated water, bursting up like a blond god, liquid silver spraying a halo around him.

David stayed where he was. Here, the soil was black, strewn with twigs and small pebbles. He could smell the must of damp earth and dense leaves. The soft murmurs and laughter of the searching girls pleased and lulled him. He lay back on a towel, saw high above him the long, waving branch of a tree, and jerked back up again. He moved the towel. A snake had once fallen on him, had fallen smack on his head, unnaturally, from out of the sky. He was only seven then, and the snake had apparently been on a branch of the plum tree in his grandfather's back yard, had eaten too many birds' eggs or birds themselves to be quick. David had stood locked in a twilight horror while the snake, fat, black, and lethargic, fell again, from David's head to his shoulder, and simply lay there. David couldn't even scream, though his entire body hummed with one. His father said, "I'll be damned," and knocked it to the ground. "It's just a black snake." He picked it up by the tail and tried to break its neck by cracking it like a whip. He was a blocky, strong man, very fair and courageous. Four times he cracked the snake. The last time, he whipped it too close to his cheek, and its fangs buried in the soft hollow under one of his eyes. He sat down, stunned. "Get it off," he yelled, and David had to do it. He had to do it and he couldn't. He stood right where he was, and his father had to jerk it out himself. His father's face swelled like boiled corn and he nearly died. It hadn't been a black snake after all. When he came home from the hospital, he never once mentioned the incident. He died in a car wreck three years later, but David always felt as if his father died of the snake bite. He thought of the two events simultaneously, so locked together they were one bit of his history, horrible and permanent.

"We got most of them, David," a girl said, and jiggled the trash bag. "Don't let Jonathan get to you."

David noted Rebecca's silence, and that she was watching Jonathan who, on shore again, bent to whisper something to his lady love. The girl slapped her small hand against his chest.

David found the next rubber snake. He reached into the cooler and saw the black curving form blurred beneath the ice. He could neither draw back nor drop the lid. Time settled still and forever around him. Someone brushed near him, said, "I got it, kid." Carl. His dark-tanned arm thrust into the ice, extracted the dark curve, and tossed it toward the trees. "I'm sorry, David. We'll take care of this." He waved at all the others. "Let's round 'em up. Jonathan, you get your ass in gear. You know where they are."

"And that's the joy of it." Jonathan squatted down by the cooler. "Want me to do that, buddy? There were twenty in all. The girls found some. You want me to get rid of them? Just say the word, and I'll root out all the little demons for you, so you don't have to meet even one. Want that?"

David shook his head. "No." He took out a beer, stood, and walked unsteadily toward Rebecca. She didn't meet his eyes. She was sunning. She had her legs stretched out, and the soft blonde hair on her thighs glinted gold. He looked at Jonathan. "Have at me," he said.

Jonathan blew a whisper kiss toward Carl. "See?"

The next was in a bread sack, its flat rubber head sticking from the end of a cored-out loaf of French baguette.

"That's it, Jonathan." Carl snapped the loaf from David's hand. "You're going to kill him. Look at him." He tossed the bread toward the campfire. "I'll see to it this doesn't happen anymore. Okay? I'll beat the shit out of Jonathan if I have to."

"It's all right," David said. "I know why he's doing it."

"I don't think any of us care why he's doing it. We care that he stops it. Now." He turned toward Jonathan. "You hear that? I want you to show me where every one of them is."

Jonathan did so, dramatically, pointing two fingers down and covering his eyes with his other hand, as if dousing for evil. Carl added them to the ones the girls had found. He stoked the camp-fire and laid the bag on top. The plastic smoldered, finally flared. Then the snakes squirmed and rolled. The air stank, turned black.

"That's all of them, Buddy," Jonathan said. "Enjoy yourself."

"I was anyhow."

"Sure you were. You held her hand yet?"

Everyone in camp knew when David eased away, toward the cars. They kept their backs to him.

Jonathan tossed a twig at Carl. "You think you've helped? The guy can't even piss without us noticing."

Dark fell. The moon rose high and silent, coasting. The woods rustled. Night birds called. Rebecca shook David's sleeping bag, spread it flat by hers, then lay down. "Your friend Jonathan's a real bastard."

David stretched out beside her. She was still dressed in white shorts and top, and the moonlight softened her lean arms and legs. "Did you know him before?"

"No," she said. "I've seen him around. He attracts attention, you know. So crude."

A sharp bark of laughter came from across the camp.

"That's him, isn't it?" she said.

"Yes."

They lay silent and motionless, as if waiting on Jonathan's voice to sound again. When she finally turned on her side, back to David, David turned away, too. Then he turned over, scooted nearer, and went to sleep with his arm over her waist.

Early Sunday morning the heat was not yet intense. A pleasant breeze floated over the water. The campers took a last few moments in the idyllic setting. Some were in the water, others stretched out on blankets. The girl in the blue halter now wore a bit of pink and lay on her flat rock, sunning. David was closing the trunk lid, ambling back to the sunbright clearing. On the shoreline, water lapped nearer and nearer the rock. From beneath it a brown speckled ribbon emerged, turned, and slithered around and up the side of the rock. It paused, blended with the stone, clung there. The quiet continued. It began moving again, curled over the top, and rested. The girl lay on her stomach, face hidden beneath her upstretched right arm. Something caused her to open her eyes. From beneath half-closed lids, she saw a narrow ledge of rock, then realized it wasn't rock. "Oooh," she mouthed, but she didn't scream. She lay inert for a while, then lifted her left wrist slightly and bent her fingers, gesturing "come here," "come here." From yards away, David saw the gesture. He knew exactly what it was. The earth stopped into sun with one floating cloud shadow, the smell of soil and water, and male strength and female waiting. It was lovely and fearful and fierce. David was not breathing. Jonathan burst into bronze action, darted forward, jerked the snake up, snapped it in a high arc. Carl, on the river's edge, gauged without thinking the flight and descent of the black curve, and he sped toward David but couldn't go fast enough and fell on his knees as the snake looped against the sun, slow and lovely, up, up, and slowly down, descending right where David and everyone else now knew it would. It fell full, solidly and sickeningly, against his upturned, flushed face, struck down into the neck, falling on against the chest where it struck again, then down, landing at his feet still alive and angry, fleeing in semi-coils and sudden, quick slithering glides away to the dark undergrowth.

"God. God." Carl crawl-stumbled forward, dragged David down.

"It bit me." David's eyes weren't fearful, but startled, wide and childlike.

"Don't talk."

"It bit me."

Carl pressed his mouth against the puncture marks on David's cheek and tried to draw out the poison.

Voices tumbled. "What in the hell were you doing, Jonathan?" "My God, you threw it right at him." "Get the car, get the car, get the car."

"Grab his legs," from Carl to Jonathan. "We've got to get him to a hospital."

David's face was swelling, the puncture wounds no longer visible. Those on his chest were still flat, red dots. "I can walk," David said, but he let them carry him. He thought the sky was the most brilliant blue, placid and kind.

"It wasn't deliberate," Jonathan said. "Jesus. I was just getting rid of the damn thing."

Carl opened the back door. "Get him in here. I'll drive. You suck out that poison."

"I can't do that. It'll kill me."

"Then you drive. But I mean drive. Fast." Carl scooted into the back seat, lifting David's head and shoulders up, cradling him against his chest. "Go, man. Go."

David's eyes were almost hidden in puffy flesh. His lips were shaped in a grimace smile, one side pulling up, the other down. He was trying to say something. Carl bent down. "You're going to be okay, David. We'll get you to a hospital." David floated in a perfect world, white pain, blue, blue, giving to dark. He was terribly loved and longed to return it.

Dust clouds rose around them, gravel spit. They pulled onto the paved road. The car raced fear and despair. They couldn't go fast enough. Jonathan's blood burned his face and body. Carl felt the heaviness of David's torso in his own flesh. He had drawn poison and spit poison and the taste in his mouth was hopelessness. The day slowed all around them no matter their feverish attempt to outrun it. They took the first exit indicating "Hospital" as if David would make it, certainly would make it, was just feigning peace. "People don't die from snakebites anymore," Jonathan said. "I mean, they got all sorts of stuff to fight it." They carried David in. He was so limp, so heavy. Sweat glistened Jonathan's half-nude frame. Gravel and sand still marked Carl's crawling fight to help.

They sat in the waiting room. Carl held a magazine open on his legs, looked at the same page.

Jonathan sat across from him. "You think he's going to be okay?"

Carl didn't raise his head. "No." A moment later he said, "He wasn't okay when we got here. You knew that."

When the doctor confirmed what they already knew, they walked outside.

"God." Jonathan got in the passenger's seat, Carl behind the wheel. The day should have been over by now. The sky should be black with night. Sun and heat danced on the car hood and the paved lot.

"I guess we have to go tell the others." Carl started the car.

"You think they're there?"

"Where else?"

"Maybe they went back to town. Maybe they tried to follow us."

"No. They'd wait."

All the world was silent although they passed other vehicles and their own movements made tentative sounds of humanity.

"I didn't do it on purpose."

"No."

As they drove up into the green hills, "But it was still my fault."

"Yes. And mine, too."

"For not stopping me."

"Yeah."

The others had packed up.

Carl explained. His voice was deep, older and suitable. And it was a sad voice. Jonathan stood with his head down, with one hand holding the other arm against his side.

They got in the cars. In the lead, Carl's group was silent for miles. His brooding face held them quiet. They leaned tiredly against doors, breathed slowly. Then the blue-halter girl, seated next to Rebecca, took Rebecca's hand. "I'm sorry. So sorry," she said.

Rebecca half sobbed. "He wasn't my boyfriend or anything."

"I know."

"I don't even know if he liked me."

"It's okay. It's okay." She, too, sobbed. "Jesus. Crazy men."

In the second car, the young people at first talked only nonsense things, like how hot the seats got in the sun, how they needed air conditioning, but each sentence was cut short, the speaker embarrassed at these futile words. Then they approached David cautiously, little by little.

"I can't believe this. I still can't believe it. Things like this don't happen."

"Twice. Happened twice. That's the crazy thing. Scary as hell."

"Does anyone know his folks? His mother's still alive, isn't she?"

"Who's going to tell her?"

"I'm sick."

Jonathan's girlfriend, next to him in the front seat, leaned her head against his shoulder. He saw his face in the mirror and looked quickly away, at the landscape receding behind them. He flicked on the radio in self-defense, found only strange clicking sounds, no music, and turned it off. He ran his hand over the steering wheel, tried to hum, and found his voice dry and stilled. Behind them, the summer day burned down over a world streaming by, muted, green, its gentle rolling hills crossed by dense trees outlining the river's course. Somewhere hidden it undulated, on and on, miles and miles, years and years ahead.

Signs

———

Lily woke up slowly, her body unhappy, as if she had binged on syrup. The sunlight on the windowpane was too rich a yellow, and she remembered, briefly and vaguely, that an eclipse was occurring sometime soon, maybe today. Whether it was solar or lunar, she couldn't recall, nor the time, but she thought its approach might explain the odd color of the sunlight and the heavy sweet lethargy she herself was experiencing.

After rising, her first act was to flick on the computer and let the impersonal star-studded black fill the screen. She liked floating stars, fake or not. Then she opened a blank document and was rewarded with the immediate, lively appearance of the little paper-clip icon. "You are adorable," she said, and as if hearing her, he leaned forward. His thick black brows raised expectantly, pleasantly, repeatedly. "Yes madam?" the movement suggested. "Yes madam? Anything." She blew him a kiss. He was ever ready to please. "I bet in your off time," she said, "you hang around with pliers." The brows lifted—her timing had been perfect. She was delighted with herself.

From the back porch area came the thumpy rustling of her three dogs.

"When I'm ready," she called.

One of them whined.

She fed them scrambled eggs with dry dog food and shooed them from deck to yard. But they wanted *her*. "I have to work," she said. "I earn our living. Remember?"

She delayed a few more moments, stealing onto the front porch so her creatures would not hear her. She sat down, pressed feet into grass. A person could ache to death from this intensity. From where in heaven did the feeling come?

In an upstairs apartment across the street, one house down from the elementary school, William Lee Harper slept shallowly, groaning and flailing in the heat. Very tall, slim, with heavy bones, he was almost homely: his nose was too large, his hair coarse and long, cut unevenly. But he had a firm jaw and well-defined lips. And his eyes, opening now to stare at the ceiling of an attic apartment, were a beautiful deep blue, soft, intelligent, inquisitive.

He didn't move because he was trying to recall a dream and he didn't want to disturb that part of his mind. But the dream fled, or dissolved—whatever dreams did. All he remembered was that a noise, a *roar*, actually, had taken him by the hand. His hand now missed that contact. He sat up, jotted the brief memory into his notebook, then stood and stretched his arms out sideways. There was no room to raise them in a proper stretch, because the ceiling of his room was shaped like an A and he could stand erect only at its deepest pitch.

In three steps he was at his kitchen table, reaching for the pack of cigarettes near the saltcellar and looking down at the house across the street. There she was. Miss Friendly. Miss Pollyanna. Miss Salt of the Earth. The kind of young woman who probably grew up on a farm, with money and history and health behind her. He placed the cigarette in his lips, struck a match, and remembered: he was trying not to smoke. Even the hot sulfur of the match smelled good, made his throat itch for that first deep inhalation of tobacco. He shook the match out, sat down before the window, and balanced the cigarette on its filter.

He liked watching his neighbor. Though she was sometimes indoors for long periods, she obviously relaxed by puttering around outside. Small, incomplete actions seemed to please her. She would water part of the yard, stop, weed a patch of lawn, hose her bare feet, smoke a cigarette, water again. Once she had attempted to capture something in a small jar and had crawled around for almost an hour, occasionally slapping the jar down, then tilting it carefully.

Now she had gone back inside, and he surveyed the rest of the visible neighborhood, the houses all blues or whites, with high elms and oaks, the leaves multigreen, wires piercing them, squirrels commuting among them all.

He knocked over his cigarette tower, picked it up, breathed that wonderful aroma deep, then inserted the cigarette back in the pack. Sometimes it was good simply to crave.

He gathered his towel and clean clothing. Already sweat ran down the center of his chest. It was going to be a blistering day. Would he ever have air-conditioning? Was his lot poverty? Did he really care? Maybe he was just a bum. Cosmic bum. He went down the folding ladder to the shower on the next floor.

Miles away, zooming directly toward the sunrise, was Dutch van Dyne. Though he had already unloaded his truck and was, in fact, driving only the cab, he was burning to get somewhere. He rolled down both windows of his truck and the air rushed in like water. He opened his mouth to gulp it in. He yelled, halloooed. The damned air smelled female. The earth itself was turning beneath him. He grabbed his CB mike.

"This here's the Dutchman, and I'm here to tell you this is one of God's great days, a most wonderful day, a day for joy and love and praise."

A moment later, a voice cracked over the CB: "Boobs headed west on I-70. Blue Lincoln."

Dutch was miles from I-70, but the notice reminded him of the other side of his nature: he who lived, lusted. He unfolded his hand-lettered sign, SHOW ME YOUR BEAUTIES, and driving with one hand, taped the sign along the bottom of the windshield. Just knowing it was there made him feel inches from a woman and adventure. He blew a thick-lipped, heartfelt kiss toward the sky it-self. "Love you, babe," he said, winking and tilting his head. "Love you to death."

In just a few moments, his religious bent reasserted itself, and he took down the sign. He beamed a gap-toothed smile at his reflection. "This here's a Christian man," he said. "If my part offend me, I'll cut it off." He both felt brave for saying it and regretted saying it. What if he was called upon to honor his word? Nah. God didn't work that way. Still, he uttered aloud, "I didn't mean that."

He was thirty-two years old, a master at jobs taken and failed, longed to be a minister, but acknowledged that a large gap lay between that goal and his nature.

On Lily's computer screen, lists of files dropped down like silver ladders. She opened one, and subfiles descended, silver with blue trim, like so many ladies in the same gown and jewels. A wedding party? A sampling of angels? Having every intention of either working on her thesis or updating her web page—where she sold essays, letters, or other wordsmithing products—she instead opened a blank document so she could study the paperclip guy. Her eyes never got tired of him. How many pixels were behind the little dope? how many frames? She could right-click and have options about his wiry little being, but she didn't. She wanted the mystery. Don Quixote. Cyrano. Yakov. Jean Valjean. Paper clip. Cutey.

From the back porch came a sharp bark and a powerful whimper. "Later!"

On the other side of the block, where college kids tried on personalities and behavior, an adopted dog, now neglected, dug deeply enough under the gate to uncover one edge of malshaped concrete mass wedged there by her latest owner. Delilah, as she was now named, began steadily, rather obsessively, worrying at that exposed edge. An hour later, hot but free, she trotted down the alley, panting, powerful, and wanting to play.

After his shower, William Lee Harper dressed in black jeans and black T-shirt, black socks and black Concord tennis shoes, and walked to the bookstore three blocks away. He was drawn to the comic section, but he didn't give in to that craving. Instead, he remained in the nonfiction section for some time, reading a paragraph or two in a number of books. By this painless approach, he had in high school read more fiction than any students in his peer group and had now a beginning familiarity with the works of Jay Gould, Carl Sagan, Lewis Thomas, and Freeman Dyson. Surprising himself, he carried a Dyson book to the register.

Outside again, a book in hand—a real cash investment in shaping himself—William felt as if he had committed to something important. Maybe practicing a virtue had actually helped him to acquire it? He even felt healthier, capable of breathing more deeply. And the air had cooled, he thought. He examined the sky. It was an odd rosy yellow, like a fertilized egg. William cut through an alley and went to the campus library, fourth floor, green sofa by the west window, read Dyson's fine thoughts till coolness and contentedness led him to sleep. He dreamed about taking action and being quite satisfied about it.

Dutch kept the semi at just enough speed to enter the truck stop safely but forcefully, pleased with the image of his JESUS LOVES YOU sign barreling into the pit of sinners, sinners like himself, of course—he was not self-righteous. Swinging down from the cab, he felt already the familiar onslaught of appetites when he neared food and companionship. He liked the prostitutes, too, adored them, actually; but he didn't really consort with them, not on the level they offered. One was smiling at him now.

"Hey, Ruthy," he said. "Quit aiming those things at me."

Her chortle was warm and melodic. "Keep hoping to knock you low one of these nights."

In bed, she'd probably be a chorus of joy. He would resist the temptation of her as long as he could.

Inside the restaurant door, he paused and scanned the room, smiling for everyone the same. His sharp gaze, though, was identifying the men he knew but hadn't yet hit up for anything, because Dutch, though a man of massive appetites, and right now twenty-eight-hours hungry, had no money and no credit. At two friendly responses, he gave a quick, flat-hand half wave, knowing exactly how that looked. He had meaty arms, really strong, and that impressed both men and women. Too wily to head directly toward potential donors, he headed for the showers, returning moments later still damp, hair slicked but curling anyhow, and his mouth fresh from toothpaste and warm from a genuine smile. He himself would share anything with someone needy, and he saw no harm in expecting the rest of the world to do the same.

He strode up to a booth where two truckers were halfway through their meal. "How's it going?" he said, slap-gripping a handshake with each man. "Where you headed?" He scooted next to the thinnest trucker.

"Michigan," from one.

"Illinois," from the other.

"Missouri," Dutch nodded. "I'm bobcatting. Gonna swing by some friends' places, visit a day or so." He glanced at the plates, quickly up, toward the waitress headed that way. "Steak looks good, but it's more'n I want right now. I'm more sleepy than hungry."

The men had ordered their steaks rare, and with each cut, a red juice seeped and discolored the edge of gravy and mashed potatoes. The man to his left, Morty somethingorother, obviously didn't like bread crust. Dutch picked up a discarded strip, munched it while he winked at the waitress. "Just coffee now, Sugar. Give me a few minutes."

Dutch didn't miss the look exchanged between the two men. They knew exactly his situation. He had intended them to—as he intended them to pretend obliviousness as he was doing. "Food lays heavy when you got a long drive and no time to sleep. I want to get home tonight. I got a personal load and a dock waiting."

The men grinned, not as much as they would have earlier, but enough. It was all going to be okay. He munched the rest of the bread crust while they talked about the boobs-on-70 call.

"I'm not going to risk my schedule just for a look, not even at a whole naked woman," one said.

"Me neither, but they sure can spice up a dull route. Wish they'd line up across that Texas panhandle."

"Give'em a reason to," Dutch said, looking outside where trucks were crossing over and under the intersection. It made him almost remember something that could be important. "Most people will respond to a genuine desire."

The trucker named Morty took out a worn wallet stuffed with bills. He extracted a five, showed it to his buddy.

"I'll add a couple bills. She kept an eye on us."

"Never mind. I got it."

"Well, God be with you, gents," he said, and stood so the man next to him could exit the booth. Then he sat back down, but sideways, as if waiting for the girl to come clear the table.

"Some other time," Morty said. The two walked away.

Dutch shifted himself to sit properly, but he didn't touch anything. He ran his fingers along the table trim on either side of the plates. When Morty came back, scooped up the bills and said, "We'll just give these to her on our way out," Dutch was offended, not ashamed. "Your money was safe here," he returned. There were rules. In Dutch's opinion, the real transgressor was Morty, who had distrusted an honest man.

Delilah trotted first down the alley, nosing into driveways and trashcans, urinating in the sight of other dogs. Occasionally she nosed the ground fervidly and then thrashed around on the spot, as if coating herself with special odors. Sleek black, large, muscular and graceful, she wove through the neighborhood, lapping from lawn-water overflow, testing trash paper and scraps. Not one can was disturbed, though, as if thus far the urge to eat was secondary to the urge to investigate wildly. Coming to the end of the alley, she turned north, then back west, eyeing tricycles, children, lawnmower, cats, squirrels. Now she trotted a bit sideways, fluid and precise, like a show animal.

William, still in the cool library, read and watched people. He admired almost everyone he saw, even people his own age, whether nerds, Goths, mainstream, overachievers, black, white, male or female. Each person was a character and was writing for himself a story and any story was worth reading by someone, William figured, even his own. But with only one life allotted, he was rather duty bound to choose one with some fire, passion, drama—if, that is, choice entered anywhere. Left to chance, he'd probably marry an ordinary woman, much like himself—respectful and goodhearted, with desires to be or to experience something beautiful. But with choice?

For a while he practiced shifting from the perception of an intellectual to the perception of a dunce and to various other perceptions, some rather tasteless. The latter did not please him, and as he left the campus, he noted that the roles he had assumed had affected the very air around him. Certainly it had changed, as had the lighting. One's mind was nothing to toy with: think on the highest level or be condemned to live on the lowest. He moved slowly, feeling as if he had stepped into a warp and must be careful.

Lily leashed up the three dogs, became twice entangled in the strips of leather until she screamed, "Sit," and the three obeyed, quivering completely, but trying to keep buttocks to the floor. She extricated herself, put the tiniest dog, who insisted on being the leader, in the center, allowed it a twelve-inch extension beyond the others, and struck off down the sidewalk.

"You guys aren't enough," she said. "You're wonderful one and all, but you just aren't enough." Now the dapple light she always enjoyed, the bright sun through moving, many-leafed branches, seemed sad and almost ominous, not at all steady or warm. Why did gardens cool? Though past lunchtime, Lily still felt as if the world were changing, as if dawn were only now occurring.

An unease shuddered through Lily. Nothing about her had been normal since she arose. Maybe this wariness was a premonition. Maybe this was second sight! What was first sight? She stumbled along, pulled like a sled over rough terrain. She adored her pets, adored all animals. Not only was she guilty of being healthy and bored while most of the world suffered hunger, violence, pestilence, and struggles she didn't even know existed, but she also fed hamburgers and grilled cheese sandwiches to domesticated wolves. Okay. To dogs. And cats. And she grieved over abused gorillas, chimps, orangutans—whatever save-the-creature cause was displayed on television or spammed on computer. There was no discretion to her compassion, no moral hierarchy. She should help humans! She was ashamed of herself.

"Quit dragging me around," she panted to her companions who were now nose to the ground, straining and wheezing to force her speedily up the incline.

Maybe she was losing natural feeling because of her obsessive time on computers. But the whole world was on computers now, on screens. Commercials were fast blips of multipictures and sounds. Infants danced, sang. Dogs talked, conspired. Cartoons and humans had merged!

Didn't she love her paperclip buddy? A cyberspace wire! She had actually hesitated to exit her computer sometimes because he might feel hurt. Absurd! Absurd! What could a paperclip feel? Much less a representation of a paperclip, nothing but pixels, each boring by itself. Unless, that is, each pixel was a star in another universe? When one emptied a computer's trash, where did all the information go? What if that trash had substance, matter, and everyone on the planet was dumping trashed ideas into the future. Humans would suffocate in their own refuse, litter the mind of God himself.

"Goddamn!" she said aloud, jerking back on the leashes so that all three animals took warning and sat still for a command. "Slow down," she said, and the recognized gentleness in her voice urged them on, though they didn't quite pick up their earlier speed. She had frightened herself into almost immobility. Now the color and texture of the air were changing again and even shadows seemed odd, like they were subtly mutating. She thought home might be the best place for her and hers. Home right away! "Let's go, fellows," she said, though two of the dogs were female. "We've had it." Now she was the one with the rapid pace and they strung out beside and behind her.

Dutch, leaving the restaurant, his body fortified with a little food and free coffee, had given a ride to a skinny cowboy who surprised him, at the next major town, with a twenty dollar bill along with a drawled "thanks." Everything about the day thus far had suggested to Dutch that a portentous event was imminent. The air was rich and heavy, though no clouds marked the expanse of solid, lowering, oddly pink sky. Maybe God was talking to him. Dutch had begun driving exactly in the direction of the sun, barreling right into his destiny with all good faith. He was a pioneer, a cowboy, a saint.

William was at the intersection near his attractive neighbor's house, waiting on the pedestrian "walk" sign. He was simultaneously watching, though, activity almost a block beyond which seemed to be the lovely neighbor walking her dogs. They made a ragged troop, and she kept looking over her shoulder as if someone or something were annoying her. William rushed the light a little and reached the other side just as a red semi, with frame but no trailer, cut the turn short and seemed near to jackknifing.

"Jesus," William said. "Run me over."

It kept traveling, pulled into the grade school lot across the street, and stopped. Across the front, blazoned JESUS LOVES YOU. Out the door came a thickset, muscular dude with a mass of tousled blond hair. He rubbed his palms over his hair and ran, quite gracefully, toward the woman's two-story blue house and rang the doorbell. Waiting, he half turned to grin and wave at William, as though he knew him.

"She's out walking her dogs," William said, indicating with a nod the direction from which she was approaching. "She'll be back pretty soon."

"I got all the time in the world."

William didn't know about this. The stranger's confidence was too much, the presence too solid, like the guy would get in the house and never leave. He didn't even question William's knowledge about her whereabouts. There was a dissipation about the man, too, as if he'd gone to the extremes of himself and might burst or something. William felt uneasy—for the woman, and for himself. After all, he dared not interfere. Nothing was happening. Yet. If it did, this guy could kill him in short order, could rip raw meat from bones just with his teeth, probably smiling all the while. This guy was evolution in retrograde. William decided to speed up a little and intercept the woman's return with a little forewarning. Now everything seemed to be edgy, dangerous. He could swear the light and shade had altered imperceptibly.

A quick repeated yelping turned his attention back to his neighbor, and William identified the problem. Another dog was following the young woman and her own creatures. It was a tall, dark, and very lean dog, maybe a Doberman mix? Wide head. Rottweiler mix? Pit bull. Damn. The woman was slowing her walk, reining her animals in closer. The little one, though, the yelper, the crazy friendly and bossy tiny bitch, was trying to go backward. She wanted some of that big dog. Let her at him. Good for her, William thought. The woman should get that tiny brave animal home fast. Save the critter. Too late. The small dog had broken loose, was running pell-mell toward the big one. Behind William, footsteps could be no other than the blond stranger, so William ran, too, from what followed and toward what waited. Just when the woman screamed and the dogs barked and the small dog yipped high and long and painful, William and the other man arrived.

The big dog had the tiny squirming one by the throat, had it down on the sidewalk, was keeping it totally immobile, and was doing this without apparent effort or concern. It was impassive, steady strength.

"Is that blood?" from Lily. "It's blood."

"Get a hammer," said Dutch, lunging forward just as William did.

William was already bending over the brute. One hand gripped skin and muscle at the shoulders, the other at the rise of hips, and he jerked up, up, up, and up. At the last, the dog was above him, feet extended toward the sky, and amazingly balanced. "Get the pup in the house," William screamed. "I can't hold this thing."

"I got it," Dutch said. "Just let it go. I'm right here."

Lily was sitting on the ground now, the pup on her lap looking simultaneously wild-eyed and dazed. "There's blood," Lily said. She pushed back the hair along the dog's throat. "But not much. Not much. Maybe . . ."

"It's coming down," William said. "Get out of the way."

With the pup under one arm, Lily scrambled up and ran a few feet away. Dutch raised his arms to help guide the descent of the brute, but he could do nothing. Once William's arms were shuddering, the upheld creature began struggling and came down at once, not smoothly, fell thump on its side, sprang up, and now focused on this street, sauntered off as if she were no dog's enemy. Lily still had the pup, who wanted down, down. "I am so glad," Lily said, "that you guys came along. I don't know what would have happened."

"Actually," Dutch said, "I didn't do anything. The kid did." He realized the word choice wasn't right. "I mean this guy here. Your friend. He . . . had the situation well in hand." Dutch smiled.

William was now appreciative of this crazy trucker. "Not totally. It came down sooner than I wanted."

"But didn't hang around to test you."

"No," William nodded. "And good thing, too, right? For both of us."

The men were happy with each other, which pleased Lily. She didn't know why, except that male camaraderie had its own mystique and she loved romance. "Look at this," she said, gripping more tightly her squirming dog. "She wants down again. Can you believe it? She almost gets killed and . . ."

"Put her in the house," William said, as if he had the right to make the suggestion and might even be familiar with the house. "I'll get the others."

Lily almost didn't comply, because who in the hell was this odd bird anyhow? Who the hell was either one of them?

"I am grateful," she said.

"You live in that blue house?" from the trucker.

"I do."

"I knew a gal lived there a few years back."

Lily could have said "lucky gal," but she didn't because she was observing the tall, younger man now jog after the other dogs. He had an easy grace. He was so lean. And his hair, jet black and thick. Rich hair.

"That your fellow?" Dutch said.

Lily made a noncommittal sound, like a clipped hum. "You're a preacher?" she asked, indicating the wide proclamation across Dutch's cab.

"Great sign, isn't it? People see me coming."

"I'm certainly glad you came."

They both watched the group approaching, William in the front, Lily's other two dogs on either side of him, as if flanking the attack. And in the rear, some yards behind, Delilah. Now part of the gang.

"My God," Lily breathed. "He's bringing back that killer."

"He doesn't even know it," Dutch said. "Better warn him."

Lily ran to her house, thrust the now yelping mass of tiny, indignant dog into the living room, slammed the door shut, and, turning, saw William telling the strange dog to go. William had one arm out, one finger pointing, and his command was evident. He strode firmly toward the creature, and it side-ran a few feet. It obviously did not fear him. Lily's two had circled back to re-identify, in their special way, the outcast.

"Come," William ordered those two and walked toward Lily's with no more backward glances. She was at the screen door and opened it for him and the two travelers. The little one tried to push out, but William scooped it up. Across the street, the odd trucker was standing, one foot in the truck, one on the guard, one hand on the mirror. He could have been a pilot or a captain. He waved goodbye and blew a kiss.

Both Lily and William felt warm at that gesture though neither mentioned it.

The strange dog was, foolishly, inexplicably, worrying at the door. It wanted in.

Lily locked the screen door.

"Dogs can't open screen doors," William said.

"Who knows for sure," Lily responded.

While Lily washed her hands and fixed coffee, William carefully checked the brave dog for injuries. The other two helped until he opened the back door and shooed them into the fenced yard. Then he tore off a strip of paper towel, moistened it with warm water, and wiped down the cuts. "If that stray had wanted to take her out," he said, "it could have. It was just establishing dominance."

"Damned scary way of doing it," Lily said, though she had thought of that herself.

"They have to be scary. Otherwise, it doesn't work."

Just then the little dog ran from the kitchen, scrabbled across the wooden floor of the dining room, barking mightily at the screen door.

Both William and Lily followed. Dutch's truck was turning onto this street again, its neon sign glowing fiercely orange instead of red. With an immense whooshing sound, the truck stopped. Dutch came striding around the cab, opened the passenger door and whistled loud and bell clear.

Delilah bounded from the porch, bounded toward him, and bounded into the front seat.

Dutch waved again as if this had been a designated time and place for this particular event. Then he hurried around the cab, released the brakes like a heavy sigh, and eased the truck away. "You hungry, kiddo?" Dutch said. "I'll see what I can round up." He and his dog, Delilah, each felt, in totally individual ways, that this was a most wonderful moment, full of hope like a door into every possibility.

William and Lily felt the same. He was taken with the light touch of red in her hair, the tilt of her nose. Somewhere in his memory was a description of a beloved heroine who was exactly like Lily, or what Lily would be to him. Lily found herself smiling at his quaint being. He had a gentle expression, good humor certainly underlying it. He winked at her when she said something witty, and she gasped at the familiar response. It couldn't be. No way. Icons were icons and men were men.

The sun was setting, and its rays fell right down that street, a street lined with old houses, odd-shaped yards, creatures making adjustments for wires and vehicles and neighbors and rare occurrences.

Alvie and the Rapist

Alvie had always been a storyteller, though she didn't always tell the stories aloud, and the rapist had always been a rapist though he didn't attack a woman till he was sixteen. Alvie began telling stories to almost everyone when she was seventeen, by which time she had difficulty distinguishing between dreams and doings. The rapist killed his first woman the month he turned twenty-one, quite by accident. He clipped her chin, but somehow her nose, too, and some kind of bone pierced her brain.

The rapist lived two blocks south of Alvie, but he didn't know her. He saw her, though, off and on for some years. When she took to coming home late at night, strolling or scurrying or sauntering along the streetlit walk, he would squint dark eyes through the parting of his lace curtains and narrow the very sight of her.

Oblivious to window-eyes, Alvie fought and won battles in the twilight and darklight hours.

"I felt like God was in the top of the tree," Alvie told her doctor.

"And what made you think that?"

"I guess it was the moon, sorta stabbed on a branch, you know, and I thought it was God."

"Actually, Alvie, you know it wasn't God, don't you? And that the moon wasn't stabbed."

"But it's a lovely image, isn't it? Stabbing the moon, impaling God on a tree in the dark of the moon."

"Yes, it is lovely. You should write, Alvie, as I've told you before."

"No, I shouldn't. People might find it, keep it."

"And then what would happen."

"Terrible things."

"What?"

"You know. I couldn't change the ending."

The rapist knew he would get Alvie, and he liked the surety of it, that he could take this one anytime, that he had this one in reserve, like on store, a cache, a hidden sock-you-dead-baby when his cupboard was empty. He thought maybe he wouldn't ever need to grab one again, because look at his restraint—wasn't he saving her daily, when she could be rolling dead? He was, man, her savior, all things considered. He granted her life nightly. Virtue too, come to think of it. *He* gave it to her, or granted it, at least. "I grant you virtue," he said from his window and thought she heard him. At least she stopped still and stared at the streetlight.

"There's a cross in my abdomen," Alvie said, "and don't you write that down. You *know* you're not supposed to write any of this down."

"I wasn't. I was noting the date and time. That's all."

"Even that may be dangerous."

"I always do it."

"Then maybe that's why I'm not better. Maybe that's why I have this pain."

"Where's the pain?"

"Here." Alvie drew one finger from the area of her navel to her groin and then across. "Like a samurai death, only it's really this cross in there—I'm not mixing my stories. I can feel it. It hurts."

"We could schedule an x-ray."

"No thank you."

"You want the cross to be in there, don't you?"

"No. But it won't show up in an x-ray."

"And why not?"

"You think he would admit to doing such a thing?"

"You mean God, of course."

"Yes. He does that, you know. Makes things and keeps them secret."

"How did he put it in there?"

"From the streetlight. I saw this light-cross and when it moved, I stepped back but it just shot down into my abdomen."

"Have you been going to movies, Alvie?"

"You told me not to."

"I know."

"I just learn from real life."

The rapist took much delight in appearing on the walk when Alvie was out roaming. She was the homeliest creature. Did she know to what value he had raised her? Her skin was grainy, her black hair thin and limp. She had a touch of mustache; her brow sloped ape-like, ending in bush brows with little space above her nose. Ugly, ugly, ugly. To rape her would be a favor to her; to save her was a tribute to the unworthy.

"Hello," he said once as he passed her, and she hunched to the edge of the walk.

He could feel her black-point eyes on his back. Such gratitude. If he slammed her face in the mud, she might respond better next time.

"He's afraid of me," Alvie said.

"God?"

She nodded. "He's got someone watching me all the time."

"Why?"

"I don't know. You think he has to have a reason? Maybe it's the cross."

"You still have that pain?"

"I'm used to it. I hug it. That'll teach him. Curse me and I'll love it."

"How do you know someone's watching you?"

"I've seen him. He wants me to see him. He's teasing me."

"Where have you seen him?"

"At night, wherever I go. He likes to surprise my eyes. He steps out real quick, you know?

"What's he look like, this agent of God?"

"Handsome. Very. He's going to hurt me."

"How do you know?"

"When doesn't he? You know history as well as I do. Probably better. You write everything down when I leave, don't you?"

"Has someone really been watching you, Alvie? Really?"

"Really."

"Because if that's true, you should tell the police."

"Ha!"

"I mean it. You should give them a description. You can describe him, can't you?"

"Sure. He looks like Jesus. Long red hair, red beard. Thin. Got these god-awful eyes, like he hurts everywhere, hurts worse than I do."

The rapist couldn't bear it, bear it, bear it, that she wouldn't look grateful, servile, frightened. She mocked him. That's what she did. Whenever she saw him, she smiled, dipped stupid ugly squat curtsies, ran that pink tongue over her hairy lip. So would he grace her with his presence? with the sign of his being? No. Let her wonder where he was, where he had gone to. Silently he would come, like a thief in the night, and then? Oh, she would repent. She would repent all right. He had so many ways to bring her to her knees.

"He wants me to be afraid," Alvie said. "He's hiding in black like a shadow so I won't know it's him."

"The man who's following you?"

"Yes. God. He wants to rape me and make Jesus again."

"If a man is really following you, Alvie, you must report it. I'll report it if you like."

"No. This is my story. Don't you tell any of it."

"Why would God want to make Jesus again?"

"Because the first time didn't work. That's why he put the cross in my belly. He's getting ready."

"Ready for?"

"To plant his little seed of sacrifice again. It's okay with me."

"You don't mean that. You don't want to be raped, do you? Not really."

"No woman has ever wanted to be raped."

"You're being evasive. You haven't actually answered my question."

"Yes I have."

The rapist wished he could fly. He wanted to stand on the height of a building and swoop down on the ugly dwarf, plummet her into the ground with the point of himself. He settled for a cape and practiced fluttering the black silk with slight movements of his arms. Then he swept down the stairs, along the street. Ah, he was fine, he knew, just hear the rustle of evil, the whisper of justice. He stopped beyond the cone of streetlight, beneath drooping branches, and breathed the thick scent of night leaves and coming pain. He was so happy that she came as he knew she would, so delighted to watch the heavy plodding of his monkey-girl, oh come-to-poppa sweet ugly one, heaven awaits you. She seemed to pause when she reached the edge of dark, so he knew she wanted him, and he ran forward, jerked her up into the shadows with moon dripping white on her ghastly face. She made grunting noises, hideous sounds. Then he felt this delicious, hot surprise and thought perhaps the grunting came from him. He didn't know how she managed to be squatting next to him, crooning.

"That was God in the tree, and he died. I was right all along."

"What makes you think it was God after all?"

"Because the other one died, too."

"The man who looked like Jesus?"

"That one."

"How did he die?"

"On the cross."

"The one inside you?"

"Yes." Alvie placed both hands on her stomach. "Here."

"How could it kill him?"

"It didn't. That's just where he died."

"What did kill him?"

"Silver. A little piece of silver."

"I suppose you mean thirty pieces?"

"You're trying to do it again. One piece of silver. One."

"Are you telling a story, Alvie?"

"Yes."

"Are you making it up?"

"No. He made it up. He kissed my palm. I put my hand over his moan and he kissed my palm. I liked that. I liked that very much. The moon cut us into a thousand pieces and he ran red on all the shadows."

"You had a knife, didn't you? Was that the piece of silver? Did someone try to rape you and you killed him?"

"Can God be killed?"

"Not God in the sense of an immortal being."

"Then I didn't kill God. But nobody rapes me."

"Why are you holding your hands on your stomach?"

"I'm certainly not going to tell you."

"I'm pretty sure I understand anyway. I hope not, but I suspect I do."

"Ha!" Alvie stood up and leaned over the desk. She took the tablet and pencil, then returned to the chair. Her black eyes had a different cast, lustrous, rather sad and gentle. She closed them.

"Alvie. Tell me what you're thinking. We have to work together if you're to get well."

Alvie was listening to the most wonderful story, a perfect one, a circle one like the world was circle. It would go on forever and ever and she could change it if she wanted because it was all her story. In the beginning there was no word and no word was God. In the beginning was Alvie, a person, a person Alvie was the beginning.

Brute

___

When I entered college, my father bought a small house for me, in an older, poorer neighborhood close to campus, where many of the residents were students. The block was small and divided lengthwise by a narrow, dirt alley. Since only one property was fenced, the yards spilled into one another, especially at night, when people gathered outside, or took walks, or cut across lawns. It was a dimly lit, warm neighborhood, quiet and harmonious.

The house was my father's attempt to provide me independence. I could choose housemates, or not, and keep whatever rent they paid. I earned extra money by helping my father train hunting dogs. He had always raised dogs, and his methods had, by default, become my own. In my backyard was a decent sized kennel, with bales of straw for windbreak and scattered straw for comfort. We didn't abuse animals, but we didn't pamper them, either. They would be sold to hunters, and for their own good they had to be oblivious to inclement weather, and anxious both to exercise their natural abilities and to please their masters. The latter was most important—a good dog should run his fine heart out if not called off the chase.

Across the alley, three black, medium-sized mutts were owned by a couple of retired professors. As the day wore on, the mutts would worry the back gate, yap intermittently, until the couple emerged, leashes in hand, ready to be tugged around by canine joy and enthusiasm. The sight of such freedom made my animals whine with longing. They didn't get neighborhood hikes, but they did get brief tussles in the yard and well-spaced hours of obedience training. Twice a week, I took them to my father's place. They were given the fields and woods and moonrise. They could roil up rapture and then sleep it off.

The new dog may have been in our neighborhood a day or so before my housemates and I saw him. We were playing horseshoes.

"Look at that critter," Jonathan said, then sighted, flicked the horseshoe, and spun a ringer. "Match that, Leo."

In the yard adjoining the old couple's, sat a huge, honey-colored dog, watching us intently.

I matched Jonathan's ringer and got another one. When I picked up my horseshoes, I strolled across the alley for a better look.

The new dog didn't bark. He didn't move, not even his tail. He was short-haired, with enormous eyes and a droopy mouth. The deep chest suggested boxer, the broad head, pit bull, the sloppy posture, Lab. But the overall impression was Great Dane, the gentle giant. I judged his height to be 36 inches, his weight to be 90 pounds. With his frame, he should have been at least 120.

A heavy chain draped from his collar and led to a pipe beside the house.

My buddies had joined me.

"Jesus," B. J. said. "That thing's got pit bull in it."

"You guys are agitating it." I turned away, easy, so the dog wouldn't misinterpret exit for flight. Fear excites most creatures.

Jonathan clanked his horseshoes, and I glanced back. The dog hadn't moved from his position, but his muscles had drawn tight. His eyes were fixed on Jonathan.

"Don't startle him, Jonathan. He's got enough trouble."

A couple of seconds later, just as I stepped onto the alley and was a short distance in front of the others, I heard a lighter clank. Jonathan, testing the dog, or himself.

Before bedtime, I came back out alone to check on my current animals, both redbone hounds. The female, Jenny, liked to overturn the water pan—any pan, actually. I refilled it, talked low to her and her buddy for a short time. When I closed the kennel gate, I felt something watching me. The new dog was perfectly visible in the July moonlight.

"You want some attention, too?"

The house behind him was dark. I couldn't see a water bowl and didn't recall seeing one earlier, so I crossed on over. He was right with me, but inches away, not nuzzling.

There was no pan anywhere.

"Water you'll get. One minute."

He followed me the extent of his chain.

When I returned moments later, carrying a battered enamel pan and a bucket of water, he quivered, but he didn't make a sound. My dogs did, low whines with a clear message: Not him, not him. Us. Us. Us.

He lapped the water so madly that the pan moved from the energy and he walked with it. He emptied it. His thirst angered me, though not at him. I filled the pan again and he drank a little more, as if to assure himself more was possible. Then he sat on his haunches. He was asking and I assumed he had been taught to do so.

I brought a scoop of dog food over and dumped it at his feet—at his nose, actually, since he was eating before the pellets had cleared the scoop. He probably could have eaten ten times as much, but I didn't test him. Overfeeding him and petting him would have been tantamount to stealing him. One man shouldn't interfere with another man's training.

In my house, Jonathan was asleep on the sofa. B. J. was on the phone—his girlfriend liked to be called right before he went to bed.

My room was in the rear of the house, with two windows to the outside. When I was undressed and the light off, I raised a blind so the moonlight fell across my bed. I like the night sky when it's sharp, when it's dense with stars. No wonder dogs bay and wolves howl. Some feelings have to be expressed.

The next morning, I started to check on the new dog but saw it wasn't necessary. The female professor was in the neighbor's yard, standing out of the dog's reach and tossing something to him. He was snapping it up as fast as she could toss it. She was crooning like women do to creatures they intend to tame. Just before I struck out for campus—a half block's walk—I saw the old gent leaving the back gate, carrying a pitcher of water.

"I saw the fellow that owns that dog," B. J.'s girlfriend said. "He was getting out of his car in front. I know him, too." She popped three pistachios into her mouth and continued talking while chewing. "He was in Darby Hall and got kicked out for selling dope and for having—guess what—a *python* in his room. A *real* python. Albino, too. Pure white sick slime."

"Snakes aren't slimy," I said. "They're dry."

"Slimy can mean more than touch," she smiled. "It's an attitude."

We didn't like each other. But she was right.

"Drugs," B. J. said. "That's it, then. That's why he's got a pit bull staked out in his back yard. It's on-site protection."

"It's not a pit bull," I said. "It's mostly Great Dane and Lab. Labs have evolved to remain teenagers, as some humans have done."

B. J. grinned, and so did Jonathan, each believing the statement described the other, or perhaps they believed it suited me. They were both smart, but B. J. was easy going and Jonathan tended toward cruelty, subtle at best.

"That makes sense to me," Jonathan said. "The guy's got the dog—Lab or bull or whatever—in the backyard, to deter misfits such as a feeble-minded burglar, and the python on the inside to deter the persistent, smarter intruder."

"Such as you," I said.

"And you, who might nose around for a higher purpose than burglary."

"I don't lightly invade property or privacy."

He didn't respond. We both knew he would invade anything for a thrill. Jonathan couldn't bear being bored. He might have been a gladiator in years past, but more likely would have trained them, to watch them kill each other. I had decided he wouldn't be rooming with me after that summer. I had told him I needed to vacate the place and upgrade it for renting. He got the drift. Upgrade the renters, too, I meant.

"I don't care what he's got," I said, "as long as he doesn't abuse the animal."

"The new guy's about six foot seven," this, from the pistachio eater. "And handsome." She cupped pistachios toward her mouth. B. J. kissed her while her mouth was full.

I lay down in my room for a while. It was a hunting night, and I had to take Jenny and Will out to my dad's. He was going to run them with our oldest and best, a full nighttime run, competition and grace. Good life. Fresh air. No people. Sky. Life. Hope.

When I loaded up the pups, the new dog was at attention. The line of his body said, "Me too?" The pan I'd left was still there. I hoped it had water in it, because now I was trapped. If I checked, he'd think he got to go for a ride with us and would moon and low for the rest of the night. Jenny and Will would madden the neighborhood over their delay. Surely the professors had seen to it the dog had water. Besides, the house lights were on, so the owner truly bore the duty.

A couple of miles down the road, I used my cell phone to call my own house and got Jonathan. He said sure, he'd check out the water pan. He wasn't afraid. "If nothing else," he said, "I'll hook the pan with a rake, fill it, and scoot it back to the old boy."

"Don't, for God's sake, approach him with a rake in your hand. I'll just come back."

"Nope. I got it. I got it. You go on."

But I went back and found Jonathan still in the middle of the alley between our houses, the brute seated in his sphinx position, Jonathan with a plastic coke bottle full of water. I took the bottle, walked up to the dog, and poured the water into his pan. It hadn't been completely dry. A hot breath might have finished off the moisture, but someone had watered him once during the day.

"Hey, man," Jonathan asserted. "I was doing it."

"I know."

"And without a rake, too. Just me and him."

"I know. Thanks. You know me. I got a burr going and had to check."

"Next time, I won't bother to help."

I drove out of the alley, zoomed into the albino owner's driveway, right behind an old red sports car, and left the motor running while I pounded on the door. I could see him rise from his sofa and see also what he left behind—a cute, black-haired girl, real thin, one tiny breast visible before she pulled closed her unbuttoned shirt.

He was most definitely tall. He had to bend down to step outside with me.

I explained that his dog must be knocking over his water pan, because it was dry, and that I had actually furnished the pan. It was a politic way of correcting someone—offering an explanation that couldn't be true, but that both parties accept in order to move ahead. He thanked me, after a fashion. A lot of "yeah, man." He explained that the dog chewed up plastic dishes, and the big metal ones were expensive. He was pushing a new job and working long hours. He had to travel, too. He had an ex-wife and she needed help moving, and . . . stuff like that.

"You are feeding the animal, aren't you?" I asked.

"Oh yeah, man. Every morning. Whenever I eat, he eats, too. We're buddies. I probably won't have him long, though. My ex wants him. Protection, you know. Her living alone and all."

In the crack of the door, the girl now stood. I wondered if she liked snakes. And I wondered where in the hell he kept the python.

I nodded toward her for courtesy and went on to the truck. Jenny and Will were now in total joy. We were moving in the right direction. They slobbered happiness all over my truck bed.

The dog was starving. Plainly. If the guy fed him, he did it under cover of darkness and in forms that would be totally consumed, not a crumb or smear left on a grass blade. I was saved from interfering by the two older neighbors, the professors. Apparently they had adopted the brute. A large yellow dishpan appeared by a volunteer tree, as if the sparse leaves could shade it. Nearby was a shallow, immensely round pan, obviously for easy dining. The couple, singly or together, moved without hesitation from their yard to the dog's. He stood at the sight of them. He ignored me, now. His gaze was most often on the professors' backyard. And the professors' dogs stopped yapping when their owners visited next door. The new dog didn't get to join on the walks, though. As far as I knew, he had not yet been unchained even for a brief romp.

Yes, that was cruelty. And, yes, I knew it.

"I've been thinking," Jonathan announced, "about letting that dog next door go. The pit bull? I'll just unchain him."

"And what will that do?"

"He can be free."

"To get hit by a car? starve to death? go to the pound and be euthanized in a week's time?"

"At least I'm worried about it. And I don't even like dogs."

He cocked one eyebrow at me, clicked tongue-against-cheek, and left for class.

My philosophy is that you don't bother anyone unless you have to. You hint, you give advice, you help unobtrusively, but you don't act unless you're ready to follow it to the end. That means an end such as fighting till blood drips, calling authorities and testifying on paper and by word, in private and before the world. You don't make little half-ass jabs that are less than dignified and may be dangerous for everybody.

The old couple had bought themselves a world of hurt, because now the dog trusted them. Now they were responsible. They couldn't skip a day or a night, couldn't take a trip. They couldn't stop. And the fellow, the owner, knew it. Maybe he couldn't or wouldn't verbalize the situation, but he understood it. He counted on it. He had probably learned it as an infant and had used it from the moment he intuited that his will could act on the world.

I, of course, had let the old couple assume my responsibility as well. So was I acting like the long legged snake? Maybe.

But a light, persistent rap at my back door changed my direction. It was night, about eight, before the real dark set in, and very hot. The lady professor had done the knocking; the old guy was squatting by Jenny and Will's pen, rubbing their noses and talking in a low voice. Across the way, the brute was up, watching us.

"I was wondering," she said, "if you would mind talking to the man who owns that dog." She turned and pointed, as if perhaps I hadn't noticed him before. "I know," she continued, "that you take care of your animals. And since you're a young man, he might listen to you. He's not going to listen to us. Obviously. And the dog's not too easy to feed. He gets excited and that chain is heavy." She looked at her ankle.

I eased on outside, so she'd know she had my full attention. "I've seen you taking him food," I said.

"We've called the authorities, too. But the man who came by, the animal patrol or whatever, says he has to talk with the owner first, unless the animal is obviously being abused. And of course the dog always has water and food because we see to it. So far, the animal patrol can't catch the man at home. We would have to leave the dog without food and water long enough for it to look like a real problem. We can't do that."

She looked sad, defeated.

"I'll talk to the guy," I said, "but I can tell you he won't change. He may act better for a day or two, maybe even a week. But a person who mistreats an animal doesn't care for animals. Every time he has a choice, the dog won't come first."

She was older than my mother, perhaps older than my grandmother, but she reminded me of one of my past girlfriends, and reminded me, too, of the girl I'd seen in my neighbor's living room, the dark-haired one with her blouse unbuttoned. All women remind me of other women. They share traits, no matter how different they appear to be.

"But you *will* talk to him."

"I said I would."

"Good." She walked toward her own yard and crooned, "no, no, I'm not coming, no, no" at the straining dog watching her every move. "No, no, no."

Now I had accepted the problem. I had let the old woman offer it, and I had taken it. I owned it. I stayed in the back yard awhile, studying the house across the alley. It was like studying a lair, maybe just letting my senses absorb what they could, start that subconscious game plan that is part of each human's survival kit, know it or not.

"I saw our dignified lady friend outside," Jonathan said, when I did go in. "And I bet I know the subject matter."

"What about the outcome, Jonathan, my man? You know that too?"

He held my gaze a minute. "Now I do," he said. "Written in blood, it is. Yours. Racing around true and confined and anxious. Anxious."

I laughed. In a way, he was right. I enjoy restrained, necessary violence. Maybe I do. Maybe I just enjoy believing I enjoy. No one can be certain of much anymore. We've been analyzed and coded into rigidity.

"She wants me to ask him to treat the dog right. She thinks man to man might make a difference."

"Yeah! You're one man. Who's the other?"

Jonathan understood.

When the moon came up and the loser's house was still dark, I cut up through his yard, petting Brute on my way, and then crossed the main street, so I could watch the front of the house without feeling like a lurker. I sat on the retaining wall of the elementary school, thought about cigarettes—Jonathan sometimes smoked and it seemed pleasurable. I thought, too, about the town itself. I liked it. The tiny traffic lights, narrow streets, patches of cobblestone, old remains of grand houses. Old men who felt superior to anybody in the world, even young men. Restaurants that served portions for the seniors and the juniors as if anyone in the middle would ever set foot in the place to order something else. Churches galore—spires so sharp and frequent maybe they held up the sky, maybe they held up the past and the future. My dad wanted me to be a lawyer. I wasn't sure what I wanted.

Outside town were lakes and ponds. Rolling hills. At night, one drove down into mist and came up into moonlight.

The neighbor hadn't come home by 2:00 a.m. I went to bed. At six, I was back. He still wasn't home. I left a note in the old couple's mailbox, telling them I was looking for the guy and would take care of things. They weren't to worry about it anymore. Then I had classes to attend, assignments to complete, and Jenny and Will, eager always for the next event.

"He's home," Jonathan announced the next evening, coming in from a sunset jog. "The red car's in the driveway and the girl is visible through the windows if," he peeled off a wet T-shirt, "one looks intently." He headed for the hallway. "Wait for me," he said. "I want to go with you. So does B. J. Is he here?"

"No."

He came back to the doorway. "Then let's wait till tomorrow. B. J. wants to be in on it."

"In on what? I'm just going to tell the guy to take care of his animal."

"Or what?" Jonathan's facial expression, and his posture, too, was one big "Well?"

"I don't know what."

"Exactly. But if three of us are there, the what is most definitely implied."

"I'm not trying to start anything here," I said. "I want to keep it low key."

"I don't want to start anything either. I plan to finish it. One swoop—key, kit, and caboodle." He shut the bathroom door behind him.

I left before he could tag along.

The girl opened the neighbor's door. She was petite and kind of perfect in all ways.

When I asked if her boyfriend was home, he emerged, as if he had been hiding—and no doubt he had been.

"You still worried about my dog?" he offered, all lanky and lazy, like we were friends. "I been feeding him regular. Water, too. He just bolts it all. Ask Sarah. You can't fill him up."

She had retreated to the sofa and had hidden most of her sweet self by clutching a decorative pillow.

"Keep me out of this," she said.

"He always dumped his food on the ground anyhow," the guy continued, "and he chewed up the last bowl. I just put his food on the ground."

"I don't want to argue with you. And I'm not going to. But if you leave him without food and water one more time, I'm going to turn you in to the authorities. And I won't stop with the first authority." I said this as calmly as possible, because tone can make any animal react.

"I told you," he said, "about my ex-wife? She wants him. It's just taking her awhile to get settled in. He'll be gone soon." He was lying. He had no concern at all and was amused by mine.

I turned to leave, but he stopped me with "Wait a minute. I want to show you something." I heard the girl say, "Don't," and he laughed from somewhere beyond the door. Then he was opening the screen door and ducking to come outside. "Look at this. See my new buddy."

With one hand, he was holding up the head and first foot or so of a huge snake. The rest of it was draped over and from his other arm. "It's my second one," he said. "I'm crazy about 'em. Pythons. Want to see the other one? It's the biggest."

He smiled in a lazy, little-boy way, not showing his teeth, and his stretched lips weren't all that different from the slice-curve of a snake's mouth.

As I walked around his house and down the dark side, I was a little scared. I had seen movies about snakes. In one, the thing could stand up the height of a man, look him in the eye. In another, a video of a real event, a black Australian snake came across a wide grassy area, half its body erect, came so fast it was like a swoop of thin death, vengeful, merciless. Whoever filmed the scene got scared, too—the last second or so was a flutter of escape.

"I want to break in there," Jonathan said when I told him and B. J. about the exchange. "Get the damned things and turn them in or something. Give them to the authorities. Isn't having snakes against the law?"

"Don't know." But B. J. was interested. Few things excited him, but he was attending this conversation. "I'd like to see the snakes, but it's not worth going to jail. Which," he cocked a hand at Jonathan, "is what breaking and entering can get us."

"Ask the guy," I said. "He'll be more than happy to show you his."

They laughed. They liked that. It put the situation on a level we all understood. I felt better myself.

Now we had set the game in motion. He made no attempt at even the appearance of caring for the dog. I had to visit the professors so they'd know I wasn't just another empty-talking young man. I explained that I'd take care of the dog—all its needs—until we could get the guy reprimanded somehow, and simultaneously keep the dog from being euthanized.

"I'll feed him," the Mrs. Professor said. "We'll do that. But could you walk him? He needs exercise."

"I will if I can get him out when your neighbor's gone."

"Maybe we should . . . ," she began, but her husband shook his head and I helped him out.

"No, you shouldn't," I said. "It wouldn't be fair to your own animals. And he's big. Training him or pulling him off one of the others wouldn't be easy."

They insisted on handling the feeding of Brute and urged me, in their gracious way, to find a solution.

My father doesn't interfere in the misdoings of others unless the acts occur on his property. He believes that right eventually replaces wrong without his intervention. We are each, he insists, to take care of our own and leave others alone.

The neighbor's girlfriend was exactly the kind of girl that caught my eye and made me stutter-walk. I saw her standing on the top step of the long stairs in the back of the house. She was looking at the chained dog in the yard below. Her arms were locked across her midriff as if she were chilled. She had on a short black skirt and a short-sleeved white blouse. Neat and trim. Probably sharp as a whip. She saw me looking and, after staring a minute, bobbed her head, turned crisply, and went back in his house.

He played with the pythons outside, one at a time. He let them stretch out seemingly free on the sparse grass, bask in the sun. Maybe he enjoyed snatching them away from freedom over and over. Whatever his reasons, he talked to them, stroked them, discussed them with passersby. Jonathan walked two blocks down and up so he could appear to be a stranger and talk with the guy about his pets.

All the while, in the backyard, staked in the sun with just enough chain to move under the straggly tree, was the dog. He heard his owner's voice, surely, and recognized a gentle tone being directed to something else, but never to him.

"I told the guy," Jonathan said, "that I knew a family that wanted a dog like his. Guess what he said."

"He said he wasn't giving the dog away."

"How'd you know?"

"He and I are on the same wavelength."

"Then I'm moving out. Two of you would poison the area."

That surprised me.

Three nights, I walked Brute between nine and ten, when his owner's car was gone. Will and Jenny couldn't bear it. Neither could the professors' dogs. Brute stopped at each fence, hiked up a leg, and left scents of his freedom. I let him do it. He walked more than he ran and stood still occasionally, his big head high as if he were dreaming the neighborhood. He nosed the edge of fences, garbage cans. If I said no, he moved on immediately. I could see the shape of his spine and hipbones. I had to get him away from his owner, but not into a worse situation.

Saturday noon, so hot and dry the dirt almost evaporated, and in the neighbor's backyard was the old professor, a shovel on the ground and a trowel in his hand. The dog had dug a shallow bed next to the house, exposed roots, and his chain had snagged, immobilizing him. He panted, head up, tongue dripping, eyes watching us.

"I've been trying to dig some of these up," the old man said, "so he could at least have a smooth place to lie. But I can't get them. I'm going to let him go, put in him our backyard."

"Then put your own animals in the house."

He looked at me rather disgustedly, and I deserved it. He was a tall, scrawny man, with watery blue eyes and a mouth that worked nervously. Maybe he was timid or had been timid. "We thought you were going to do something," he said.

"I am. I will. Leave him, all right?"

He studied me, shook his head. "No. I won't." He reached down to unfasten the chain, then fumbled at the collar when he couldn't get the chain unsnapped.

"Please," I said. When he stood up, he brushed the back of his arm against his eyes, maybe to avoid looking at me. In a moment, he took up his tools and walked away. I saw his wife at their gate. I waved but she didn't return the gesture.

"We could kill the snakes, feed them to Brute," Jonathan said. "Ironic justice."

"Or kill the guy and feel him to the snakes," from B. J.

"God! Even better!" Jonathan's eyes rounded at me. Our housemate had out-performed himself.

"It is the dude," B. J. said, "that we want to get, isn't it? not the snakes?"

We talked about the amount of drugs likely hidden in the house next door, about feeding snakes, about regulations for dog care and maybe regulations for snake care. The darker night came in with my two friends supposing this and supposing that. It was a good time, analyzing a problem in the midst of beer, fireflies, and futures. I loaded up Will and Jenny and drove out to my Dad's. He was ready with Omie, a blue tick, and he and I followed the baying under a yellow moon with a night breeze light and laden with honeysuckle and grass.

My dad, who owned banks though he liked his farm best, knew all the old-money people and many of the new-money ones. He wanted to approach Taylor Buchanan, who owned the lot of houses across from mine, with the problem.

"Taylor'll give the man notice," my father said. "He won't want someone like that on his property. But he'll have to see the situation for himself. There's a big difference in protecting and invading."

"I'd rather you didn't tell Buchanan anything," I said. "If the guy just moves, the dog will starve outside my eyesight, but not outside my knowledge."

When I went home, Jenny and Will stayed, not without some sad yipping at me. Their new owners were lined up and I had done my duty by them.

Jonathan, all on his own, had been hunting, too. He had got in the guy's house that very night, and the report spilled out of him. "He's got dope everywhere, coming out of cracks. But get this, only one of those snakes is penned up. The other one's loose. I was looking under a bed, you know, and damn, that shadow moved, and I did, too. Boom, bam. He didn't come out. Nobody would poke around much if they knew that thing was on the prowl."

"No one but you."

"Right. You got it."

"You broke the law."

"Yep. Somebody had to do it."

Later that morning, I watched the professors carry a tray of scraps over to Brute. The old guy watched the house like an enemy might emerge. The woman, thin and a little masculine, glanced over at me occasionally, then at the dog. When he had finished eating, she took up the tray, handed it to her husband. Then she rubbed and scratched along the dog's spine. He loved it. He leaned into it. When she walked away, he stretched after her. Her husband veered toward me. "We're going to file a complaint with the police, get the dog taken away. Then we'll adopt him."

"The guy's wife might take him instead. Or somebody else."

"No. We'll ask to get our names in first."

"I can get him out of there in a week. Maybe sooner."

"I don't believe you."

"Give me three days. Just keep feeding him. Or I'll do it."

Though he was a thin man, he had heavy wattles, like an old turkey's, and they trembled as he breathed. He was agitated. Understandably.

"When you were my age," I asked, "what would you have done?"

He didn't answer. I could tell that he'd never been too physical a man. A good one, though.

"You'd have gone to the authorities, right?" I said. "Like you're doing now."

"It's better than doing nothing."

"I am doing something. You just can't see it."

"All right." He nodded, walked off, a little stiffly. He went through the gate, had to twist and talk his way through the excitement of three loved dogs, and went up the grassy yard to his own high deck, where his wife awaited him. I think maybe he felt very good right then.

So, I talked to my buddies.

Two nights later, B. J. was dressed all in black. "I got on red underwear, though," he said, and snapped the elastic of his sweatpants. His girlfriend was dressed in black, too, though she was headed to work, swing shift. She had brought him a gift, a thief's toolkit, all the tinier instruments in a roll-up vinyl band that would fit around the waist, held tight by Velcro. "Am I bad? Bad." He turned in a circle, his homely face transformed by this borderline risk. I'd trust him with me in a war. Jonathan, too, actually.

"Ugly as sin is what you are," Jonathan said.

B. J. left to drop his Miss at work, then station himself where he could follow the red car. In B. J.'s possession were two bags of pot I'd paid for. If possible, without risk to himself, B. J. was going to give them to the neighbor, by just placing them in the rear-seat floor of the red car.

Jonathan, meanwhile, waited with me. When dark descended, we whispered past Brute, pried out a screened window, pushed up the old-fashioned sash, and eased in.

Only a small blue light showed us passage. One huge aquarium, in the living room, held its occupant, the large python. The other aquarium, in the kitchen, was significantly empty, as Jonathan had explained. I kept lookout while Jonathan dropped a couple of baggies into the empty aquarium, easily visible if anyone were to enter the house. Then we went searching, gingerly. We found the albino in the same bedroom where Jonathan had seen it, only now it laced the inner frame of a window—nice surprise if we had chosen to jimmy open that particular one. Jonathan gripped the neck, I the body, and we carried it into the other room and out the window we'd opened. We stuffed it into the plastic garbage can and struggled the can across the yard, across the alley, and put it where we usually kept it. I held the lid down while Jonathan went inside for heavy tape. We used the whole roll, but we didn't jerk the trashcan around.

"You think it's mad or scared?" Jonathan said.

"I don't think it makes much difference."

"Can it breathe in there?"

"We won't keep it that long," I said. That had been a decent question.

Car lights swept around, then down the side of my house, and clicked out. B. J. was home.

"I did it," B. J. said, sauntering up. "If they look in his car, they're going to find evidence of one of his hobbies." He looked at the garbage can. "Is it in there?"

"We hope so," Jonathan said, and spit to his left, laughing.

"Nobody saw me, but I'm going to change anyhow." Without pretensions, B. J. walked behind us to avoid nearing the can and slammed his way inside. The backyard lightened as B. J. progressed through the house, obviously flicking on every switch.

When he returned, dressed in slacks, sandals, and a short-sleeved shirt, he could have passed for a fraternity boy. "You ready to call?" he said. "I want to drop in at the police station and listen when the call comes in."

Jonathan set him straight. "You stay here, got that? We're just do-gooders. The thing got out and we caught it. We don't know what to do with it, and we don't know how many may have gotten out." He looked at me. "Isn't that right, Leo?"

"That's the story," I said. "And it's true that we don't know what to do." I got a lead and collar from my trunk, then walked across the narrow alley, to our friend in the backyard. He quivered. He could smell something wonderful on the way. I released him from his collar, then fastened it empty, but larger, and dropped chain and collar on the ground. For all anyone but us knew, the dog had just pulled out of it and had taken off. I slipped the new collar on him, clipped on the lead, and headed down the alley.

We traveled the neighborhood, slow, fast, pause, look, start. Streetlights and yard lights played false moons for us. Jonathan would have called the police by now, by now cop cars from different boring sections of town would be rolling toward the strange call of dangerous animal on the loose. Maybe the animal patrol guy would be heading for his wagon, one of the real heroes this night.

Soon, I saw the lights. There were no sirens. Though it wasn't easy, I stayed on my own course and followed Brute, let him nose himself through the neighborhood until my curiosity took us back. I put him in my house and gave him some bologna. Then I went out the front door and walked around to the old school, where other neighbors had gathered.

Three police cars were in the street, only one cutting the night sky with whirling lights, maybe like the aurora borealis but from down low and headed north. Then that one went dark, too. The professors were on the sidewalk in front of their house. He was behind her, but very close, as if to put a hand on her shoulder if she dared to go closer.

Two cops went into the house. Two went down the side, toward the alley where Jonathan, as good neighbor, would be guarding the trashcan. The word passed down the street or the lights drew people, because our number increased. People blocked my view. Voices blurted, hushed. A baby cried. A woman about my father's age, with a cane in her hand, said, "They said a boa constrictor got out of its cage. Somebody caught it, but nobody knows how many were in the house. You know, if one gets in the plumbing, they'll never get it. A woman in Florida had one come out of her commode. They're probably breeding all over the country."

Inside the house, the officers had found the python in the aquarium and were searching for more. Surely they had found other obvious things, too.

Luck was with us.

The guy came home. The red car drove up, just as it should have, and I moved to stand slightly behind a tree. He was alone, for which I was grateful. From the car, he stretched out and stood up so calmly, lazily, like maybe these people needed his greeting. He started forward but two officers detained him. He bent his head to listen to them, and when he raised up again, he looked around at the gatherers. When his gaze swept the school, I wanted to step forward all the way, into the curve of light. But I didn't. Let him think the world had just caught him. The officers put him in one of their cars. This is a small town and they had to make many phone calls, check many procedures, and give the drama its due.

I went on around the school, down by the railroad tracks, and then two blocks over. When I arrived home, B. J. had taken off to get his girl, and Brute was sitting in front of the sofa, fixated on Jonathan.

"I gave him a pound of hamburger," Jonathan said. "I thawed it in the microwave."

"Where's the python?"

"At the animal shelter. The cops called them. I let the agent take the can, too. Made sense to me."

"Good thinking."

"He said they've had snakes before. They get adopted faster than dogs."

"And if they don't?"

"Zoos, Leo. Heard of zoos?"

Three days later I saw the pretty girl in the neighbor's backyard. She was standing where the collar and chain had been and maybe still were. She wore an old-fashioned print dress, one with square, padded shoulders. I had horseshoes in my hands and was waiting on B. J. and Jonathan to find the energy to join me. They were arguing about summer courses, whether they were harder or easier than regular semester. Neither of them had to worry. They liked challenge.

I let one horseshoe fall, linked it, dropped it, linked it. It was a heavy sound, but musical still. She looked at me and so did Brute. I don't think she could see him from her position, but it didn't matter if she did. Brute could have turned up at my place on his own. I thought maybe she'd walk over and we'd fall in love for a few months. But she turned away. Obviously she was a woman who liked snakes.

My buddies and I played horseshoes for two hours or so. Fireflies were rampant, in a hurry as they have to be. The night cooled. The professors' back door opened, and they came out on their deck, walked down the stairs while one of their black dogs keened so fiercely the woman clamped her hands over her ears. A ringer hummed. Their three dogs barked intermittently. The strange family came through the gate, and the professor went on by, three dogs pulling him along. She came into our yard like being around a group of young males might make her nervous but would never stop her. B. J. and Jonathan called a halt, kind of listened without nosing.

"I know you did all that," she said to me, nodding toward the neighbor's place. "And I want to thank you and to apologize for what I was thinking about you."

"I didn't do anything," I said. "He did it all himself."

Jonathan snorted.

She smiled. "Yes, he sure did."

A few feet away, sitting at rapt attention, was Brute.

"He's such a dear," she said, and left us for him. She squatted down next to him, rubbed his massive head. She kissed him on the nose. I've seen that done before, usually by a man to a good hound. The new ones in the pen whined their jealously and misery.

There he was, now my dog.

"Does he sleep outside or in?" B. J. said.

"In Leo's room," Jonathan said, which turned out to be right.

I had to learn how to train Brute. I could never know what the pure animal, the pup, might have displayed, or how that beginning creature could have negotiated his training. But I knew for certain that he had become painfully willing. His heart strained to please. My primary duty was to teach him a pleasurable anticipation, one aroused through a just reward, however small.

He liked to sleep in front of doorways. "I'm going to plow right through him some day," Jonathan said, but he didn't mean it and he didn't do it. Occasionally, when Jonathan was reading and his hand dangled from the chair arm, Brute lumbered over and pushed his head beneath the hand. He was stroked every time. So Jonathan stayed until recently, when he entered a law school over two hundred miles away. "You better come along," he said. "Keep me on the straight path." B. J. switched his major to Criminal Justice, moved in with his pistachio girl, and is meandering toward a degree.

My father now argues that if law doesn't attract me, I might make a good veterinarian. He wants to guide me. Meanwhile, I have bought another rental and plan to buy another one. I'd like to move to a larger house, from where I can see the university's east gate, and the courthouse clock, and walk downtown for the specialty lunches. Often, I take the dogs out for a run. They whoop and bay and fire themselves through the hills, after a scent or a hope. Brute keeps up for a while, then he wanders off and eventually back to me. He likes to be touched. The stars stud the sky.

A Fragile Life

Amelia delayed approaching the bird section, though a parakeet was exactly what she wanted, a green or blue one, with yellow markings. They could learn so much so fast. She had heard one actually speak. It belonged to a neighbor couple and was free to flit throughout their home. It would alight on the man's shoulder, nip his ear, and say, in a string of watery, warbly sounds, "I want a drink." The man or his wife would offer a glass of water and the bird would peck-sip, always four sips, and then say something else. It had five sentences in its speaking repertoire and could perform innumerable stunts, among them hanging upside down on command, from the man's finger.

"Why not from yours?" she had asked the neighbor lady.

"I tremble too much, we think."

Now she studied gerbils, mice, an iguana, a python, fish. One group of fish disturbed her because their fins, all transparent gossamer, were frayed, like they were dissolving. Maybe they were eating one another? She shuddered. Life was ugly.

"Could I help you with something?"

The man, whose shirt pocket bore the pet store logo, seemed genuinely friendly. She recognized the familiarity of male to attractive female. It made her comfortable. "Not yet. I think I want a canary or a parakeet, but I'm enjoying your store."

"Is this your first time here?"

"Don't people just come once? How often does someone purchase a pet?"

"They purchase supplies for the pet."

"Oh," she brought fingertips to lips. "Of course. I'm being stupid."

"No. And actually, some people do come in for another pet, a different one or an additional one."

She asked about the fish with the wispy fins and he bent down to look. "No, they don't eat each other, but they don't hold up well. They take a lot of care, exotic fish."

"I thought fish were the easiest pets in the world."

"No pet's easy. Not even worms."

"People keep worms?"

"I'm joking. People raise them. For fishing. Or selling for fishing."

He had work to do and she had a bird to find and obviously he wasn't all that interested in her.

She thought of her husband and felt her heart wrench, like a contraction that wouldn't end. He didn't love her anymore, if he ever had. "Deal with it," she whispered.

She strolled toward the birds, letting her hips roll and her long skirt swish. Womanly ways. Mundane steps. One at a time. She passed another iguana, whose color was grayish and whose left eye—the one visible from her vantage—was cold if not hostile. "I don't like you either," she said, but low.

A pleasant hour later she was at the cash register, writing the check and hoping the clerk noticed the beauty of her handwriting, the fullness of her breasts, the brightness of her eye. Anything.

"You'll enjoy the parakeet," he said. "If you have any questions, feel free to call."

She still thought his gaze met hers invitingly, but he hadn't suggested she *stop* by with questions, only phone. Still, the sun was shining and she was in good health. "Petey Boy," she said to her new pet. "Are you my Petey Boy?" Maybe she would be okay. She liked the bird, colorful, joyful little thing.

At the school, her daughter was one of the last stragglers. Only seven, she was already a remarkably beautiful girl, with the olive skin of her father's family, with large dark eyes and reddish lips. She clambered into the front seat heavily, let her books slide around her feet.

"You have a good day?"

Vehement headshake no.

Around the circle drive, behind other cars, and down the long, straight shot to Main Street, Amelia queried Why? Why not a good day?

Marianna shrugged, which alone meant nothing, but combined with eyes awash with imminent tears meant she was too overcome to explain. Overcome with what?

"I have a surprise for you at home," Amelia offered.

This did not change the world.

Amelia continued, determined for the two of them that life be good. "Actually, it's a surprise for the both of us. Each time I look that way—it's in the kitchen—I am so delighted. It's like a piece of rainbow. It's like a piece of . . . sky. . . . It's like a floating ribbon."

"You got a bird."

The voice had no excitement at all.

"What makes you think that?"

Another shrug.

Amelia felt a touch of resentment. "I guess I described Mr. Hatshaw's parakeet that way."

No response. She allowed Marianna the solace of silence for the rest of the drive.

Children had powerful and unfair memories.

Home, Marianna took one long look at the parakeet. Then she marched, deliberately heavy-footed, to her room. Amelia heard the door close. She could follow, but children needed their privacy, too, and Marianna was a proud child—even so young, she interpreted concern as invasion. Besides, Amelia didn't want to follow her daughter right now. Anger and sadness were wearying and contagious.

She pulled out a stool from the kitchen island and sat enjoying the parakeet's presence. All he had to do was *be* and he brought pleasure. Life was simple for that kind of creature. She lighted one of her rare cigarettes, but immediately snuffed it out and waved away the wisp of smoke. "Sorry, Petey," she said. "Marianna may not be in the room, but you are. Right?" Then she remembered that she hadn't put seed and water in the cage yet, and hurried to do so, relieved at the need to be near the delicate thing and to take care of it. She washed and dried the glass containers, clicked them into the plastic brackets on one side of the cage. "You are *so* fine," she whispered. "I'm sorry you're caged, but that's why you were bred, probably." She fastened a mirror onto the other side of the cage. The parakeet came to it immediately, pecked the reflection. She ran one finger down the soft blue back. "You like that, Petey?" He was occupied with his reflection, but she stroked his back again. She wanted him to associate her with happiness. She lowered the barred door. "When you get accustomed to us, I'll leave it open. Meanwhile, eat your dinner and sing us a song."

She missed her husband, who was gone, and her daughter, who was home. And herself.

She loved the parakeet, his tiny sounds, his bright flits of joy, his upside down peering into the mirror. He was obsessed with the mirror, and she considered removing it. Instead, she hung a miniature bell at the top of one perch. "A present for you," she said. She didn't understand his eating habits. He strewed a few seeds—some were always on the paper, even the floor beneath—but he didn't empty the dish. Just like a human child. Picky. Temperamental.

"Amelia," she said toward him, enunciating clearly the syllables of her name. "Amelia." She gave him a red thimble, and in a day's time he delighted her by rasping it against the bars. Buying him had been the most foresighted act she could have taken, because everything else in her life turned ugly. Nick threatened to leave his job and leave the state rather than pay much child support. "You earn as much as I do," he accused over the phone, "and I'm letting you have the house. That puts you way ahead of me."

"This isn't a one-upmanship situation," she countered. "This is our daughter's life we're discussing."

"It's *your* life. I've got bills, too."

"What bills? School clothes? Books? Dentist? If you leave the state, Nick, I can follow you. You have to work."

"There are ways around any regulations. I don't have to have a well-paying job just so you can get more. If you want to fight, have at me." He hung up.

She lied about him to Marianna. "Your dad's so busy, honey. And if he *did* come by here, he would be even sadder. It would remind him of what he's losing."

"Then he should come home."

"He should never have left us."

"He didn't leave *me*."

Amelia felt that like a blow to her own heart. But what could she do? Tell her sweet child that her father was a selfish, conniving bastard? "Don't blame me, hon," she said, and hugged the resistant little body. "Please, don't blame me."

"I'm going outside." Marianna stepped clear and, with her new walk, that odd march, crossed the kitchen and dining room, and went out the patio door. She left it open, as usual, and Amelia slid it closed. Everything about Marianna seemed new, strange. She didn't play. She waited. Now she walked along the low retaining wall to the corner of the yard, where the wall was higher, holding firmly a magnolia tree. She maneuvered the extra two feet nimbly and sat beneath the tree, from where, Amelia understood, could be seen the first turn onto this street—the direction from which her father used to arrive.

Hope, the sustenance of children.

As far as Amelia could tell, Marianna never looked at the bird cage. She might, when urged, look *toward* it, but never at it. Amelia's attempted conversations about the creature elicited only silence and that impassive, tense withholding that was another trait of Nick's family, as if they held back the most powerful part of themselves.

"Maybe I should take Petey back to the store," Amelia said. "Or set him free."

Marianna raised her glass of orange juice and sipped, her eyes round pools of not caring.

Amelia persisted. "I got him for both of us, honey. He brightens up the kitchen. Talk to him. Get him to say your name. He'll love you."

"I don't want him to love me."

Amelia wondered if perhaps her own mood and troubles kept Petey from adjusting. He had eaten so very little in two weeks' time—a scattering of seeds on the lining suggested he had eaten a few, and spilled a few, but the glass feeder was still almost half full. "Eat, baby," she said. She moved the mirror near the food dish and added another mirror on the other side. "Happy bird?" she said. When she bent down to check the angle, she saw facets of herself. "See, Petey? A little group gathers here when you do. Make merry. Sing."

Nick managed to leave a note in the mailbox without her seeing him drive up. "I really will leave. Settle for the amount I offer. I'd like to see Marianne every now and then, but not if it means paying everything I make for the privilege. I'd rather never see her at all."

And me? Amelia wondered. She had arranged her schedule at the hospital for shorter hours, to fit her daughter's needs. What about her own needs? Why couldn't people want the same things? Learn from one another? At least stop loving at the same time? Or simply be kind? Nick had always been unpleasant when crossed. Maybe that sprang from his upbringing, but was she supposed to forgive him? To excuse it?

What she really wanted was to show Nick's note to Marianna, to her sulking, angry, daughter, but she didn't. Children should feel loved, safe. Beautiful. Cherished. Little girls were fragile.

Marianna wanted no bedtime stories, no help with her bath, no night-light.

"I'm not afraid of the dark," she said.

"Since when?"

"I'm not afraid of anything."

"You don't have to be brave, you know. You get to be mad at me and your dad, to be scared, to ask questions. Just tell me what you want, honey."

"I want you to go away."

Amelia closed the door quietly. She wanted Nick to come take his child. No she didn't. No, she didn't. She went in her own room with its gigantic, ridiculous bed. She slept in a silk nightgown for the sheer waste and power of the act.

On the newspaper a few seeds floated, fell again. Amelia folded in the corners of the newspaper, removed it. She wiped down the cage with a mild antiseptic, lined the bottom with a sheet of white paper towel. "What's the matter baby?" His feathers had lost a smoothness, a richness. Maybe he needed something more, a vitamin of some kind. Medicine. "You have to try," she said. "Eat, damn it."

She stopped at the pet store. The young man, though helping someone else, called, "Welcome back. Be with you in a minute." He remembered her. She browsed, waiting. The python still slept behind his false, pale tree. The gerbils hurried and trilled. The isolated iguana still hated her.

"He was abused," she heard from behind. The young man pointed to the iguana. "They don't usually bite, but this one does. If they're mistreated, they can get pretty nasty."

"That's true of all creatures," she said, embarrassed at saying something so trite.

"Right. How's the parakeet?"

"Beautiful. But he barely eats."

"What are you feeding him?"

"The seeds you sold me. Maybe it's the tension in the house." She regretted the personal tidbit immediately and was grateful he didn't pick it up.

"Do you talk to him? Play with him?"

"Of course I talk to him. I gave him a bell, a thimble. And a mirror. Two, actually."

"Now that could be a mistake. If they have a partner, they don't interact with humans."

"You didn't tell me that."

"Sorry."

"So I should take away the mirrors?"

"Maybe. He's just flirting, courting. Maybe he'd pay more attention to his food without the distraction."

She felt slightly guilty, though it didn't make sense. She was trying all she could to make the creature happy. The young man seemed less friendly now that she represented a problem. In defense, she sought out the possible defects in his own person, stumpy toes bared in sandals, frayed collar—on a lavender shirt. Perhaps he was gay. Only a foolish woman, she reminded herself, interpreted lack of interest in herself as evidence of homosexuality.

He found a dropper bottle with a supplement that might help. Momentarily, she had no faith in his knowledge or his taste.

"If it doesn't work," he said. "Let me know."

She didn't respond because she had recently learned how very apt silence could be.

At home, she approached the cage timidly. She gave him fresh water, tapped the food dish. The seeds shifted. "Petey," she said. "Petey, baby. You've got to eat." He bit her. She assumed he just didn't like her, which was the world's attitude. She tried to woo him. How could she fail in this simple caretaking, easier surely than marriage and motherhood?

Days later, Petey was dead—three weeks from the purchase day. He lay tousled and not yet stiff when she entered the kitchen. At first, she wondered if Marianna had killed him to express her anger and sorrow. But she knew better. A pall settled over the kitchen, seemed to disperse outward, like a cloud beneath the ceiling. Everything was heavy, overcast. She felt weak and lightheaded. She sat at the kitchen island, unlighted cigarette in her hand, studying the cage. Why did it matter so? It was just a bird, and not even an established, beloved pet. It was still new, not hers at all. And her daughter hated it. Maybe this was for the best. If she wanted to change things, she should change what truly mattered. She could lose some weight, maybe look into braces for herself. Think differently. Think differently. There were surely worldviews that could get a person though life with less pain. With the cigarette in her left hand, poised for lighting or drawing, she rummaged through two drawers for a match, found one partially used book. She tore a paper match loose, started to strike it, and remembered that miners had used canaries to find gas, to check for oxygen, to verify that conditions were safe for humans.

"My god, Petey. Have you saved our lives?" She went to the stove, expecting to smell gas. Nothing. She bent down. The pilot lights were on. Everything was functioning normally. She struck the match, held it to the cigarette, drew deeply. No great tragedy or sacrifice here. He had just died.

She stood by the cage, looking long at the dead, once lovely thing. She did feel some sadness, but also curiosity, and a bit of anger. It could have *tried* to live. It could have cared something for her. She committed to memory its position and muted colors and knew that were it to revive now, she wouldn't want it anymore. It had betrayed her and frightened her. She wrapped it in paper towels and put it in the garbage can outside—that seemed so terribly common and ugly, but also the most sanitary and practical. What more could she do?

She showered, dressed, and woke her daughter.

"Pancakes?" she said. This was a Sunday favorite, never allowed on schooldays.

The response wasn't actually an acceptance, but it wasn't no. Amelia decided the ambiguity was progress and was good enough. "Pancakes, it is," she said. "Ready in two minutes."

Marianna, perched on the stool facing the living room arch, obviously looked at the empty cage, but Amelia didn't know what to say, how to handle the whole thing. Her daughter finished the pancakes without comment. She finished her milk, wiped her lips like a satisfied gourmet, and tossed the napkin in the plate, exactly as Nick had always done. She slid off the stool and said clearly, "I want to live with Daddy."

This was so unexpected, so foreign a tongue, that Amelia responded in a tone she would never have used. "Well you don't get to choose."

Marianna got her books and stood by the garage door, waiting for her ride to school as though nothing had transpired.

"Why did you say that?" Amelia demanded. "I'm doing the best I can for both of us. I'm lonely, too. I'm miserable. Your father left me for another woman. For another woman. Do you hear that? Do you think that's easy on me, to know he loved somebody else before I stopped loving him? And now you creep around like some dead block of tissue, acting like you hate me when I'm the only one who's been true to anything at all . . ."

It caught up with her like the hideous, unnatural stream it was, and shame overtook her pain and rage. She ran to her room, as if Marianna could get herself to school or become the adult and comfort her mother or complete the divorce negotiations, or just ease the future or just stop being a problem herself, altogether stop being a problem. Amelia hid among pillows shared by her and Nick, on a bed meant for a long life of loving and some leisure, maybe other children. It was white. The ceiling was arched with a skylight, and she could see that proverbial patch of blue that most people never attained, and she certainly wouldn't be able to. Her anger eased almost immediately, because she had to listen for her daughter. Mothers shouldn't express their pain, not to their children. She hoped Marianna would come through the doorway, contrite, loving—at least concerned. But that didn't happen.

"Marianna?" she called. Nothing.

Amelia quickly arose, ran into the kitchen. It was empty. Of course. If you have problems, just take off. Like father, like daughter. Amelia got the car and caught up with Marianna one block down, her sturdy, beautiful little form determinedly headed elsewhere.

Amelia leaned over, opened the door, and crept-drove along, stopping every few feet to offer enticements: "You don't know the way to school, honey." "When your father wants you to stay over, you can." "I would miss you, but I would understand." "We both love you, Marianna. We just have different ways."

Near the intersection, her daughter slowed down, and without seeming at all frightened, came to the car. Since she didn't speak, Amelia didn't either, even though she preferred chatter in tense situations. She wanted to tell about Petey, because that seemed a perfect way to bind them, to offer his tiny death as a port to her and Marianna's future. At the school, she leaned over to kiss her daughter's head and felt the hostility that might never, never dissipate.

"You have a wonderful day," she said, as brightly as if she were a happy, contented wife and mother. She waited till Marianna had crossed the schoolhouse walk and disappeared inside. Then, breathing shallowly and fearfully, Amelia drove off, sped onto the freeway leading to her work. For the next short distance, she wove through heavy, unbearable, and constant traffic. In the midst of it, when any distraction would be inopportune, the last image of Petey came to her. There had been an oddity besides death. Something. Then she remembered the seeds near him. They had been pale, translucent, like the skin of pearls. A few had lifted from the simple force of her breathing. She remembered seeing that before, how the seeds shifted from his movement, from hers, so very very light. Oh.

They weren't seeds. They were hulls. Hulls. She hadn't known that seeds that tiny could also have hulls. They were delicate because they were empty. She had starved him.

The knowledge threatened to sicken her. Her best intentions had turned into cruelty, needless cruelty. It wasn't the bird, not just the bird. She was struggling in the dark, caught in a life that was going too fast for her to learn what to do and how to be. She gasped at the magnitude of her mistake. What else had she done wrong? Would do wrong? She tried to slow down, searched the myriad signs for the closest exit, but they blurred. She eased over anyway. She needed a respite, a safe moment. She loved her daughter, her strange, terrifying daughter. She had to think. She had to stop, to grieve. She had to forgive herself.

The Bully's Snake

Going home from school on his bike, Lester cut over the footbridge in Weiser Park. A particular color in the gravel creek bed brought him to a halt. He dismounted and skittered down the short bank.

It was a glass jar with a blue and white lid—old, but fairly clean. Inside was the green ribbon snake that Bob Pfister had brought to show-and-tell earlier.

Lester held the jar gingerly, one hand on the top, the other on the bottom, and scrambled awkwardly up the bank, freeing a hand only briefly, eyes locked on the jar as if the creature could turn the lid open. He thrust the jar in his backpack, zipped it in tight, and resumed riding home. He was too uneasy, though, and stopped again, fixing the backpack on the rear rack, and even then running and pushing the bike.

At home, he stuck the backpack in the closet, then jerked it out and put it in the corner, where the floor was clear. He knew none of this was needed, but he was diminishing the possibility of surprise.

He wanted to keep the snake and he wanted Bob Pfister to know he had it.

Bob Pfister was the school bully. He had sandpaper skin and orange hair cut short and gelled stiff. His scalp was pink, and a white scar ran diagonally across it. According to his mother, he had fallen onto an old-fashioned lawnmower when he was a kid and had had forty stitches, but he told people a man had struck him with a sword.

"I got whip marks on my back, too," he bragged. "Been whipped with a chain, and a belt, and an umbrella."

It was crazy enough to be true. A liar would have stuck with the chain.

Bob called Lester "Lady Louise." He let the air out of Lester's bike tires, removed the seat, and wiped some stinky, oily gunk on the handlebars, the tubes, the crankset, the chain. Everywhere.

At home now, Lester told his mother he had no homework. He needed time to think about the snake. About what to do with it. He watched a television show with his sister, went outside and caught a few fireflies, saving them in an empty jar he kept for such purposes. Spiders, praying mantis, grasshoppers. He'd catch a creature, study it, then release it. He considered feeding the fireflies to the snake.

No. He let them go. Blinking eyes all over the evening. He wasn't afraid of fireflies, but he didn't grasp how their light worked. He knew it wasn't magic, but it was like magic.

Off and on until bedtime, he peered into his bedroom. The backpack looked the same.

When bedtime came, he worried about two things—if the snake had died from lack of air, which made him breathless himself, and if the snake was alive, quick and angry.

He thought he should take the jar outside. But then? Could he take the lid off and release the snake without getting bitten? He wasn't sure it had teeth.

His sleep was plagued with thousands of ribbon snakes slithering over his bed, across the ceiling, lacing together. When he woke, light through the blinds and streaming on the floor, he felt relieved of the night's fear. He sat up, only to see the backpack. A shiver reminded him of responsibility. He got out of bed, dressed in jeans and double shirts, and cautiously opened the pack, first one side then the other. As he lifted the jar, the green snake slipped up and down and over, and stopped with a frozen look at Lester. Lester hurriedly stashed the jar in the corner behind the pack.

At breakfast, he asked his mother if snakes had to eat three times a day. When she said she believed they ate only once or twice a week or a month, he felt as if he could breathe. The sun seemed to flow fully into the kitchen.

"They need water, though," she said, looking at him quickly, then back to her task at the sink. "Why?"

"Bob Pfister had a snake at school. I don't know if he gave it any water."

"They shouldn't let children bring snakes to school. Shouldn't let them bring any live animals."

"Dead ones all right?" his dad asked.

He and his dad laughed. His mother hid a smile, Lester knew. She had rules and didn't laugh when matters were serious.

Before leaving the house, he carried the backpack, jar inside, into the bathroom. There he set the jar atop the sink and dripped water from cupped palm onto the lid, so droplets gradually seeped through the holes. The snake eyed him wickedly. "You're going to live a long life," Lester assured him, as he had sometimes been assured. He felt immensely good. Not brave so much as responsible. He wouldn't let any harm come to this creature.

Lester rode toward school in shards of light and green, thinking of Bob Pfister who would be surprised. He slowed down at the rickety bridge from where he had yesterday seen the snake. He glanced behind him and around, expecting to see Bob Pfister looming up, searching for his snake. But only short grass and woods were visible, a little breeze whistling. He was anxious to get to school and begin the process of returning the creature.

He recognized Bob's bulbous shape outside homeroom, but wasn't ready yet to relinquish the prize, his purchase for, if not friendship, a mark of unexpectedness, maybe honor. Some almost thought nagged him, made him delay. It wasn't a pleasant anticipation he felt, but more a guilt.

He took out his notebook and books carefully, ensuring the jar remained upright. He patted the jar, felt a bit foolish. Still, he slipped his fingers around the cool glass. It was like having a movie in the classroom, or a friend, a different kind of friend. The day couldn't be boring. He couldn't be lonely. Just the secret was company.

Bob seemed to remember Lester's presence in the world and turned, upper lip raised in a sneer. Lester couldn't keep a smile from touching his lips briefly, but he sobered immediately, and nodded, as if a conspiracy existed between him and Bob.

In the lunchroom, when Lester had planned to return the snake to Bob, he instead kept it hidden in his pack. Bob came over, wordlessly scooped up and ate all of Lester's french fries and his two cookies. He smiled a loose blubberlip smile that Lester found ugly and sad.

"Burp Face," Bob said.

Lester nodded as if saying, "yes, that's me." He studied Bob's bushy red eyebrows and droopy earlobes. He wondered if Bob really received beatings.

"Did you lose your snake?" Lester asked.

"What?"

"Did you lose your snake?"

Bob didn't answer. He looked at Lester's backpack and got up from the bench. He deliberately tipped the bench and picked up the end of the table enough that it rattled the plastic tray. A teacher started over, but let it go as Bob moved off.

Lester wondered why Bob hadn't responded to the question. If he had lost the snake, he'd want it back. Wouldn't he? What if he had tossed it down to the creek bed? Thrown it away to die in a jar? At one end of the cafeteria a huge red shield hung, a coat of arms donated by a former graduate. A snake curled over a printed word, "victus." Lester memorized the spelling. He didn't know if it meant vicious or victor or victim. But it meant something. So did the snake. The cafeteria lighting was milky, like a dream coming on in daytime. Lester opened the backpack so the air would surround the jar, too, since he and the snake were in this together.

After school, Lester pedaled slowly toward the bridge. Still some distance away, he saw someone descending down the bank, a hulking red-haired figure. He guessed if Bob knew where to look, he could have looked yesterday. Maybe he wanted to find it now for a different reason. Lester rode his bike into the center of the bridge and dismounted, kicked down the stand. He opened his backpack, lifted out the jar. Light glinted from the glass and the green inside seemed like light, too, liquid light. He carried it across the rest of the bridge and down to the gravel and grass where he'd found it.

Bob Pfister had already crossed over and was halfway up the other bank.

"He needs some water," Lester called, and walked down the creek bed. He listened for any sound indicating Pfister was coming after him, but he didn't look. He kept his eyes to the ground, seeking a puddle of water or a dampness in the soil, a place that would be suitable for a small snake. He found both near a recess in the bank, beneath a clumpy bush. Close by were other bushes, and further down was a stringy tree with young leaves on it and a few white buds. Lester squatted, resting his skinny hips against his heels, then just sat back on the ground. He was pleasantly uncomfortable. Above, from one end of the bridge, Bob Pfister watched him. His features were visible, but no hint of what he might think or do.

Lester loosened the jar lid enough that one little turn and it would lift free. The snake might be able to read his intent. It had the strangest way of going rigid and looking at him as if out of the corner of an eye. Instead of tilting the jar down and pulling the lid back over the top of it, Lester placed the jar next to him and nudged the lid off and aside. The snake stayed where it was, then streaked out, alongside Lester's leg, over his ankle, and straightaway in the opposite direction of Lester and Bob Pfister and the bridge and the jar.

Lester was elated and shocked immobile. That was a great snake, he thought. Real brave little devil. Lester breathed deeply. He wished the snake had hung around a little, hissed at him, coiled up. Maybe not all snakes coiled. He wanted the time to go on. He looked directly at Bob who had not moved closer to Lester's bike. He might any minute, though, or tomorrow, or the next day.

Lester nodded at Bob, just as he had earlier at school. In a few seconds, Bob nodded slightly, turned away, and went on somewhere, disappearing into the soft shine of Lester's afternoon.

The Dancer's Son

Milosh Lukovich finished mowing his grandfather's lawn, which had been kept in perfect order even though various tenants had inhabited the house since the old man's death. Then he pushed the mower the two blocks to his parents' house. He had done the mowing, and myriad other chores, since childhood, under his father's tutelage. Now he hummed the whole way, wiped off the mower and stowed it in the garage. He took the steps in two groups of three and banged onto the back porch. "Hullo. Done and Done. When's lunch? A man's got to eat."

"You do Grandpa's?" she called from the kitchen. "Behind the garage, too? That little strip?" Bang a pot onto the stove.

His mother was a good cook, but when she was sad she seemed lost in the kitchen. He strode into the room, opened the refrigerator. "What we got here?" Cimać. Beans. Bologna. He put the pan back. "You want a sandwich, Mom?"

She twisted her hands, poofed him away with a wave. "You eat. I'll finish your Dad's bureau. Such a mess. He saves everything."

"Better not throw out one thing. He knows every piece."

"I'm cleaning, not throwing away. Putting things together."

He ate four bologna sandwiches spread thick with cimać. At twenty-eight, he was bigger than his father, six foot two and 230

118

pounds, but felt dwarfed in that man's presence. Today, with his father visiting a brother back East, Milosh sang while he straightened the kitchen. He liked Elvis and delivered the lines with gusto, attempting to twist his lower half as he belted out the final phrase. He looked, he knew, ludicrous. "This, Ladies and Gentleman," he announced to the sink, "is the Serbian King of Rock and Roll. Milosh Dragisha Lukovich. Eat your hearts out ladies."

"What did you say, Miloshka?" his mother called.

"Nothing. Singing, Mom."

She had left the pan on the stove and he put it away, too. The sink curtains were orangish and stiff from accumulated smoke and oil. He removed the rods, pushed the curtains free and stuck them in the washing machine in the laundry room, and strolled down the hall to his parents' room.

"I'm heading back to Tucson. I put the curtains in the washer."

"Look here what he's got. Still got this."

In her right hand was an old photograph, creased across the bottom and with frayed edges. A young woman stood next to a wire fence. She had on baggy slacks and a white blouse. Her black hair was rolled to frame an oval face with wide-spaced eyes beneath dark arched brows. She was smiling just enough to reveal the edges of straight white teeth behind full lips. She was lovely and sad.

"Put it away," Milosh said. He lightly pinched the edge of the photograph and tugged.

She resisted.

"You want to cause trouble?"

"*He* causes the trouble," she said. "I don't hide pictures." She let him take the photograph.

"So where was it?"

She gestured toward the corner of the drawer. "Under the socks. Clean socks." Milosh returned the photograph to its place. "Don't say you saw it. That's what he wants. Don't say anything. Quit cleaning now."

She continued to stand by the bureau, looking like a squirrel momentarily startled still. Milosh took her hand. "Out of the room for a little while. What's your hurry? You have some tea and lie down.

You worry too much." He led her to the kitchen and filled the teakettle with water. "She's probably dead a long time," he said.

"Not dead enough."

"Listen to yourself."

He stayed to fix her tea and to talk about his brother who had once lived with the grandparents and now, at thirty, sponged off relatives in Chicago, too fat and lazy to support his own appetites. "I got a job, he can get a job," Milosh said. "Don't send money to him. You give him my money, it stops coming. I mean it."

"He's not a worker like you. He has no confidence."

"Got no pride, that's what he's not got. He's a woman-man. Pop says."

Then she wouldn't talk. He had wounded her motherhood. Milosh put forty dollars in her hand and kissed the top of her head. "For you only. Got to go. Things to do, people to see."

"You could fix the garage door. He would like that."

For a second, he felt compelled to stay. Then, "Pop can fix it. This is his house, as he says."

She stood on the porch while he drove away. He wished she weren't so timid. His dad had done that, Milosh supposed. Maybe not. Maybe she had always been that way. How could sons know what their mothers had been? Sons should believe their mothers are beautiful and their fathers are strong and good. Believe it. He turned on the car radio, tuned as always to the community station, where he was also a volunteer deejay, and wondered who was performing. It was live, right there in the studio, and the mix wasn't right. The guitar was drowning out the fiddle. "What is that song, what is that?" He caught his reflection in the mirror and cocked one brow, as if he were on stage. "'The Humors of Lisadel,'" he said, then forgot himself for a while, listening to music.

At least twice a month, Milosh drove north on Saturday afternoons to stay with his parents until late Sunday. He would take meat or cheese to them and do whatever work had been saved for him.

He took his mother to the hairdressers. She couldn't drive and his father thought the beautician an "American extravaganza."

"Why no cheese this time?" his father said, or "Why no ribs? This family likes ribs." Always a few words about what was missing.

"Do you have a girl yet?" his mother said. "If you come up for the dances, you'll meet nice young women. The doctor says your father can't smoke in the house with me, so he takes your room for his. He can smoke in there, he tells me. I feel it here all the time." She clutched at the base of her throat. "He says I make it up so I can rule the house."

Milosh approached his father man to man, jovially, slicing bread for the dinner. "You have to quit smoking around her, Pop. I can smell it, too. It comes through all the vents."

His father splayed the fingers of one big hand. "I smoke only five cigarettes a day now. That's my gift to her. She wants me to stand outside so everyone sees she's queen of the house."

"You could smoke in the garage."

"No. *She* can go stand in the garage. I pay the bills."

"Actually, Pop, half of any money you got is hers. According to law."

"We'd be broke in half a week."

His mother called him at work. "Now he smokes in the garage. He took the best chair from the house, and a lamp. He reads the paper out there."

"Be happy."

"He won't come back to the bedroom. You tell him that's no good."

His father cooked with other men for the big monthly gatherings. When the food was served, he changed his clothing, came into the huge room a different man. He joked with the musicians and the ladies. He wore black slacks, white shirt with flared collar, a red sash around his thick torso. When the music started, eyes followed him. How could they not? In the moving circle of men and women, he was the master, the most graceful, most grand. Milosh had sat on a folding chair, hypnotized by that man, who was his father, who hacksawed a bicycle and left the parts in the basement for a year, who smashed a guitar that had been hidden beneath a bed. "You break a rule, you lose something. It's a law of the world."

On some Saturday mornings, Milosh rose at 4:00 a.m., staggered sleep-drugged and resentful into the living room, and flipped on his stereo. He dressed to something fast by Bill Monroe and heated a mug of leftover coffee in his microwave. Then he drove to the plant and opened the gates for the delivery men, as he had for four years. He had to supervise the unloading and check off the inventory. Afterward, he drove back home, showered, sang, and loaded up his albums and tapes for the community bluegrass show that started at seven. He never shaved for the show, and he wore bummy, comfortable clothes, because who could see him? Nobody in the world. He sat in the swivel chair with his big body slumping happy at this free, nowhere job. If he could spend his life doing this, just this. But a man had to work.

"Good morning, you bluegrass aficionados. This is Milo the man—the man-about-town and about everything else good in your lives, with your WAKE UP CALL. How about Del Wood with 'Taking That Georgia Train'? Let's choo-choo you into the table."

"It isn't fair," Milosh said to his boss at the meat plant. "I did a lot of work I didn't have to when you started this place. I laid the tile in the storage room. I helped knock out the walls, put in the water heater. Somebody else can meet the truck now."

"No. We all have responsibilities we don't like. People get paid for what they do."

"Nobody works more hours than me. Nobody."

"A lot of that wouldn't be necessary if you were better at your job."

Milosh couldn't look directly at Mr. Turner then. He stacked some papers, cleared his throat. He glanced up and away quickly. "You got more?" His words were wavery and his lips were trembling. He told himself it was anger.

"I think you understand me, Milo. And cut down on the music when you're working. This isn't the radio station."

Milosh stood up, took his jacket from the hat rack. "Excuse me, sir," he said.

"Where you going?"

"If I have to be here at 5:00 a.m. every Saturday, then maybe, sir, kind O Mr. Employer of Mine, I can leave at 4:45 p.m. on Friday. Or would you rather I quit than give me fifteen minutes I already earned?"

Mr. Turner threw up his hands. "Take your fifteen minutes, Lukovich, but you'd better think about your goals. You can't act like a boy and get paid a man's salary."

"I'm Serbian. A man the minute I was born." He swung out his door, past the secretaries, and through the exit. Was it true what the man said? No good at his job? True? His face was flaming. He needed a war, a place to redeem himself.

Milosh's father began appearing at Milosh's house. Usually he arrived only shortly after the sun, sometimes before. He boomed through the front door with a "you up?" even if Milosh was standing right before him or in the shower or still in bed. "You up? Breakfast in one minute." And Mr. Lukovich would carry the one or two bags of groceries into the kitchen.

"You okay Pop?" Milosh asked the first time.

"What's not okay? I come to fix my son breakfast." He went about slicing bread, onions, cracking eggs into a bowl, stuffing things into the refrigerator. "This refrigerator should be damned."

"Condemned. Should be *condemned*."

"Right. Should be in the garbage."

Milosh showered, then stood wrapped in a towel watching his father.

"You sure you're okay?"

"You eat with clothes on or you don't eat."

Milosh dressed hurriedly and wished the phone were not near the kitchen, so he could call his mother. In the kitchen, he sat where his father motioned him to sit. The curtains were now open and cof-fee steamed from cups on the table. Hot sudsy water filled the sink. An orange-pink dawn illuminated the alley and the neighbor's fence.

"A working man should eat a big breakfast," his father said, and they ate together with comments about the grape vines that needed watering in the back, about grapes don't grow in Arizona, need water all the time, all the time, all the time.

"I'll mop this floor this morning. Been six years since somebody mopped this floor."

"I mop it every week."

"Sure you do. You need a wife." His father began clearing the table.

"You're acting real crazy, Pop. Does Mom know you're down here? You leave her a note or anything?"

"She doesn't care where I go. I slept in my bed. You go to work. No Lukovich is late for work."

Milosh called his mother the moment he got to the office.

"How should I know?" she said. "He gets out of his bed, says he'll fix Milosh breakfast, and he's gone. He does what he wants to do. Don't let it upset you. You do your job. Your father is okay."

At lunch he drove home. His father was gone. No dishes in the sink or on the counter. Everything wiped down and put away. Rake circles in the dirt yard. Grapevine trench soaked.

He called his father. "Just seeing if you got home all right."

"Of course I got home. I drove one side of the road, fifty-five miles the whole way. Who's going to stop me? Did you eat lunch? I put food in your refrigerator. Don't call so much. It costs money and makes your mother worry." He hung up the phone.

The next week he came twice; the next, three times.

In. Cook. Clean. Go. Poof.

"You got nothing better to do than clean my house?"

"I got nothing better to do."

"So clean it."

"I will."

Milosh liked it. Crazy man. Crazy Serbian man. At work, he punched his chest and told the secretary. "You think Americans got customs? *We* got customs. We got customs I don't even know about. Customs up to here." He gestured to his eyebrows and swung back to the office.

Milosh was so stunned by his employer's statement, so acutely hurt and angry that his body reacted as though he were the boss-man. THIS for Turner, with a sweep of his hand to the heavens. THIS for loyalty. THIS for a slap in the face called a generous gesture. "You don't know generous," Milosh said. "You don't know generous worth dung."

"You get full pay, full benefits, full everything until you get a job or for six months, whichever it takes. But I don't want to see your face in the office anymore."

"This is the same face you hired. My father's face. Don't say anything against it."

"Don't play games, Milosh. I owe you, and I admit it. You were a solid worker in the beginning, but you don't grow up, fellow. You penny-ante your life and it's affecting the business."

"How affecting the business? You quadrupled business the last two years. You alone grossed onehundredthirtythousand last year."

"You weren't part of that. You just did the books. The sales-people did it. I did it."

"And they got bonuses. You, too. Me? I got shit. Shit."

"You didn't earn a bonus, Milo. You're the accountant. Basic stuff."

"You think I'm stupid, huh? I got everything on computer for you, you don't need me. You save my salary now. Use what good a man's got, spit him out."

"You're not a businessman. You spend half your time in the office talking about music, dances, dates . . ."

"Haven't had one. Women are dangerous. Don't talk to me about dates."

"See? You can't be serious. You're on stage all the time. Like I said, you have full pay for six months or until you find a job."

Milosh opened his office door and called the secretary. When she appeared, he said, "Now we got a third-party here. Tell *her* I get six months' full pay."

"Don't push me," Turner said, but he repeated it for the secretary.

"You bear witness," Milosh said. "It's important to bear witness."

He shut the door behind them. He intended to gather his things together, but he couldn't determine what and where they were. In this room, yes. He flipped the radio on loud. He needed a box. It was shameful to have to walk to the secretary's desk. "Please," he said, "get me two boxes."

He carried both boxes when he left and thus couldn't hold himself as erect as he wanted. He kept his head up, his gaze straight ahead.

"Mr. Lukovich," the secretary said, "I hate to do this, but Mr. Turner said I should ask for the key."

Milosh didn't respond. She got up and opened the door for him. "I'm sorry," she said. "You're getting a raw deal."

He nodded to her, embarrassed that he was touched by her sympathy.

He put the boxes in the back seat of his car, then returned to the building. He went to Turner's door, opened it without knocking, and tossed the key on the floor. "Six months to the day mistermanofhisword."

Tucson streets because he couldn't go home yet. Talking to the Turner ghost in his head. Come the day Turner stretched out his hand, this hand would not rise to take it. Come the day Turner lay in a gutter, let urine rain down on him. Come the day Turner died, bless the dirt of his grave. May every Serbian saint guard close the doors to heaven. May the man never make a dollar, never have a son. May his wife leave him. May his wife never leave him and never love him. May he live in hell before he dies.

The next morning, Milosh laid his clothes on the bed, but when his father didn't appear, he didn't dress at all. He kept the blinds closed and he listened to records. At noon, he brought the bottle of Slivovitz into the living room. He got one shot glass. Man-to-man-to-himself, this life was a crock of shit. American saying.

The next morning, he dressed as if he still had the job. He planned what to tell his father, who maybe would not come after all, would stop this foolish careering down the interstate to fix a loser son breakfast.

But he came, swept into the house like he delivered the dawn. "Today we got also bagels and cream cheese. Breakfast dessert."

"Turner and I haven't been getting along lately," Milosh said, second bagel in hand.

"You doing your work?"

"Of course I'm doing my work. Doing my work, huh!"

"Too much music. All the time music, music, party talk."

"Five days a week, up every morning, out of here, stay late. You think Turner cares? He cares about nothing but himself. You stop coming. You make me nervous showing up here. Who can think about work with his father running all over the country."

"You get fired?"

Laugh, scornful look. "Me? I run that company." Slide the chair in slowly and carefully. "I got to go to work. You go home, okay? Okay, Pop?"

Milosh and his mother sat in the waiting room. "You should have told me he was sick," he said.

"I didn't know. You think he tells me anything? He tells me to mind my own business."

The chairs were too small and Milosh couldn't get comfortable. He thought waiting rooms should have televisions. Or windows. Anything. He went down the hall to the men's room, splashed cold water on his face. His reflection was of a scared man. He loved his father. In the waiting room again, he was gruff with his mother. "You're his wife," he said. "It's your job to know when he's sick."

They put his father in the hospital that afternoon, operated the next morning. He called his brother. "You got no choice," he said. "This is your father. Don't talk to me about problems. You got one problem only. Your father." Milosh wired his brother the money, but he still didn't come.

For the next week, Milosh drove his mother home late in the evening and returned to sleep on a cot by his father's bed. The cot was also too small, but he relished the hardship. He could hear his father's breath and wanted to hear it all his life.

"So am I dying?" his father said once. He was unshaven, and the muscles of his face fell slackly back. He didn't look like Milosh's father anymore.

"Who said anything about dying? Don't talk dying. Eat and sleep. You never had it so good."

He drove to Tucson. He had a check from Turner. "So okay," he said to his gritty porch. "The man meant what he said." He did the bluegrass show. He was subdued because a man couldn't joke at a time like this. Nothing in the world was funny. He played back-to-back songs so he wouldn't have to talk. He felt such steady pain he thought he might himself die. At his sign-off, he said "Thought you'd enjoy hearing just music for once in your working-man lives." The station told him later he got a lot of calls about what a good idea that was.

"He was in the resistance," Milosh said, though all the people in the living room already knew that. "Couldn't ever go back because his name was on a list." Somberness filled the house. The drapes were drawn, the living room filled with dark wooden chairs brought from throughout the house. All the men and women were dressed in black, as they should be. Milosh answered each knock at the door. No one entered without hugging him, then searched for the wife and mother who would be seated in the living room and not expected to greet anyone.

A good man.

Wonderful dancer.

Could sing, too. Used to.

People came and went, brought food. Remembered one more thing about Drago Milan Lukovich.

The relatives' cigarette smoke drifted everywhere, but the mother didn't say a word. She was sedated but looked angry and grief-stricken. Once she blurted out, "Never kissed me after Milosh was born." One of the women dampened a handkerchief from a small vial in her purse and pressed the cloth against the widow's temples. "Two sons I give him and he loves a dead woman."

Milosh led his mother to her bedroom. "Say only good things," he said. "You don't want to remember bad stuff today. People are listening. He was a good man."

She shook her head vehemently. Milosh pulled her against him, held her head firmly against his chest. When she finally quietened, he took tissue from the box by her bed and wiped her face dry. "Where's your inhaler?" She gestured toward the dresser. He handed the inhaler to her. "Use it," he said. She didn't respond. "Use it," he said hoarsely. "Please. I don't want anything to happen to you." He guided her hand to her mouth. When she closed her lips around the dispenser, he pressed the plunger for her. "Try not to cry so much," he said. "Makes breathing harder." He followed her back to the living room, seated her, and spoke to the room. "Please go outside to smoke," he said. No one protested. Milosh returned to his own chair near the hallway, where he could easily hear someone arrive. Sometimes the pressure in his throat and chest made him gasp, and he would pretend he heard a knock so he could leave the room a moment or two.

The big fat brother wore a black suit, had a plate on his knee constantly. Didn't cry but looked as if he might. Other people cried, men, too.

Good man.

Good man.

When the house closed for the night, Milosh lay on the sofa so his brother could have the second bedroom. Oppression weighted him. No matter how he tried to avoid them, memories of his father's looming presence rose again and again. His father with a belt, striking the pudgy, bare thighs of his oldest son, till the mother, screaming, snatched the boy by the arm and dragged him outside. His father on the inside of the house, refusing to open the door for a tardy Milosh. His father eating, smoking, cooking, singing. Dancing. A strong and beautiful man.

After the funeral, Milosh sorted through his father's belongings, gave small items away to family members and friends. Good clothing, he folded neatly, packed in boxes, and delivered to the church. This his mother could not do. She would have become ill herself. All her protests meant nothing. She had adored Drago. She grieved for more than his death. Milosh pocketed the photograph of his father's Old Country wife. He took it to his uncle. "Tell me about her," he said.

"What's to tell? She was a looker. Probably fat by now."

"When did they marry? Was it in a church?"

"Married? Make sense."

"Pop. This is his first wife, right? The one he left behind to come here, to escape?"

"Who told you that? Drago? Your father?"

"Yes. No. He told Mom. She told me."

"Bunch of lies. He was kidding her. This woman," he poked the photograph, "just one of the young girls around. A dancer. Drago always danced with the prettiest."

"He told Mom it was his wife. He said he had to leave her behind to save his life."

"In his dreams, maybe, he married her."

Milosh kept the photograph a day more, then threw it away, feeling another kind of grief, as if she was someone he had known too.

"Why did he give Pravi to Granddad? Why didn't he want both sons?"

"He said Pravi was too scared to live in this house. He needed a momma for life."

"Why'd you let him do it?"

"No one stopped your father but himself. He did what he did."

"Because Pravi was fat, right? Not a proper son for Drago Lukovich."

"Because Pravi wanted his Grandmamma. That simple. Don't make more of it than it is."

She had to use the inhalant often. She was small and homely, grieving for a man who hadn't treated her well. Now her happiness fell on his shoulders. And his brother's. "Pop loved you," Milosh said. "That woman? In the picture? All made up. One big story to keep you guessing. Just ask Uncle Vule. He'll tell you."

She would have none of it. She clasped her arms against anything good this late.

"Maybe you didn't want to know?" The question surprised even him. He didn't wait for an answer, but stood, moving behind her and bending down so his lips brushed her hair and his arms completely enfolded her. "You'll be okay, Mom. I'm going to take care of you. Me and Pravi."

"You're a good son."

He raised up but stayed behind her. "It's not true what you said, is it? Pop did kiss you, right? After I was born, he still kissed you sometimes?" When she didn't answer, he felt anger not toward his father but toward her. "Come on, Mom. He's a dead man. Don't hold onto a lie." In the continuing silence, he came forward. She looked so sunken inward, so beaten, so differently fragile that he feared for them both. "It's okay," he blurted, "either way, Mom. You did the best you could."

He wanted his father to have loved his mother, to have loved her dearly.

He talked his brother into moving back from Chicago to live with their mother.

"I'll pay all the bills," Milosh said, "till you get a job. Then we split."

"I'll wake up here every morning, go to bed here every night."

Milosh understood the brother's argument. "As long as you live in the house with her, I'll pay more than half."

Milosh went to work for Hartford Distributors. They gave him his own office. He didn't bring one personal thing into the building. He wore black slacks and a white shirt every day, with an armband on his left bicep. He might wear the armband all his life.

His mother called. "I asked the priest. He said go ahead and make music. Join your friends. No one can be quiet a year anymore. That's the old way. Just don't you be loud, Miloshka. No loud music."

"You tell the priest no exception from honoring my father. Okay? No excuses from grief." He stored his instruments in a back room closet.

Milosh continued the volunteer radio show. It was early morning dedication, no pay, struggling up from sleep with a purpose in his heart. He talked the station manager into an ethnic hour on Sunday afternoons. He punched music from the world into the fair desert city. "Miserlou" was his theme song. Just before the first note, he could see his father strike the proper pose, arms wide, ready for joy, and though Milosh didn't leave his chair, he would move with the big man, the huge man, the man who was in the resistance, into that dance from the Old Country, *miserloumiserloumiserlou* step, turn, slide, kick, stepstep pause, *miserloumiserlou miserloumiserlou* step, turn, pause, step step, slide turn slide. Turn.

Dating in America

There is the most beautiful man with a guitar across his legs. And he can *play*. He could woo widows and wives with that strong stroke. This he obviously knows. And so knows the woman watching him. Oh. If she could play as he does, that would be enough. But she can't. Around them swirls the sun-heated light of a Southwest summer day. Couples dance, their sandaled and moccasined feet spinning dust like threads of song. Anyone's laughter is so welcome, like the hope of being single again and lovely forever. He has black eyes, intelligent eyes, and when he sets the guitar aside, gently—it must be a female—he ambles to the prime listener who would move him, yes, to her side, maybe for an entire future.

They talk, easy words, who plays with whom, what song won where, how harmonies are held. When the day descends into pine shadows and camp sites, they walk, making themselves silhouettes above the valley, against the moon—or so she sees it—perhaps he's thinking of food or sex, one-time stands, or even, below the level of pearls and magic, a condom? But he tries nothing! Absolutely! She wills it! wishes! He's a chaste hero. Are there such? They stroll back and before he leaves—yes he must, having to work next morning, festival or not—before he leaves, like fall, like spring bloom, like pages from a book or letter she'll save as proof of something almost remarkable—before he leaves, he gives her a slip of paper no wider nor longer than his thumb, and it has a number, a phone number, a most wonderful number, where he can be reached if ever, ever, she were to pass his way.

Which she does less than a month later, because the moon has waxed and she's near craters of despair at such a dead life, a madness gone numb. So she calls him, punch punch like making a cardboard fellow only onto the keyboard of the phone and there rises that voice, melodic, male. Yes he remembers her. Certainly. And he would like to see her. So he shall! he shall! all of her, perhaps truly beautiful this one time, this one last grand stand against the boy who did not take her to the prom, against pale eyes and freckled skin, not angel kisses, no, a pigment problem, just this once, overnight beloved and for eternity. She packs lightly, because she will soar, nothing of hers will touch a molecule of reality. Into the car midafternoon, racing from that city sun that would blaze all romance into concrete, sweat it to a smudge of oil on the pavement. And she wins. Outside the limits, on the freeway, speeding faster than the whole goddamn galaxy toward her own little sun, that fellow, that guitar fellow, with his lower lip working with songs, and his fingers coaxing the finest melodies from threads of metal twisted so thin if they burst, they could shred even memories. Around her and through the car and out over the desert whips and whines and whispers the wind, hot and breathy, gusting, lowing, touching her throat and eyes, and she gulps it in, swallows the whole blasted summer and everyone. This maybe-hope is so miraculous, one could live on it, eat it, drink it, sleep in it, love it to death.

But something, something is wrong. By her feet, by the pedals that control travel and arrival and all arrests in between, a spider web has spread. Oh, it's white, all right, and silky and empty, but it clings and stretches and winds against itself. It has sealed itself across a stretch of space and is home to something, only the something is not at home. She zooms into the city, trying to think and feel a separation between herself and the car, herself and the spun trap she shifts with every change of speed. How big will the damned thing be? And is it poisonous? Of course it is! It's the first obstacle, the first test.

Why hadn't she anticipated this? No one makes it through unchallenged. Well, come on babies. Come on fellas. Give it your best shot. Her dainty foot, white and smooth as alabaster but strong as oiled leather, thrusts down the accelerator and she impels herself to his address, reaching it while the late afternoon radiance is still golden like an age gone past. She slips out, stands, looks back and down. The web strands are wadded and soiled, one thick and trailing against the mat, like a cloud turned crude and falling from lethargy. But no spinner, no creature in view. From instinct, she looks up and around, too, because what nests underneath might hide up above. Then, she's on his porch and knocking demurely and breathlessly. Will she be lovely to him? Will this evening be like a story she could have written in her sleep, even when she was three or ten or seventeen?

He is the same. Exactly. Strong. Handsome. Confident. His speaking voice is her entire trip in symphony. And his home! So cool! All shadows and neatness and cleanliness. Here the air is filtered, she knows. It must flow over water or ice before entering the house. He controls atmosphere. And skin. And heartbeat. And he himself is so calm. So pleased to see her. Truly. Even his lips are firm, delineated, as though etched. Words from there must be perfect, learned. To hear love from such a source would turn the text into cuneiform, runes, all her past made legend. Let him like her! Let him like her!

He presents her to the rooms. They are cared for, oiled, coordinated. Nothing dares move. On the wall, framed, and framed, and again framed, like moons saved for a future spending, are butterflies. Yes. Maybe moths. But beautiful, and so very, very dead. Butterfly-mothbabies. Yep. He puts on an album and music spiels around her like invisible wings. Wings of everything that no longer flies. Still here. He smiles so greatly, so truly, that his teeth are horrifying because they are rows too uniform for human admiration. She refuses to like his teeth. And perhaps she could dislike his hands? Are they monstrous? scarred, misshapen? Worse. They are unmarred, sleek and sinewy. No melody could ever stay hidden from them or deviate from the score. There would be no freedom. He does like her, of course. He asks many, many questions, and the scrutiny of his eyes makes her weak, shamed, because he couldn't miss the map of life on her face, could he? Pores. Her skin shows pores, doesn't it? She can't remember, but now she's too pliable, absorbs water and air and scents and powder. So she isn't foolproof or safe or even special. She's simply—a horrible word, an undoing word—simply one of those who come to his door. One who floats in on tendrils of night and clings to the black screen of a closed entrance. One who leaves little wishes like moons for him to collect, to make art from, or scrolls, or himself. Damn him. Damn him.

He guesses it isn't going to work out after all, because he's experienced at these things, having entertained creation stories before, and he can, of course, predict the end. They are not meant for each other. But the evening has been pleasant, hasn't it, like a tale around a dying campfire, the sky red from some god bleeding somewhere, and night on its way. He is rejecting her most gently. He walks her to the car, and she forces her feet—winged though she believed they were—to stroll, as if she will circumnavigate the world and spread her own gospel and have no dirt cling to her soles, and he happens— is it really by chance? does he really not know what he will find?—he happens to open the door and see the web. It now holds a black round shiny spot, but not for long. The spot disappears beneath the pedal like a blink of nothing. He is alarmed, distressed, must save her, win the grail, and she tells him to forget about it. He insists, names the poison, and she tells him again to forget about it. This is her problem and her creature. Ignoring even her attempt to salvage a modicum of grace, he runs for a can of something mundane. He is going to help her out. Prosaic and pisspoor help her, her ass. So she departs. She straddles the little pinch of death, cries, and races the night sky and all its wee winking lights all the way home. She wants a fairy tale. A kid's story. Something violent and just and glorious for her to slide in on. But she has only herself and a fucking spider, a black widow baby.

They reach home when the moon has turned absolutely pale from exhaustion and too many centuries of the same thing. She whispers goodnight sweetheart two or three times as she drags her wounded self from the car, and then, out of spite and some kind of fierce spirit, she blows a series of kisses upward, waves them higher and higher. She suspects they will fall, like notes, like dead song, but they don't. No. She is certain they float away, as if on invisible silk. Perhaps they will defeat seven monsters, open a drawbridge, choose the lady door, outspin the gods. They might net the entire world, the moon, too. She stands in the heroine's moonlight, which is the only light available, and breathes in the cool, clean night air. She may be growing very beautiful, may be worth a golden apple, or a dip into purgatory. She hums. If she could play the spheres, oh, that would be a wondrous skill. She becomes aware of the heavy shadow that is the car, isn't a chariot, and she strolls over to leave the door ajar, so the creature may escape if it wishes.

Small Courtesies

The Fan-T-Sci conference descended on the Delmar Hotel on a Friday afternoon in November. The Missouri sky was already shading toward its winter gray, moist, and low, but shimmering, as if a colder layer moved above. Inside the hotel, the employees, though all decent people, were tired and harried, and felt disconcerted by the nature of the guests. The clerks tried not to stare, but they covertly assessed the arriving group. The night supervisor called the manager and moments later was instructed to provide extra security for the duration of this conference. Costs would escalate, but possibly food and drink sales would more than compensate. Hotel security contacted the police station and requested five of the city's finest for an off-duty job at good pay. Just in case.

Truly, this was no common conference. A new world mingled in the lobby, then dispersed in singles or small groups toward the stairs, elevator, or bar. One woman was dressed in silver sequins that clung to her torso and limbs as if they actually grew there. Only her face and her pale hands—the latter with silver nails at least three inches long—indicated that flesh lay beneath the sequins. She rippled when she moved, a most mesmerizing sight for everyone in the lobby. She noticed the attention and laughed. The sound brought chills to one clerk, and glances among them all. Another female wore flowing red chiffon—with nothing underneath but billowing body. Huge and rolling, she registered using her own pen, and the red ink name sworled violently. Most of the women were in black; most were buxom; all were on display. Male gazes could move from breasts that peeked, perked, to those that swung or hung pendant like sinking moons. The men seemed less colorful, but more ominous overall. Only a few were proportioned or attractive, and they highlighted their best features: A young man with the body of a dancer wore tight briefs, from which narrow silk bands led down his legs and over his upper body, creating the illusion of shirt and slacks; another wore form-fitting silver, not sequins, but with the sides missing, the front and back laced together. Most of the males, though, were misshapen, too tall, or too thin, obese, squat, or perhaps with skinny legs beneath a pear body, or narrow shoulders above a globe of rump. A cadaverous man in black leather had somehow shaped his long orange hair into spikes, so no one could stand near him. Beneath the jutting front spikes, his eyes appeared like black holes. His teeth were orange or had been painted so.

A gnomish man in green velvet looked up at the doorman and said in a low, soft voice, "We're not freaks. During the year we're just normal people with normal jobs. This is our holiday. Our chance to be different."

The doorman, who had a nice home in the suburbs and two children in college didn't understand why this guy was explaining to him. He didn't know whether to feel threatened, because maybe the dwarf was flirting, or complimented, because he looked like a man one should explain to. "Well," he said, "we all need a vacation from time to time."

"We won't be causing any trouble or anything."

"Well, that's good. You might tell the manager that."

"We will. We're always good guests."

Behind the desk, a night clerk mumbled, "We're in for something different this weekend," and read a few names to his coworker. "Dala Coflera, Zi Ki Lai, Larry Lech, Mylaika Rakon." He scrolled down the computer list. "Hey, a John Brown. Probably a spy." He was pleased with himself and had managed to pass from trepidation to anticipation. Usually he was bored at work. "Let it rain, let it pour," he said, sat on the high stool by the desk, and watched what was shaping up.

One of the night staff told the supervisor she needed to go home. Her babysitter had just called, and her son was ill. "My God," she said to herself, hurrying across the filling parking lot, "it's like hell opened up." She was afraid of her own imagination and what such guests could induce in her. Even in the car, she felt unsafe, as if something horrible would pop up over the back seat and speak to her. When she got home, she asked the babysitter to stay for a while, but the girl couldn't. The woman and her son watched a comedy on television. The frantic, crazy humor made her tremble.

Meanwhile, on a one-way road from a small university, miles away, a midwestern couple who had been dating only a month or so and were already struggling for conversation or a tinge of passion, drove toward the conference. Their headlights turned the heavy mist into sparkle, but they couldn't see much beyond the light, just black shapes that must be a house, or barn, or closed country store.

"Where do people in this country go?" she said. "The houses are always dark even early in the evening, like people are already in bed. Sometimes it's like the world has died and I'm coasting alone."

"People save electricity. If you look close, there's probably a light toward the back of the house."

"I leave every light on when I'm home, and some when I'm not."

"I've noticed."

She didn't like that statement, and he knew it. Both understood the implication, that he found her wasteful with money. He was a saver, a healthy man who worked out daily, read much, and had a strong sex drive. She was older, thin, chain-smoked, loved fat and chocolate, read much, and also had a strong sex drive. Both were headstrong and lonely. She liked houses that were warm, that glowed at night like an invitation to life, and she resented this bleak moist country of homegrown tightwads and tiny spirits. "I think," she said, "a house should look warm and inviting."

"Yours does, that's for sure. It's a nice effect." He meant that. Although he would never waste electricity in his own home, driving up to hers always made him feel the lights were for him especially. He thought perhaps she had a generous spirit and he hoped he did, too. "I'm always comfortable at your place," he said.

The moment was saved, and they settled back into their new lovers' closeness.

She was the one who had received notice of the conference. It was in her mailbox at work, with "FYI, Keith," signed at the bottom. Keith was a fellow professor from another department, who sometimes smoked outside with her, where they talked of writing and individuality. When she told him she might attend the conference, he said, "Good, but let me warn you that it's not traditional, not academic like you're accustomed to. These people are into science fiction and fantasy. I think you're pretty liberal and will enjoy yourself. I know you're bored with the normal routine here."

That she was. But, being also wary of new things alone, she had invited along her friend, the thick-set man who had recently proven they were compatible in bed.

Now, she worried. "What if we don't like it? I'd hate to cost you time and money for a bad weekend."

"At the worst, we can stay in our room for two days." He took her hand and placed it on his thigh, then patted it. "You worry too much."

They felt very comfortable the rest of the drive, very much together and ready to risk a step into the unknown.

One wing of the hotel had been reserved for the Fan-T-Sci guests, but other guests were certainly aware of them and grouped closer together when entering the dining room or bar. A few ventured into the special wing and read the legend of events posted in that registration room. It seemed bland enough, listing introduction, icebreaker, awards, dance; for Saturday, readings, mixers, games, stage play, special sessions. One brave brown-suited man managed to swipe a fuller program from a table near the bar, guarded by a green-dressed gnome.

"Just checking it out," the guest explained. "Looks interesting."

The gnome seemed saddened. "Those programs are for members only. You don't look like one."

"I may be by morning," the guest laughed, and waved the program as he walked away. It made for good reading with his wife: "Listen to this. 'Condom prizes, Fleur-de-lis Room, 8:00 p.m.; Cross-dance by Leonard the Lionhearted, 9:00 p.m. Saturday sessions, 10:00 a.m.: Leather, Centurion Room; Metal, Skyline Room; Silk and Softer, Dahlia Room; Surprise, Charleston Ballroom.' God," the man said, "I'd like to go."

"They'd kill you for smirking."

"Probably." But he wondered if he could somehow dress to pass, just sneak in for one session. He wanted to see this other life.

The policemen, having conferred with the night supervisor, stationed themselves discreetly apart, covering elevators and exits. One had a full view of the rear parking lot, where lights were dimmer, especially in the heavily descending fog, and anyone dressed in black would be indiscernible. That policeman would occasionally have a smoke while he strolled the lot and sensed anything inappropriate. He was told by a green gnome, who startled him by appearing silently and suddenly at his side, that "We're just ordinary people, you know. We assume a role this one weekend of the year. I'm an accountant myself. We're a courteous group, overall. We don't tolerate poor behavior." The policeman found that little guy somewhat sinister, maybe because of the fog, maybe because he had a slight lisp, maybe because he was too damned ingratiating. Sort of a protests-too-much guy.

Having become lost in the city streets, where signs were in ridiculous positions, and two-way streets became suddenly one-way only, without any indication of the direction of the one way— north, east, south, or west—the midwestern couple arrived later than they planned. Both were slightly embarrassed that she had used a green garbage bag for a dress-carrier. He felt a little more worldly than her, because he would never have carried such a contraption into a nice hotel. He would have left it in the car and brought it in later, draped over his arm. She held it up so the bottom of her pink dress wouldn't touch the carpet. It seemed to him like a flag of mediocrity, perhaps low-class. She, however, quickly decided that it was a sign of her true individuality, since the really wealthy, the really secure, broke all the damned rules. Only middle class worried about correctness and they were who made the world truly monotonous, because they were cowards. He signed them in, registering by two names but one room, because what-the-hey, they were what they were. Unmarried and together. Modern enough to be blunt about it. He steered her toward the elevator. "We couldn't get in the reserved wing. It's all filled up. Might be best anyhow, to be separate from the main group since we're not really fantasy writers."

"I am. One of my published pieces is a fantasy."

"Okay. But we still can't get in that wing. The clerk said the introduction has already started. We can drop our things off and get right over there." He carried the suitcases and thought briefly about liberated women. She hadn't offered to carry her own suitcase.

A cop by the elevator said, "Good to see you folks. Thought there weren't any normal people left in the city." He had a good-hearted laugh that brought crinkles around blue eyes. He was too heavy for a policeman, but then, the woman thought, a good nature was a strong force. She sure liked that trait.

"I got a feeling," her lover said, "that we're not going to fit in."

"Why?"

"Didn't you hear the officer?"

"Maybe it's a young group."

"Maybe."

In their room he wanted to make love before they began the evening. The wide bed with the gold bedspread sank deliciously when he fell backward, and he wanted her to immediately be taken by the manliness he presented, lying on his back, hands behind his head, so his broad chest expanded even more. If she would just unfasten his belt, unzip his pants, without his having to say a word, she'd be the woman for him, but she was worrying aloud about whether to change clothing now or just get to the meeting. He reluctantly rose, and put his arms around her from behind, cupping her small breasts. "We could skip the first meeting," he whispered. "Why don't we shower together and then change? We can go for drinks afterwards and meet the crew."

"I want to see what's going on," she said. "We can make love later."

"Planning things ruins them."

"Spontaneity can ruin good plans."

So now neither could be truly happy with the evening. He had been postponed and devalued; she had been made selfish and staid. Both felt guilty and in risk of loneliness. Why didn't anything ever just work out right? They left dressed as they were, in search of the conference registration room.

And there, though all but one of the conferees had gone on to the introduction, leaving one member to man the table, and though all the other tables bore the familiar paper cups, coffee urns, beer cans, and plastic glasses of conferences all over the world, the midwestern couple knew they were at the edge of a decision, because the one person had orange spikes for hair, and eyes buried deep in shadows and sinking flesh.

She strode up to the table, and her lover, though hesitant, followed, feeling that he might be enlisting which he had avoided during the last war. He didn't like confrontations of any kind.

"We want to register for the conference," she said.

"I don't think so," the orangehead said. "Are you already members?"

"No. Do we have to be?"

"If you've ever been to one of our conferences, you are. If not, you can sign up. But you don't look as if you're into sci-fi."

She couldn't bear being told what she could and could not do, and the chagrin brought her connection to mind. "Keith Parmenter suggested I come. I write fantasy."

The dark holes seemed to shift to her partner.

"He's with me."

"I don't think either of you will be very comfortable."

"I want to register."

He allowed them to. He gave them blank lapel cards to fill out, and obviously read the names they wrote. "You better wear the cards all the time," he said, "so people will know you've paid to attend."

Her lover was amazed anew at her fortitude. For a few moments he felt that he traveled in her wake, which he didn't particularly like. He did like the sway of her hips and the curl of her hair and that stride that was nothing less than bold. He held the door open for her to enter the gathering room.

Actually, there was no silence when they entered, though both felt as if there were. And both felt the prickle that comes from unseen eyes, though each, if turning, could have seen all the eyes. No one missed the couple's entrance. The speaker, laughing, had a brief lapse of sound, then launched off into the grand introduction of the guest entertainer, none other than Leonard the Lionhearted.

The couple had to sit up front, near where they had entered, because the room was full, full, full, to standing creatures in the back, and they had seats only because a small man dressed in green carried forward two folding chairs. "Welcome," he said, and the couple felt warm toward him for a human gesture and a familiar word. They sat.

Now the speaker was joining the audience, and music rolled out from behind them, fast and rumbling, a rock boogie, and people clapped and hooted and squealed. The couple didn't turn, because whatever was coming, was coming their way. A man gyrated past them into the space before the podium. He bumped, high-stepped, turned, wiggled that bottom, flipped his wrists, manly wrists, with strong hands. He was tall, muscular, with wild black hair falling mid-shoulder, and with a black beard heavy enough for two hands to get lost. His long legs were hairy, too, so very male and strong, but the feet were encased in black stiletto heels that never faltered in intricate turns and quick, cute little twists. His tight buttocks were covered by black lace stretching to a bodice top, above which his chest hair curled ludicrously or sensuously. His red-painted lips synched the boogie words and he wooed the crowd with winks and kisses, all to a boogie beat. Keith Parmenter. Leonard the Lionhearted. He stopped one moment in front of the couple, his hips and hands in rhythm, and capped each head with one of his hands for one beat, switched hands for another cap, then was bouncing off, swishing past, shaking that bodice top as though breasts might fall out. The couple now felt better. They had been touched and welcomed and were special guests, not outsiders. They were the anointed. When he danced back down the aisle, the couple applauded as loudly as anyone and even turned in their seats, surreptitiously skimming the crowd and meeting a few glances. Not all were cold.

They had to sit for another few minutes while awards were given to the conference planners. Black and orange condoms, blown slightly full, some with faces painted on the ends.

She wondered if she would be sickened by herself later, for having not walked out, for being pleased at the dancer's recognition. She hoped her lover didn't blame her for the coarseness of this meeting. He wasn't suited for this kind of thing. He was more conservative. A nice guy. Beside her, the lover thought by god he might not be happy, but he hadn't sunk this low. He was going back to the room and maybe back home. He had nothing in common with these crazy loons. Sick cries for attention. Losers all. Jesus. He didn't know what to make of her, sitting there so calm. But maybe she wasn't. Maybe they'd laugh and get the hell out of here together.

Keith, now dressed in a gold-mesh jumpsuit, was waiting on them by the door and drew them aside. "I'm glad you came," he said. "I hope you're not shocked. I warned you."

"You did, but I didn't know what you meant. Now I do."

"And you're offended?"

"Maybe. I don't know. I've never seen anything like this. I tell you what, though, you were really good. I was fascinated. You can dance like crazy. I never knew that."

"I'd prefer no one at work know."

"I'm not going to say a word."

Keith glanced at her partner who shook his head. "Don't worry. This isn't the kind of thing I would talk about."

"You two," Keith said, "are a little noticeable. If you've got some more casual clothes, you'd feel less conspicuous."

"We both brought conference clothes," she said. "Will they kick us out?"

"Of course not. Just wear your name tags. And have fun." He patted her hand, while nodding at someone yards away, a lovely black girl whose body was painted the same array of colors as the chiffon scarves she wore, so that she looked like a wispy tropical bird or a blossom coming into being. He hurried to her and the couple watched this perfect match impossible anywhere else in the world they knew.

They went back to their room and made love with the lamps out but the drapes open, so the window was all moonfiltered gray. He poised himself above her as if he were a bird and would swoop into her forever. That's how they both felt when he entered her, like they rode a fierce warm wind together. Then they lay side by side, sweating, tired, and each still charged like the night wouldn't let them rest.

"You want to go home," she asked.

"Was thinking about it."

"I'd like to see the dance. Just for a little while. Then we could go if you want. Or we could get a good night's sleep and leave in the morning. Or maybe shop awhile."

He thought it odd that she could think of shopping. What was shopping, anyhow? His head wouldn't clear enough to get hold of that thought or any thought equally common.

Across town, the night staff woman let her babysitter go home, and she checked on her little boy who hadn't been sick at all, but who wasn't sleeping easily now, maybe from popcorn and cookies so late at night. Maybe from her own tension. Certainly she herself wasn't feeling well. Her breath was ragged, which meant she needed to calm herself or she'd start hyperventilating and get panicky. She hated her damned nervous nature, having to guard against her own tendencies. But she'd had sense enough to take off work. She'd be vomiting by now if she had stayed there. Crazy people scared her to death.

The back-lot cop had an intuition about which one would be the troublemaker. It was that creepy green runt. He was too damned friendly. The other cops said he'd talked to each of them, gave each the same line about being normal people all year and just acting out fantasies during this conference. What kind of fantasies? Maybe there'd be a murder from someone thinking he was goddamn jack-theripper. Heaven knows the women were dressing like they longed to be victims of something.

The silver-sequin lady had to take six pills before she could attend the dance, and apply fresh makeup. She was a mass of pain and sometimes nausea. Beneath the silver, surgery scars crisscrossed her abdomen. Her breasts were foam and she loathed them. But she loved the reflection of Mylaika Rakon. She could swim there, in that vision, because visions never took treatments, felt terror, never lied, never died. She was her own mantra.

The midwestern lover refused to dress any differently for the dance, and besides, he couldn't if he wanted to. The change he brought was dressier than what he had on. Well, she asked, would he attend with her if she was wearing only a slip? Because that's what she was going to do. She had a black, long, half-slip, and if she wore it pulled up over her breasts, wore black stockings, let her hair down and put on gobs of makeup, she'd fit right in.

"What about shoes?"

She solved that. She pulled house slippers from her suitcase and waved them at him. Silver slip-ons, with elastic pulling them tight. "Will you go with me dressed like this?"

"Why not? We're never going to see any of these people again."

Now each felt superior to the other and were separate as they walked down the hall to the elevator. When they emerged, he avoided the cop's eyes by lighting a cigarette and falling a little behind her. He was with her when she entered the elevator to the other wing.

"Ashamed of me, I see," she said. "You don't need to accompany me."

"Somebody better. You're acting strange."

"I'm the same woman you came with."

"Maybe, but you're not attracting the same kind of man."

She thought that was astute, that he was caring for her in his way. "I do feel ridiculous," she said. "I mean, this is obviously a slip. Maybe I should change back."

"You've done it, let's go. Or let's go home."

"You're right. I made the choice. But if you get the least bit uncomfortable," she said, "we'll leave."

"I can take it as long as you can." He put his hand on the small of her back to guide her down the hall. "Whatever you do, don't stare. You don't know these people."

The small ballroom had a fountain in the center, with a low wall on which some guests sat. Others danced on the square-tiled floor. The music was haunting and frantic, metallic, like wind through huge flutes. Colored globes hung like moons across the room. The couple sat on the fountain wall. Near them, a tiny, fragile blonde, who held a posture so rigid she looked like a statue, spoke with a brown-draped monk. He turned to assess the couple. Moments later both left, followed by the others, and the midwestern couple was alone by the fountain.

"I never felt so naked," she said. "I'm having chills."

"It's the water. Did you know you forgot your name tag?"

"My God, I did."

Across the dance floor, the statue and monk had stopped by Keith Parmenter. Now he crossed to the couple, smiling slightly. "So you found something to wear after all."

"Is it okay? I feel foolish."

"No. You're trying to fit in. That's good. Why don't you dance? Show everyone you want to mingle, not just watch."

"So people *are* noticing us."

"Yes, but that doesn't matter. Relax. Dance. Laugh. Get acquainted with the members."

They did dance, because they were certainly no worse at it than most of the others, better in fact, except for Keith and his lovely flower, for whom the dancers applauded. The couple envied that grace, though when they considered the source of the appreciation, were glad enough to be just competent dancers. He wished she had not worn the slip, because the excitement flushed her neck and chest a funny bluish-red color that made her look older and more worn, and because with no waistline in the slip, and with her tiny breasts, she was a slat woman, not feminine at all. He wanted to feel some appeal for her, even if it were just protective, but he felt she was asking for ugly attention and that made her ugly. She felt terribly alone in his arms, because he was so judgmental, and he had a way of with-drawing that she could sense, even when he denied it, so he was like a force against her. It was wearying. She couldn't bear the weight of his discontent. Her own was heavy enough.

Someone stopped them from dancing by touching each simulta-neously. It was a small man, dressed in green velvet. His shoes were green, too, with curling tops.

"We have to ask you to leave," he said.

They were both taken aback, partly from his statement, but mostly from the lisp in which it came, childlike and soft, but from such an aging face.

"Why?"

"You obviously don't belong here, and you're making everyone uneasy."

"We're just dancing. Minding our own business," the lover said.

"And we paid our way. I'm a member now."

"You're not wearing a tag."

"I couldn't pin it to this outfit."

"Still, it would be better if you left. Everyone thinks so."

"You got it, buddy," from the lover. "This isn't my idea of a good evening anyhow."

"I paid and I'm staying."

Keith appeared again. "What's the matter here?" The green man bowed deeply, backed up while still bent, and spoke toward the floor. "I've asked the gentleman and lady to leave so the guests can be at ease."

"They're friends of mine. It's okay. Leave it to me."

The little man backed up a few more feet and turned before he stood upright.

"That's Pietro, the Peacekeeper," Keith said. "He tries to make everyone at ease."

"Why did he bow to you?"

"He bows to anyone he respects. That's his only direct commu-nication other than peaceful greetings."

"Well, he sure didn't make us feel any better," she said.

"I'm sorry it's not working out for you two. I didn't know when I invited you, that you'd bring a guest. I should have been more explicit."

"I, fellow," the lover blurted, "am perfectly willing to leave right now."

"You don't have to do that. But you might skip the dance and come down for some of the games tomorrow. Though, if you haven't enjoyed yourselves thus far, I don't imagine you will tomorrow either."

"What are the games?"

"Depends on the room you choose. The titles are suggestive. You're both intelligent, and I imagine you can guess fairly accurately. I can't just stay with you. I hope you understand. It might cause hostility and these are my friends. They buy my books, they feature me at conferences. I have a responsibility."

"Why did you invite me? Why me and no one else?"

"You seemed different from my other colleagues. Are you sorry?"

"No. I just want to fit in." She and they knew that wasn't true, but it couldn't be *unsaid*, and she couldn't be uninvited. Now he had demolished any of her worlds.

Her lover felt the other man, Keith the Creep, had somehow violated the woman he was with, and though she wasn't truly attractive and wasn't as intelligent as he had first believed, she was with him and therefore his charge. "We're leaving," he said. "You can count on that."

"And on your discretion, I hope."

"We'll see," the lover said, and felt he had retrieved a little pride.

In their room, she cried deeply, so that makeup ran her face into a dissolving mask. "I must have looked *so stupid*," she said. "Damn. Goddamn. Like such a fool, showing up in a slip. I insulted them. That was it. I made light of their costumes by pretending a piece of underwear could make me one of them."

"Why do you care what they think? They're a bunch of sickos. Crazy people who can't lead normal lives, and you're crying because of them?"

"But if even they reject me, what in the hell am I?"

"You rejected them before you even entered."

"Then they're better than me. Can't you see that?"

"No. What I see is a college professor who's tearing herself to pieces over a crowd of jokers. You must want to dislike yourself. You have to really twist things to take the view you've got."

"You don't care about anybody but yourself. You never see what's going on. You even make love like you're watching your own body, or watching me watch it. You're as self-centered as any of them."

The possible accuracy of that stopped him cold still. He had thought she appreciated his body. Now he wasn't certain of anything about her or him.

"Are we leaving?" he asked.

"Let's do."

She showered, dressed in a suit with padded shoulders, the one she had planned to wear to a conference session. The rest of her clothing, including the pink dress, she folded, wrapped in the garbage bag, and stuffed into her suitcase. When they checked out, her hair was still wet and her reflection was pretty ugly, as if her head were too small for her body. In her heels, she was taller than him.

"You want to carry your own suitcase," he said, though it wasn't a question.

"Glad to." She teetered toward the door, and in a moment, he swept up, grabbed the handle, and carried her suitcase, angry but oddly grateful at the same time. In the back lot, the policeman recognized them as having arrived only a short time earlier and felt he should investigate.

"You folks get driven out by the creep show," he said, trying to be light though he meant it.

"Yep," the lover said, stuffing the suitcases in the trunk. "We were actually asked to leave by a green runt."

"Bet I know who you mean. He's a troublemaker. We spotted him early on."

"We didn't know what kind of a conference it was," she said. "We made a mistake. They didn't do anything to us. We shouldn't have come."

"You shouldn't be driven away, though. If you don't want to go."

"Believe me," the trunk was slammed shut, "we want to go."

"That right, lady?"

"Yes."

They rode off into the fog together and they welcomed it. It seemed actually warm, and the vague, filtered lights along the highway seemed like suns that would guide them home and rise tomorrow on a new day. They held hands and felt genuinely close, forever close. Even when they entered the backland leading to the small university town, even when the road was one-way, and absolutely dark, houses and stores closed down against the night, they felt good together.

"We're hitting it off really well, aren't we?" he said.

"Yes. More than I thought we would."

"We had to team up tonight. That was an experience, wasn't it?"

"Yes. Scared me somehow."

"I'm glad I was with you. It wasn't pleasant, but you needed someone."

"I did. And I'm grateful."

He squeezed her hand. She held on and thought about the houses along the road, how people turned in early, snuggled against one another, maybe whispered in the dark. She sighed. "I guess life is easier if you're not alone."

"Maybe we won't ever have to be alone again."

They both thought that sounded right and good. They were suited to one another. If they hadn't attended the conference, maybe they would never have known.

In town, the night staff woman paced the hall. She had taken two tranquilizers and still her heart was buzzing. She could feel it, like someone had an electric charge going through her. She was going to die. She knew it just as she knew it wasn't true. This was a panic attack. Nothing more. She wouldn't die. She couldn't leave her boy alone to go the hospital, and she couldn't very well drag the child there again. Poor thing, with a neurotic mother, a crazy mother. She should've stayed at work, faced it. Then, if she went crazy, her son wouldn't see, and she couldn've gone to the hospital and then come home sedated, and he'd not know the ugly, terrified woman who wanted him raised with none of her fears. Still, she had to wake him up and get him in the car with her and drive to the hospital, because now breathing was difficult and her heart was going to stop. She wanted it to. She wanted to die rather than to feel fear like this. Unshakable, horrible, rushing fear from absolutely nothing, nothing.

The back-lot cop called his buddies for support because something was brewing out here, something big. A spikehead had kicked the green dwarf to kingdom come and now had a knife out threatening the little twerp. The cop headed that way, where the two were moving shadows in the misty light, but he didn't run, because this was a strange crew and he wanted his backup.

He heard the spikehead repeating a grunted "Bow! Bow!" but heard nothing from the shifting, smaller form till he moved nearer, and then the sound was soft, a steady mumble. "No, never, never, never."

"Bow!"

"Police," the cop yelled. "Hey! Assholes! Police."

The tall spiked man kicked out, caught the short one in the face, and then ran right over the fallen man, the sole of his shoe pressing against the throat. The cop called STOP, but he didn't really care if the guy stopped or not, and besides, his friends were now on the scene, one taking after the running man. He himself knelt by the green velvet punk, checked his pulse, though obviously he was alive—he was turning his head back and forth as if still saying no, while he struggled for breath. The cop called an ambulance and wondered if he were capable of cutting a breath hole in the guy's throat. He'd seen it done, and it looked easy enough. The struggling ceased and he thought there goes one little loser, but he was wrong. The paramedics arrived, said the man was alive, carted him into the vehicle, and sped away to a hospital.

The cops had a talk about the group of weirdoes, about never being able to identify the orangehead if he washed out the paint and wondering if he would or not. They ambled back to their stations, feeling pretty damned good about how well they did their job. It was even sort of fun as long as no one got hurt. Pity about the little creep. He didn't give in. Had some guts, at least. The back-lot cop was glad he'd been wrong about the guy.

Inside, the night clerk thought this was the best evening he'd ever worked. Excitement every place he looked and no trouble to speak of. These people tipped, too, or so he'd heard. And one woman obviously was drawn to him. She didn't talk at all, or maybe she did, but it was through lips that didn't move. He wondered what making love to a statue woman would be like? It gave him quickened breath. Life was damned good most of the time.

At the hospital, the night-staff woman turned on her table, sedated now, slightly guilty about her son sleeping in the visitors' lounge. Through pleasantly blurred vision, she saw a green twisted dwarf wheeled past her, insisting that he was not harmed and should be released immediately, please, immediately. The sight didn't bother her at all. Poor ugly creature. Her life at least was better than that.

The couple went to her house, where all the lights glowed welcome to whatever moved around on such a night. She unlocked the door and he carried in the luggage. He turned out all the downstairs lights and she didn't protest, because she knew what he was doing. He undressed her slowly and lovingly, like he enjoyed unwrapping this surprise for his body, and then she undressed him. They twined together standing, while the streetlight outside softened the dark enough to recognize each other. Then they lay down together, still twined, knowing that this wasn't love, but it was the best they could make together and would have to do. It might be enough.

On Sunday, the sky had settled into stillness, lowering over the city and the rolling countryside the muted gray of a common midwestern winter. In the Delmar Hotel lobby, the Fan-T-Sci group said goodbyes amidst the amused or frightened gazes of incoming guests. The silver-sequined lady was the first to actually leave. She was wearing a tiara with three diamonds sparkling a triangle just above her wide brow. It had been presented to her at the last session, in honor of her many publications of high fantasy. But she was no fool and recognized compassion behind the gift. Now she gathered her waning strength and with a haughty laugh, strode boldly toward the exit, so their memory would be of grace and happiness and determination. The doorman found himself bowing as she passed, though he never stooped to such servile behavior—it wasn't one of his duties—and wondered why he felt that courtesy not only appropriate but most pleasant.

Recovering Integrity

It was the cutest dog he'd ever seen, just a pup, and *so* fat, so fat it was adorable, with a wide, rolling, pink belly underneath and everywhere else this black, coarse hair, very thick. The eyes were black, too, and when the pup was curled up sleeping, it could have been nothing but a ball of hair. With the eyes open, though, it was a wonderful, trusting, lazy lump of puppy love.

"Leave that dog alone," his wife had said earlier. "Let it rest for a while. The kids wore it ragged yesterday and last night." She was removing her nightgown and the word "ragged" coincided with her face being hidden by the gown and her stomach being bared completely. She was tanned and in good shape for a woman who had borne three children. But the last child had been by Caesarian, and a wide, ugly-red, irregular scar ran from belly button down. She sometimes worried about it, but he thought it a mark of courage at the very least. "Let the kids enjoy it while it's small," he said. "It sleeps more than it plays anyway."

"Which is natural. Babies eat and sleep."

"This is a dog."

"A dog *baby*," she said. She was totally dressed now, standing before the mirror. With one smooth movement, she coiled her long black hair around her left hand and wrist, then raised her arm and released the coil down into a thick, silky ebon circle. Her right hand deftly pinned it into the perfect position, exactly between the top and back of her head, leaving more sharply visible her temples, cheekbones, and lovely neck. And eyes. Luminous, arresting eyes.

He knew she was more intelligent than he, maybe more wily, too, and certainly more ambitious. But he truly loved her and hoped that made them equal in some kind of spiritual way.

"Yes," she said, smiling and coming to kiss him quickly goodbye, "just a little dog baby, no different than babies the world over. Eat and sleep. Cosmic law." She hurried down the stairs. He stood at the top and called down.

"Baby sharks don't sleep," he said. "Even in the womb. They hatch inside and zap! gobble up siblings as they're born."

"Ugh!" She didn't turn around. She walked across Persian rugs—genuine ones, she bought them on site herself—through the dining room, then out of his sight, through the kitchen. He studied the stained glass arch above the front door until he heard the garage door open and, moments later, her car.

"Wifey's gone," he said, as if someone small were nearby. "And we is alone." He rubbed his hands together like a mischievous kid, but the mood wouldn't take, and he slouched back into lethargy. "So, Allen-me-boy, what to do?" The absolute quiet of this perfect home, the mosaic of colors, the perfect temperature even, and with a housekeeper three days a week, drove him back through the bedroom into his private study. Hers was on the other side, but she rarely used it because she had an office at work.

"Job search," he said, clicking on the computer. A series of sad yelps from another part of the house split his attention, but he persisted at his task long enough to check for messages and to look at his listing status—he had a placement bureau at his beck and call and on his wife's paycheck.

"On my way!" he yelled back and ran down the stairs as he enjoyed doing, a kind of ripple-skim he had learned years ago, maybe naturally, maybe from movies.

The pup obviously believed it had been abandoned. The cries were piteous. In the kitchen, gloriously sunlit through many windows and a generous skylight, he scooped the happy creature up.

"You're ruining my shirt," he said, not caring at all. It squirmed so wildly to reach him, or reach the floor, or simply to be reaching, that Allen put the pup down. He didn't want it to wriggle loose and fall on the tile. Then the pup was slipping and clicking, trying to climb Allen's leg, sit on his foot, become airborne. Allen scooped him up again. Such life. Such a great feeling in his hands and arms, almost as he had felt with his children when they were still babies. Now he felt responsible around them. Or, rather, irresponsible, since his wife's salary was five times his own. With the pup secured under his left arm, Allen headed for the garage. He was taking the baby to the park. Parks were as much for pets as kids, or should be.

An hour later, Allen was sweating profusely, sitting on a bench, eating a strawberry ice cream, and watching the black bundle of joy scatter a couple of ducks and delight one little girl. Pink drips marred Allen's nice shoes and one knee of his trousers. His fingers were sticky. He walked to the fountain to rinse his hands and turned moments later, feeling refreshed and perhaps ready to go home, to find the pup not in sight. There was the little girl, the ducks, an elderly gentleman, a boy on a bike, a hippy couple, and a trail of small children led and followed by women who were likely teachers. Allen whistled sharply, and everyone in his view looked at him. It was a piercing whistle, made so by the quick and artful placement of thumb and little finger. No puppy came running. Allen strode onto the pebble path, called, "Hey Pup, Pup," as he moved around the enclosures. Kangaroos lay on their side, propped on elbow, like lazy teenage boys. A smaller female stood by the fence as if she wanted out, and Allen thought perhaps she did. "Hey Pup, Pup." The path inclined and he followed it, turning around often to scan in a circle. Some young kid had probably picked the pup up, and would, if Allen was lucky, put it down somewhere along here.

At the top of the hill was the railed walkway around the polar bear enclosure. Allen could feel the cooler air and wondered at the foolishness of bringing here, to a moderate climate, a creature meant to live in the arctic. He glanced down the sloping cement wall, toward the water below, and saw a black object bobbing. A wet, straggly, small object bobbing.

"My God. That's a dog down there," someone said.

Allen climbed over the railing immediately, held onto it while he tried to position his feet so he would not simply slide down the concave curve. He had begun a tentative descent—against protesting sounds from above—when the polar bear came lumbering into the open. It was not white, but an off-yellow. And big. Big and rolling. The bear's head was cocked, turned slightly toward the left, in the direction of the struggling pup. Allen accepted that of course the bear knew the dog was in the water. Obviously the brute hadn't come out for nothing. There was an alertness about the sloppy body.

There was also that bobbing, foolish, bedraggled, soon-to-be-dead creature.

Allen slid, not as much from volition as from gravity and from a vague, generalized hope that he could save something from willpower alone, or perhaps with his belt or his pants.

Voices were now all around Allen. They were indistinguishable and almost lovely, like the sound of sparkling ice, like quicksilver bursts of pain. The fingertips and heel of his right hand were scraped, and maybe his elbow and hip.

"Don't move, mister," he distinctly heard. He didn't plan to.

The pup had gone under.

Allen, suddenly, was under, too. The water was like liquid ice and Allen sank down, down, down into the blue cold world, his clothing making silk swirls of color, and on his way up he caught the surfacing black ragmop and pulled it to him. Then he felt a massive misplacement of water and expected, with no fear—because it was frozen in place—an equally massive blow to obliterate him. Instead, a loud noise stunned him just as something jerked him backwards. It jerked him again, and again. He had the pup in both hands, held to his chest. He burst back into the world. Before him, near the false bank, was the bear, netted within a red, ropy, mesh. Four men had lines to the net. Someone had Allen, tugged him to the sloping wall, around the end. Allen floated, or almost floated, and the pup, eyes open, remained still, as if it knew something had a deathhold on it. Allen was numb in body.

Two men lifted him to the lowest rock near the bridge.

"You okay mister?"

Allen thought about nodding but couldn't do it.

"You're absolutely crazy."

"You may have to pay a fine, too."

"Don't tell him that now."

Other men came with a stretcher. They lifted Allen and pup. His hands were not about to release the recovered object. The men carefully, with great skill, or so Allen thought, maneuvered the stretcher over the rocks, into the bear's cave, and on into safe daylight. The crowd was interested, alarmed, and genuinely thankful for his rescue. The pup whimpered but lay still, right on Allen's abdomen. For all Allen knew, they would each die if separated. Allen wasn't frightened, though. This was one seamless reel. This is what life was supposed to be like.

"We've got a towel here for the dog."

He didn't let go.

"We can warm him faster if you'll let go."

He didn't obey.

They put a warmed blanket over his hands and therefore over the pup.

Allen felt himself rallying while they were still in city traffic. He could hear the jarring metallic business of life as usual. It was distantly comforting. So was the streak of rust on the ceiling of the ambulance and the near concern of the two men. He was neither afraid nor relieved. He was in awe.

"You're looking pretty good," one medic said, nodding satisfaction as if he had accomplished something wonderful. Allen didn't begrudge him. He concurred.

When they rolled the stretcher table out, the pup tried to stand, and Allen, with gentle steady pressure, held it fast. "We are fine," he said, in real, spoken words, and the medic heard him.

"Yes, you are. I think so."

The other man said, "Did you really jump in after that dog or did you fall?"

The option had not occurred to Allen. "I don't know," he said, surprised that his voice wasn't strong and that speaking wasn't easy.

When he woke, he wasn't sure if it was that afternoon, that night, a day later, or years later. He felt cheated, certainly, of whatever moments he had slept. A few feet away, back to him, was his wife. She had the saddest set to her shoulders, to her nice, broad shoulders. Her pinned braid had loosened, lowered, now lay at an angle just above the nape of her neck.

"Hi," he said.

"Oh." Immediately she was right next to him, leaning down, burying her face against his neck. "You sweet idiot. You crazy idiot. I am so glad you're okay." He could feel her crying, and when she raised up, he could see it. She was lovely when she cried, too. "The kids are going to love this," she said. "You're going to be on the evening news."

"Good," he said, flippantly, in one of his best, impressive, sophisticated, bantering tones. "I deserve it." His hands remembered the pup. "Where is the fellow?"

She pointed down. "Under the bed, in a basket."

"Hand him to me."

"He's asleep. You want him crying again?"

"Did he cry?"

"I mean like last night." She hugged him again, kissed him again, before scooting from the bed and lifting up the pup which continued to sleep. He slept while being dangled into position beside Allen, lowered, petted, and covered with the sheet.

"You really jumped in after him?"

"I think so."

"You don't know?"

"No."

"You jumped. I know you." She kissed him a little longingly. "You jumped. The kids are going to go crazy."

He got to go home, though first he had to talk with three patient reporters. He and they drank tepid coffee and joked a little. His wife stood by impatiently but indulgently. Her good shoes were dusty. Her skirt was twisted so a seam went down almost the front of her thigh. The pup woke, yawned, and she took him outside to a patch of grass by the walk.

"We gotta get home," Allen said to the reporters. "He's going to forget he's a dog."

"What's his name," one reporter asked.

"I don't know yet," Allen said. "And don't make any suggestions."

Another reporter grinned. "Call him . . ."

"I meant it. No suggestions. It will come to me."

At home, Allen sat in the family room, in a huge, circular red chair big enough for him and at least two children or with a wife and one. They took turns. The pup ran and plopped. It fell into dozing in the midst of being loved.

"That's you, Daddy," one child squealed.

Allen looked at the television screen. "That is not me. That's the bear."

"It's big, really big. Really, really big."

"Oh Allen," his wife said, and sat at his feet. The film was of the bear on the rock ledge near the water, still covered with the red net, but not awake, obviously drugged. It was rather slovenly, he thought, but impressive.

Two people were interviewed. They both said the man had deliberately gone over the railing, down the wall, and leaped into the water.

Allen's youngest daughter clapped her hands. His son made a peace sign. His oldest daughter, nearly eleven, came over and kissed his hand, as if he were a king of some kind, which he knew, momentarily, at least, he was.

They had macaroni and cheese because the children proclaimed a celebration. They offered a small serving to the pup who nosed it around, stepped in it, then fell asleep with his nose yellow from cheese. They moved him and his box into the bedroom.

Allen showered long, in hot, forceful water. It beat and sluiced across the glass doors, pelleted his skin. Then he lay down naked on white sheets.

"I'm going to shower, too," his wife said. "You go ahead and sleep. You need it. I'll be quiet."

"I'll wait on you," he said. "I'm fine."

The pup was quiet, sleeping. The lamplight fell in a wide soft circle on the rich carpet. The bedroom was very, very huge. Allen had the distinct impression that the bed moved. Or the room did. The outer edges of the room were dark, like maybe everything ended right there. He sat up, rose, and with firm steps strode to the box, lifted it and occupant, and placed them by his side of the bed. "This is your place," he said.

He intended to talk to his wife before sleeping, but his body wanted to be alone. He felt it drifting toward rest and he needed to capitulate. It had served him well. Still, he remained just alert enough to speak one lucid sentence when his wife eased next to him. "I'm going in a different direction," he said, feeling that the statement made perfect sense. She said, "I know you are." He fell asleep, then, comforted by a great need he was meeting, had met, might meet again.

A Rising Silence

W hen the lightning cracked, Paul Hardy woke immediately, not because the sound frightened him, but because it warned him, threatened him with Leona's fear. Any moment now, particularly if the lightning came again, she would moan or whimper. Then, brought to the rim of wakefulness by only a slight thunder roll, she would startle up and begin a day's descent into terror. He didn't understand it, though he knew it all too well.

There came the lightning. There rose Leona.

He feigned sleep.

The sharp light came again; even behind his closed lids he sensed the whitened bedroom, Leona slipping from the bed with a gasp. He could see her without seeing her, the movements furtive, her body rigid, tensing against itself. Her eyes would be wild, her lips parted.

She had gone to the living room. She would take a pill first, wait moments for it to have some effect, then turn on the Weather Channel. They were her preachers, those prophets of natural doom, with their red warnings of deadly lightning, flash floods, severe thunderstorms, giant hail, lethal tornados.

He loved her most of the time; he detested her at times like this.

He knew she wouldn't call for him. She would either leave the house, driving madly across town to May's where she would unlock the back door and hurry down the stairs to the basement, still dressed in her nightgown; or she would concoct some emergency magic shelter, move the sofa perhaps, lay it on its back, seat side now a buffer toward the southwest. The sofa was heavy, though, and she balanced her methods against her blood pressure—what would make her safest the fastest. He had encountered her topsy-turvy worlds at times, when he came home during a storm or rose at night to try to calm her. He didn't bother anymore.

If he happened to be at home and awake, she would do nothing except cringe, more and more cringe, until he said, "Go ahead. Run to May's." Then she would leave, shamefully, but quickly. Sometimes he wanted a tornado to strike the house, to leave him a survivor, sitting placid, laconic, philosophically always happy, safe or not.

He let himself drift back to sleep. She would probably leave soon. If the house was empty, why shouldn't he sleep? And when the weather was bad, his house was always empty.

It was 10:00 a.m. when he heard their car turning onto the street, and he stepped outside before she was fully in the driveway. The rain had stopped, but the wind was brisk, moist. Dark clouds roiled in the southwest.

"I just came home for a little while," she said through the rolled-down window.

"You said you'd go out to Cave Hollow with me on Sunday."

She didn't unlock the passenger door immediately.

"Leona," he said.

She lifted the button. He slipped in beside her.

"We can't go out there today," she said.

"Sure we can. It's not even raining now."

"But it's going to."

"If it does, we'll sit in the car till it passes. Best kind of summer morning. Everything cooled down."

"I just came home for a change of clothes."

"You look fine."

"This is a nightgown, Paul. You know that."

"Good enough to wear across town, wasn't it?"

He waited in the car while she went inside to change. He felt like a bully, but he wanted her to trust him a little and to worry about his opinion. When she emerged from the house, she was dressed in old blue slacks, a white pullover top, and white tennis shoes, as if she were seventeen instead of fifty-seven.

"Got your running clothes on, I see." He couldn't help it.

As he eased the car out of the drive, he patted the back of her head. "It'll be okay, Leona. Relax and enjoy the drive."

She was quiet a few moments, hands daintily over her purse, one atop the other. She had delicate ways most of the time. She even crossed her ankles when she sat, and her calves were as shapely as when they married.

"One touched down in Oklahoma," she said. "It was on the ground thirty minutes. Thirty minutes. It was a mile wide, and on the ground for thirty minutes."

"It wasn't a mile wide, Leona. It probably cut a mile swath, and you got it mixed up. And this isn't Oklahoma. It'll blow itself out before it gets here."

"They said it was a mile wide."

She was looking out the window away from him, and he knew why. Her eyes were terror stricken. If she met his gaze, they would be shamed, too.

Paul drove slowly. From the turnoff to the park, the road wound thinner, the tall, roadside brush encroached onto the gravel. Paul liked this place and he didn't understand why Leona resisted it so. She was afraid, he supposed, of the surprises that could dart from the shadows, from beneath rocks. She liked open spaces so she could see what was coming; *then* she wanted a close, safe harbor.

"You'd probably be safer at Cave Hollow than any place in town," he said.

"But I wouldn't *feel* safe," she said toward the window. "I don't want to stay afraid like this. It's dangerous for me."

"You can stop that anytime. Just don't give in."

She shifted ever so slightly away from him.

He whistled.

She opened her purse.

"Got your pills?" he said, and she closed the purse gently. He wished he had taken her hand instead. He could change his attitude, too, he supposed, make her life easier. But her fear didn't make sense. She was deluding herself into misery.

Cave Hollow was not a manicured park, with regular caretakers to clear the path, to thin the verdant undergrowth, or to prune the too many trees. It was on the outskirts of the small college town, where, some years before, an alumnus had funded the preservation of the few caves in the area. The money had sufficed to lay a concrete pathway two miles into the small hills, with smaller gravel paths leading to each cave. They were not even true caves but sloping depressions beneath overhangs of massive stone. Water accumulated, dripped, ran; lichens colored the water and stone. Some semesters a few students congregated in the depression, lighted candles, and recorded their immediate moods in paint or chalk, so the daylight revealed names and vulgar incantations, young wisdom in primitive scrawls. Now, in early spring, rains had sparked an outburst of growth; wild grass, young saplings and bushes branched high, domed the air green.

Paul parked in front of the wooden sign with its black "Cave Hollow," and got out of the car, stretching.

"Best time of year and best time of day," he said. "Sunday morning, no one around."

The air was heavily moist, but very still. He glanced at the sky quickly. The dark clouds were scudding fast, toward them. But he wasn't buying into Leona's fear. He had told her that once. "You go along with things too long, you own them or they own you," he had said. "You be as afraid as you want, but I'm not buying into it. It's yours." Now she stood by the car. "I'll just wait here," she said.

"The one place you shouldn't be is in a car."

"The storm's moving at thirty-five miles an hour. That's what the man said."

"We got time to walk to the caves and back three times even if it is headed this way. I wouldn't let anything hurt you, Leona. You know that." He was pleased with himself for trying to be gentle with her even though she made him so angry. When she came forward, he put his hand on the small of her back. He wasn't a big man, but she was a very tiny woman, and touching her so made him feel good. He believed she felt the same.

He liked the very sprawl of the place, an unkempt Eden. He often came here alone and kept a slender but sturdy branch secreted a few feet from the entry path, with which he brushed away twigs, vines. He overturned stones, cracked them against each other. And he named everything for Leona, who knew nothing about the natural world. He identified the grasses for her, and the trees. He identified birds. He stated these identifications casually, but absolutely, since he had learned long ago that the slightest doubt made Leona feel he wasn't trustworthy and made her, somehow, more nervous. "You can trust me, Leona. When will you learn to trust me?" It became more and more important that she take his word about a serious matter, just once to take his word.

"That was thunder," Leona said, stopping dead still in the narrow gravel lane.

"Miles away yet."

Leona studied the sky. The black line was nearer, meshing together, forming a long, wide bank.

"The temperature's dropping."

"Good sign," he said. Look."

He had walked ahead, now stood on the low plank-bridge leading to one of the overhang recesses. He held his walking branch by the center, pushed one end forward as if to knock someone away.

"Take that, varlet," he said, "and that." He checked to see if Leona was watching. "And so the troll beneath the bridge was vanquished."

Leona had returned to watching the sky.

"I'm going home," she said.

He stepped off the plank. "We got time. Besides, we're safer here than anywhere, even May's basement."

She had sat down on the gravel, opened her purse.

"Don't take a pill, Leona," he said. "Just this one time, don't take it."

"My heart's racing. I don't want to have a stroke."

"Your heart's racing because you're scaring yourself to death. It's adrenaline. Just walk. Run it off. Don't take a pill."

She tilted one of the pink tablets into her palm, and he flicked it away. He was as surprised as she was by his action. It had been automatic, a simple step forward, then a swat of her hand with his own.

Her head was down. Her hair was more white than black now, but still very curly. Her back was somewhat bowed and her shoulders narrow, but she was precious to him, a little plump and old, but with translucent skin, and very precious.

"I'm sorry," he said. "Take your pill."

He threw down the branch, turned his back to her. He walked across the plank, into the shadow of the overhang.

"I can't get it down," she said. "My mouth's too dry."

He knelt by the water. "I guess this is okay to drink," he said. He thought it was a concession. "A handful wouldn't hurt you, anyway."

She didn't move for a moment, then came forward gingerly, as if she had never been to this place before, had never seen him before. She didn't get on the plank, but knelt where it touched the bank, dipped water to her mouth, sat back, bowed her head.

The air had taken the color of green shadow, heavy, almost palpable. In the distance, a piece of cloud seemed to be thinning away from the rest.

He put his hand on Leona's shoulder.

"Did you get your pill down?"

She nodded.

"Come on. Let's look at the cave."

He took her hand, helped her to her feet. When she started to look upward, he jerked her a little. "Let's go."

"My God," she said. She had looked anyhow.

"It's miles away."

"Let's get in the car, go to May's."

She tried to pull away, but he held her fast.

"Don't be stupid, Leona. If it comes this way, we're better off here. Come on. I'll take care of you. I told you so. Come on." Even tugging her, he could feel the shakiness of her, the weakness in her body. She wavered, stumbled. "There's a ridge," he said, "around the town. Makes them skip. Makes tornadoes skip." He tugged her into the recess, bending down beneath the heavy stones, then to his knees. "That's why one's never hit here." That was true of the town. He didn't know about this place. He pushed her in front of him. "Here," he said. "Lie down, lie against the rock." He could hear the roar now, still distant, hear the wind whipping through the hollow, the snapping of dead branches. He felt minute stings as if the wind were peppered, splintered.

Leona groaned.

"We're okay, babe," he said. He curled against her. He could feel her fear as if it were a sound humming through his body. "The pill will work, honey," he whispered, unable to hear his own words above the roar descending on them. "Let that pill work, baby," he said. "Just let that pill do its business."

He wasn't at all frightened, just fiercely alert and curious. He wanted to turn around, but he held onto Leona. He could hear it bellowing down, around them, pressing angry, angry. He felt a quick, heavy blow to his back, a sharp pain in his rib cage. He was buffeted, hammered. Hammered into Leona. The sound roared through him, tons of sound on rock ceilings and floors, and Leona.

Then it subsided, whined away, not suddenly over, just less.

He had won.

He was lightheaded, had to concentrate to stay conscious. "Leona?" His side hurt. He thought perhaps he had had a heart attack, was having one, but the pain was on the wrong side, and too low, his right rib cage, front and back. Inside something was trickling, gurgling.

"Leona?" He pulled back slightly and the pain intensified. He groaned.

"Don't move," he said. "Not yet." He slid his right hand from her hip, up to his ribs. His fingers touched something round, hard, held between them, or holding them together. He sickened at the very idea of it. "Are you okay?"

She didn't answer. He lay perfectly still a moment, then moved his hand across her chest, pressed it flat. The motion brought such pain he moaned. Her heart was beating, though. It was beating. "Thank God," he whispered. "Thank God." Then he said her name again, with no response. Again. Something was wrong with her.

He lay waiting for enough courage to pull backward, away from her, to wrench free whatever held them together. Her hair, lovely swirls, smelled sweet, a flower he didn't know. The stone they faced was pitted, the pits filled with dark green—mold, he supposed, some sick, dank life. He closed his eyes, counted to three, pushed and jerked backward, and swam in red and black vision for long moments. He was bleeding, that he knew. He scooted backward till the stone ceiling was high enough that he could sit up straight. Before him, some feet away, his wife lay still, the back of her blouse bloody. But it was likely his blood, not hers. He saw the gray stone that must have struck him. His fingers touched the shaft of rib protruding inches above his waist.

"I'm going for help," he said. "Leona?"

She didn't stir.

"Don't be afraid, baby. I'm going for help."

A few feet from her someone had painted a red heart. He could read, "PAUL LOVES," but he couldn't read the lower name. He supplied one. "Leona," he said. He crawled slowly, till he could stand. The plank was gone, but the water shallow. He sloshed across. Leona's purse lay on the ground where she had knelt. He thought that odd—such a tiny object to remain. He walked on. He didn't hurt, either. He wondered if he were in shock. Shock was a blessed thing. The air was cool, shadowy, but he sweated profusely.

"No Eden this," he said, reassured at his own voice.

He thought his car would be gone but it sat where he left it, unmarked. It started easily, like always, drove like always. He wasn't sure where he was going. He stopped at the first place he saw, a white house with red shutters. A child's swing set glistened in the front yard. The woman made the call for him. He insisted on waiting on her porch so he wouldn't soil her furniture.

The ambulance came for him first. He directed them but had to stay with the ambulance at the entrance to the park. He refused to lie down, watching the path till the crew appeared, carrying Leona on a stretcher. Her body rolled with the movements. She was a round little thing. A man carrying a bottle walked by the stretcher. A tube ran from the bottle into Leona's arm. They lifted the stretcher into the ambulance, onto a cot across from his. One side of her face was slack, a crushed flower, wilting and transparent. He knew she saw him. He knew the vision of her right eye was all right. The pupil had contracted. "I'm sorry," he said. "I am so sorry." He reached over the legs of the attendant beside her, and he thought she pulled away.

"Just lie back, sir," the man said. "You shouldn't be moving."

"I just want to tell her she'll be fine," Paul said. "I just want to take her hand and tell her that."

"She hears you."

"Does she? Leona? Honey, you'll be fine. You'll come through this. We both will."

She was moaning. He knew that sound came from her. It wasn't a pretty sound. It was the ugliest sound in the world. He felt wretched, ashamed. He turned sideways. Through the small rear window, he could see the trees of Cave Hollow receding. The tops whipped, bent low, rose again. He wanted to tell her she had been right, right all along, but he just watched the trees till they disappeared, tiny flecks of green light, flickering, flickering, gone. Pine trees, he believed, ancient ones. He had read somewhere that people used to burn the needles to ward off evil. She was still moaning but it was more distant, blending with the whine of the wind. His mouth was dry, and he licked his lips, wanting to whistle, to dissipate a terrible, rising fear.

Mother Post

Factory workers and the service station guys were the first to see the lone mailbox post established before Oida Leban's house. It rose like an ugly weed with sturdy stalk and oblong bloom overnight. It was the only black mailbox for miles around—guaranteed, because didn't they know every inch of newness in their home ground? The only solid-black mailbox. In a few days, dawn revealed a night artist had been at work. On the side, in the middle of a flurry of hand-painted yellow and rose and lavender flowers, was the name *Flora Metcalf.*

The name caused a stalemate in discussion of rights, because though Oida Leban, who owned the modest house behind the gaudy post, had a right to the conservative, neat façade she had maintained all her years, Flora Metcalf was a very ill woman, in the sunset of life, and if she wanted to get her mail in town, what did it hurt Oida?

What if Flora wanted her mailbox set on the easement space before the mayor's property?

She didn't, so the question didn't apply.

What if she did?

That would be the mayor's problem. He could deal with Flora.

More than a few people asked the mail clerks about regulations, and various versions of the truth passed through the ranks at lunch counters and in factory break rooms. Any person could choose a spot for a mailbox if that person needed access. The post office could inset the post. But they couldn't take it down willy-nilly. Once it was in the soil, it could be moved only by permission of the person who received mail there. The post office personnel couldn't move it, and neither could the owner of the property it fronted. Oida, for example, could not lay a finger on that mailbox, and neither could her son, daughter, son-in-law, or any henchmen she hired. Only Flora Metcalf or one acting in her stead could move it.

And a post office authority! Surely!

Nope. The regulation was a botched up job, but on the books into perpetuity—if convenient, as things went, so to speak. When Flora Metcalf died, though, the box would disappear, and things would return to normal.

Flora didn't die right away, and given the Lord's penchant for thwarting expectations, especially about when something would occur, she might outlast judgment day.

Odd occurrences began. The city manager received a pressed toad leg in a properly stamped envelope, no message. The county clerk received a curled tress of hair, very old and dry, that looked familiar, but then most humans had hair, and many of the elderly in town had curls pressed in bibles and keepsake books and boxes. One woman passed the word down the pocket-seaming line that if fingernails started showing up in the mail, a curse was being spread through town. Instead of a voodoo doll, they were getting piecemeal magic. It would all add up.

Nothing like this had transpired for years and years, and then it hadn't been exactly voodoo or magic. Voodoo was foreign, not American magic anyhow. There had been a handsome older guy settle in the area, a man who was fond of the prettiest girls and had a way with them, just like the vagabond lover, the rambling man, the gypsy rover. He got three of them pregnant before women got angry and began buzzing around like hummingbirds, those tiniest but most fierce defenders of territory and brood.

Then, horror. Not small town fare at all. The ladies got the guy out somewhere, made him drink some brew until he was doped out of his gourd, and while he was out, they tied him up with clothesline wire, and with medium-sized stones smashed his own soft stones to pieces. Didn't cut him or kill him. Ruined him.

Like he ruined ours, one of them had reportedly said, meaning the girls.

No one in town was kin to any of those women who, at worst, were very distant cousins, and all dead, anyhow. It was just a nasty old story.

The guy had moved on.

That incident was not like the little violences occurring in town now, like the mere mailing of toad legs and dead, disposable body parts. Hair got cut, didn't it? So did fingernails. There was no mayhem involved in obtaining them.

Oida herself went to the post office to plead that the post be removed. She was seen sideways-walking up the edge of the main street into town. She was terribly humped, more than a dowager's hump. It was like her spine and one shoulder blade tried to rise up out of her body and forced the other shoulder blade down, so she was bent double but with one half of her torso turning up. It had to be a torture to walk, even that crabwalk. She'd take about four steps, rest and breathe. Four more.

She must have wanted to confront the post office people by herself, with no older children butting in. She wanted the brunt of the argument in her face—as much as it could be—and wanted her vocalizations to be the ones ringing in the ears of those public servants who chose one public to serve and one to abuse.

She got into the post office and into the main room. There was no line. She tried to talk but she wheezed so badly, especially as she got angrier and angrier, that they called her son, which made her even madder. She tried to push out the door and stride off, but poor woman, old warrioress, she couldn't stride or scream. She huffed and then punched someone away with her bony elbow and then fell down on one knee, couldn't hold it, and tumbled onto her side. She may have had a minor little accident from the stress.

Another post popped up, in front of the mayor's house. It was black, too. Then another one at the city manager's place. Then another at the Methodist minister's. Was this the handiwork of a cult? Were the posts identifying evil or attacking good? If the latter, they were doomed by the solidarity of the townspeople, a solidarity now increasing. A post showed up not planted but leaning against the center seat of the center row of the movie house. The show that night was *The Haunting of Audrey Rose*. The floor felt different, suspiciously sticky, and the air was filmy, like oil had been burned off. The whole evening there was preciously vile. Some teenagers from Dexter claimed the theater post, passing the word that they had slipped it in through an exit. Just wood, they claimed, no slimy stuff. But the other details persisted as fact, thus suggesting a ritual not as wholesome as teenage prank. Satanic or sexual, possibly both.

A dead cat was found in the anteroom at the post office and a dead dog on the hood of the mayor's car. They had evidently been dead for some time, and maybe someone had just hunted roadkill for this purpose, but it was ugly all the same. Escalating. Things were escalating. Next time, it might be a recent dead animal, you know? Recently alive dead animal.

Someone was just buying into the violence to open a door for maybe longtime built-up thoughts, longtime sheer nastiness made possible. People liked to have a little war when a big one was going on, you know? This was a way of easing tensions in the human community, little dribbles of bad.

No, evil was mutating. That was a fact. Couldn't kill it. Even in movies, the dead evil just popped right back up, showed its face in the feathery off-stage night, glowing like a little moon.

A fellow said the men should get together one night, maybe with a few of the ministers, and should dig up the first post, the mother post he called it, drag it through town and burn it, burn it to ashes and bury the ashes. The specificity of his passion created a pocket of champions who would defend the post to the death.

"Mother post"—the phrase chilled the skin but fired the heart.

A bunch of small pets were killed, poisoned. In one week someone had wiped out much of the little love that people counted on. Although that happened every three to five years—some crazy nut around town who got tired of the stench of cats and the yapping of dogs and took it upon himself to reduce the population—it was a piece of the current situation. The ugly stuff was growing outsize. People suspicious of mail, fearful for their animals, wary of irritating a neighbor. The trouble with this world was that evildoing was rampant and sneaky, and gooddoing was afraid to go out in the dark. It was better than television and movies, actually. Didn't cost anything. A roadside attraction. Like a corpse that could be you.

Someone turned in, anonymously, the name of the possible animal killer, and a police officer took it upon himself to begin charting the man's activities. Even if it was three or five years before he caught the culprit, the time would be well spent. He would end the who-dun-it speculation. Other citizens took credit for a bit of playful evil. Someone had mailed a postage-stamp-size piece of her underpants to another woman's husband. Someone had dropped two aspirins in another's warm cup of coffee. Imaginations dared to consider what might have been done but *not* admitted.

Then Flora died, quick, like her illness had promised from the onset. She was on view at the funeral home for one day and evening and was considered quite lovely considering her impressive age and long illness. A dark blue dress accentuated the powdery translucence of her skin. The prominence of her bones leant fragility to her self, and regality to her death. She had worn well. People remembered her.

Oida came during the end of visiting hours. She signed the registry, maneuvered her crooked self to a chair, and stayed there for a full thirty minutes, the minimum time if respects were sincerely given. That was the rule. She had taken a taxi, people assumed. By the time she died, she'd be as misshapen as a cricket and putting her in a casket would require a fine touch.

All the odd mailboxes were gradually removed so that the remaining presence of the first became most significant. Anyone could take it down. Who would protest? But by default, at best or worst, it was now Oida's, wasn't it? She sometimes sat in a metal chair on her porch as the sun was setting. That was a lonesome time in town, the way the sun went lower and sort of lifted its rays up from the ground so the land got darker first, before the sky. Someone was pulling off the daytime. Oida, all hunkered in the metal chair, would seem to be dozing, but who could tell? She was toothless, wasn't she? Her hair was almost white now but red tints still glowed. She had been a fiery woman when she was young. So had Flora been, and gorgeous.

When Oida died, the guest list in the funeral home was impressive. The town had long admired her fortitude and were admittedly curious as to how a body so misshapen might be laid to rest in a standard casket. They noticed the silk cushion was a little thicker. She herself was simply human and lovely, old and finished.

Hadn't she and Flora been young girls together, and rivals for that man? The one less-man run out of town by a bunch of mothers?

Nah. That's an old story, didn't take place anywhere near our time. Nobody around here was connected to such craziness. That was a different lot, rougher times.

A vine grew up around the mailbox post, started like a weed, one of those field vines that some people called witch vines. They didn't really root. They just grew, taking their sustenance from the very air. This one grew slowly at first, like it was testing the safety of the environment, and then sped along, curling tendrils here and there. It had a reddish cast, the vine did, green but with a thin red line on the underside and with a reddish hue. The vine grew up and over the top of the oblong container and then sprouted the most delicate yellow blossoms, big, butter-yellow blossoms with red centers. The vine didn't, though, grow around the pull-down hatch.

It knows, someone said, that the mailbox has to open. It's not going to interfere with function. It's just redecorating the voodoo, so to speak.

It's not voodoo. This is American magic.

American justice.

Oida had been a redhead, they recalled. So had Flora. The old 'twixt and 'tween—could be one or the other, or both. Maybe they had finally made up.

One of the musicians in town worried out a song about the mailbox, trying for a ballad with old-time heart. He was a little different from most of the town breed and wasn't comfortable in the public eye.

He planned to move, run away someday. But meanwhile, he was so taken with ballads and lore and especially with the straight, sturdy, lastingness of the post, with the vine that shriveled a little in winter but clung on, clung on, and then blossomed again in spring and summer. It trailed out a little, bunched up, but always stayed clear of the closed hatch, which could be pulled down at any time, revealing a message in there, from someone, to someone.

Bay at the Moon

Evans had always liked the Missouri Bootheel, and often wished he had been reared there. In just a few miles, the landscape could change quickly, from flat cotton land to rolling hills with rich, black soil, then to low swampland, stretches of water with skeleton trees like old soldiers at attention, then to flatland again. Sometimes, returning to the city after a circuit court hearing, he would linger in one of the small towns. He would eat in a local restaurant, read the newspaper—if there was one—and he would listen. He liked the Bootheel vernacular and the way the locals guarded their stories by telling them piecemeal. "Catch this," they might have been saying, as if everyday life were an important riddle.

Now, at the second dirt road north of Aquilla Junction, Evans turned west, and the landmarks he had heard about became real: a barbed wire fence, a cattle crossing, a lightning-struck tree, more barbed wire, then dense trees, still denser, and a road that forked—deceptively, since both branches would lead to the same house.

He took the right branch. Trees crowded the road from both sides and flickered waning sunlight across the windshield. He could see small birds flitting among the trees, a hawk gliding in the distant sky, but the early evening felt silent.

According to the story, the woman of the house, Lorena Welker, had been found on a lane behind her home, wearing a full-length cotton nightgown, her long black hair pulled back and tied with a yellow ribbon. She lay on her stomach, face to the side and hands drawn up. Near her, a slight depression held rainwater from earlier in the week.

The cause of death was not a mystery: an inherited weak heart had claimed her, though she wasn't much past forty. The mystery was the site. Why was she outside in a nightgown? and why walking *away* from the house?

She had been a very lovely woman. More the pity, people said.

The brick dwelling sat back from the circle road, at the end of a stone pathway. Grass and clumps of weeds, some with fragile blossoms, grew among the cracks. A wild, high grass covered the cleared yard and swayed to a sudden breeze, shifting colors as the paler underside turned up. The house appeared airy, as if windows were open, and clean, spacious, intended for a large family. A deep concrete porch spanned the front and partway along each side.

The husband had built the place and brought Lorena here from a nearby farming community. Shortly after her death, he had moved to another county, yet had never sold the house. That, too, people wondered about. He hadn't been much liked.

Evans took his thermos from the car, along with matches and a partly crushed, unopened pack of cigarettes. He hadn't had a cigarette in three days. The possibility and proximity of tobacco had thus far gratified him, though a cigarette would have done so more to his liking. He wasn't fond of discipline.

He followed the stone path around the house, past the final room—a screened porch. A few yards away stood a slant-roofed, wire kennel. The husband had owned hunting dogs and had obviously sheltered them decently. Old straw lay scattered across the dirt floor, and bales of hay sagged along one side, providing windbreak. Three doghouses were aligned against the back of the kennel. A large rectangular plastic pan, cracked and weather-streaked, was tilted upside down in one corner, by it two empty metal pans, one of them with an oxidized rainbow in the bottom.

The last shaft of sunlight illuminated a dirt lane leading from the backyard. On either side of it, a wide strip of land had been cleared, the distant edges dark with trees. The high grass had claimed patches of the clearing. In another year or two, the lane itself would disappear.

Evans sat on the back step, poured coffee into the thermos lid. Lorena had died on this day two years ago. He wondered if the scene itself retained a memory.

Night settled. A birdcall, hollow and plaintive, wafted from the woods. The grass whispered. The moon slid down, large, nearer, infinitely out of reach. Evans, with knees drawn up to brace elbows, turned the cigarette pack over and over. The resulting rustle was familiar and reassuring.

The husband had been hunting with friends, over sixty miles away. He had borrowed a buddy's phone to call his wife shortly after 10:00 p.m. No one had overheard the conversation, but phone records proved the call, about two minutes long, had actually been made. He had commented to his fellow hunters that his wife wasn't feeling well, and he probably shouldn't have come. He was enjoying himself, though. The fellows understood that the relationship had been tense for some months. He, the husband, liked women and spoke of them as he did game, as if that kind of hunting, too, were a sport.

The husband had not been involved with anyone at the moment. His most recent lover had been seen from early evening until past closing time at a western swing bar on the county line.

Details from the investigation suggested Lorena had bathed and scented herself with a lemony powder. She had sat down in the living room, curtains open, but only to an expanse of trees and narrow roads. There were no neighbors for miles. She had read. She had put the book face down on the chair arm—probably to answer the phone. Maybe she had again sat down. But very soon after the phone call, she had gone outside.

With no flashlight? No weapon? No robe? Why?

Evans' attention snapped back to the present. Something crossed the lane, far enough away that only shadow and movement were visible. He heard an owl, heard a hollow, lonely call. Perhaps a loon? A rabbit appeared nearby, and he wondered that he hadn't heard it approach. How could anything be silent with someone listening precisely for the movements of any life, however small? Before him, the moonlight glinted a dip in the lane, and he realized that was likely where water cached, and was where she had been found.

Maybe small animals came to drink. Maybe larger ones. Surely, though, the forest had better, safer caches.

The white nightgown did not square with a lover. Neither did the book. None of the stories suggested anything that would sully her reputation. People had liked her, perhaps loved her. She was a true gentle woman, given to charities and kindness.

They suspected her husband had won her by seeming to need her.

A low howl began, undulated to a higher note, stopped. Repeated. Evans had expected to hear hunting hounds—this was, after all, the season—but he didn't know what he had heard, dog, coyote, wolf.

His sharpened vision swept the cleared land, the far reach of the lane, and again the kennel—nothing could have entered it. The gate was closed, and the kennel held nothing to entice an animal.

The rabbit passed him, trembled on hind legs as it sniffed the air, and hopped on. With a few more pauses, it crossed the lane.

The night was likely filled with such searches.

Evans leaned against the screened door. She had worn white terrycloth slippers. They had been found between here and the body. She may have tried to run. Only the front of her gown was soiled, from the fall, from lying stomach down in the lane. Nothing had accosted her.

The moon, truly yellow, a deep yellow, hung heavy above the fields, against a blue thick night.

When the husband arrived home, the dogs had alerted him. They found her body first and bayed so that he feared before coming around the house that something terrible had happened. He had rushed to her, realized that she was already dead, and had called for help even before penning up the animals. He had left his trophy, the deer, in the truck until much, much later, when one of his friends had gathered the other men to help clean it up. He was dazed and sick.

No one doubted the grief was genuine. His appearance at the funeral drew sympathy, though no one had liked him. They wondered when he would sell the house. They were still wondering.

Something now appeared briefly from the woods, darted into the clearing, low and fast, stopped, then ran on? A dog? A coyote.

Moonlight filled the kennel floor. Evans noted again the two metal pans, the large plastic one, the three pet houses. The plastic one was likely for water. Where, then, was the third food pan? He walked around the corner of the house. The basement windows were shallow, but wide, the kind that opened inward. The first was latched, but through it he saw a utility sink. He tried the next window, went around to the other side, where moonlight lapped up the darkness. A large raccoon, startled, lumbered across the yard. One window here was locked, the other closed, but not flush with the casing. Evans knelt, pushed against it. It didn't give. He sat down, pushed against the frame with his feet, and gradually forced a gap, wider, then wider.

He slipped inside. He expected to hear the scuttling of mice or rats, but he heard only his own breathing. He waited a few minutes before closing the window. When his eyes adjusted, he saw the basement was almost empty. In its center, beneath a hanging shop lamp, was a large, square table, the wood darkened and splintered. The utility sink he had seen was against the rear wall and situated above a floor drain. To one side, a long plank table held myriad containers sorted into smaller groups. Evans walked there, tilted one can to read the label. Then he struck a match and scanned the other labels. They were all poisons: insecticides, herbicides, pest baits and pellets. Liquid concentrates.

On the other side of the sink was a rolling rack, bare except for the bottom shelf. There, right at the edge, was a metal pan. Evans squatted down, struck another match, and examined the pan without touching it. It was the same kind as the two outside. It was clean, but marked with the dark, rough streaks of much use and little washing. It had been a food dish.

He blew out the match, waited until the retained glow no longer blinded him. The air was close and musty. Something above him creaked and he imagined the woman of the house hurrying toward the back door.

She had been alone and this pan, this dish, was outside. Evans was certain of that. The husband brought three dogs home, but only two dishes were in the kennel. If two of the hounds had a separate, metal dish, the third one likely did, too.

She hadn't brought the dish inside.

The husband had.

Evans went up the stairs, into the kitchen. It was spacious, with a high ceiling, chilly. It would be a nice kitchen for a good husband and wife to share.

She had gone outside *because* of her husband's phone call. But she hadn't been afraid for herself. There were guns in the house. She would have armed herself if necessary or called for help. She went out quickly but for something else.

She was going to help something that might come near the house when the dogs were gone. Perhaps she had left food. But this time, the husband, too, had left food. He had called to tell her exactly what he had left waiting.

She had come through this room, lighted then, and rushed out across the porch. She had hurried down the lane until she had found the pan he left, probably already empty. Or perhaps she had found the creature itself, sickened or just now eating. Maybe she had wanted to take the food away, to coax the animal to her, had chased it. Maybe it had run to the water and she followed. Her heart would have been beating dangerously.

Evans stood on the porch, the landscape now diffused through screen. From far away came a true bay, then another, and another, the calls weaving around each other. The group hunt. The masculine game. And she was here, tending to shelter creatures. She had sheltered an unkind man. Had he meant to harm her?

He went outside, sat down on the steps. The raccoon was now going down the lane, cutting across the field. Evans poured another thermos lid of coffee. He wondered if a test on the metal pan in the basement would reveal a poison and a trace of the food that had held it? Even if it did, what would that prove? That someone had left poison for some creature. This was a country house. That practice was common.

If, come daylight, he scouted the land, circling out from the house, would he come upon the bones of a wild creature that had not made it back home? A wolf? A coyote? Something weaker? Stronger?

Possibly. But finding the wild victim wouldn't answer all the questions. Why hadn't her husband thrown the pan away? why had he left so quickly? and why had he allowed the house to remain vacant, surrounded by meandering creatures and moonlight?

Because he hadn't meant to kill her. He had meant to wound her with a cruel joke. He had sent her flying into the night and had ironically stopped his own heart as well.

The conjecture felt true.

Evans sat for hours in the still, cool, night, only slightly hopeful that something would happen to seal the tale. He was a city boy and a professional man, and this, he knew, was just an interlude. Twice, close to dreaming, he thought he saw a white gown fluttering from the quick movement of a graceful woman and a desire to protect welled in him. He wanted the feeling to remain. Just before dawn, in the sudden stirring the local people called the night wind, he opened the pack of cigarettes, lighted one, and drew the familiar hot taste through his mouth and into his lungs.

The Stuff of Ballads

She wasn't a musician, though all the men had hoped she was, certain they could feel the magic of a voice about to be released, or perhaps a body. Not that she was beautiful, nothing like that, but comely, yes. Small, striving for height in spike shoes that perched her precariously and delicately always thrusting forward.

Her husband was a banjo player, not very good, but handsome in a regular way—a bit muscular and tanned, and obviously in control of his woman. When he jammed at the local bars with the other musicians, she was audience for all, but she talked with none of the men unless one approached her, and then she was friendliness and daintiness and purity, too. The husband's brown eyes would flit toward her and keep her pinioned chastely in that chair until he was ready to leave. Even so, even so, something was amiss with those two and hopes dallied around her. When she left with her husband, she waved at everyone in general, like wishing the whole world merriment, and her disproportionately long legs were enticingly firm, arched for attention. And her smile—slightly bucked teeth, just slightly, always a sign of a woman who could make a man happy—suggested she was fond of them all and very sorry to be leaving.

The women liked her, which amazed both men and women. She chattered a great deal, laughed winsomely, became flustered easily, and always had a nice comment about her female companions' appearance.

Rumors about her and her husband were common, particularly because the couple seemed perfect, so devoted to one another and to their two children. Sooner or later something spicy would emerge, because no one was truly that happy.

Then someone noticed that another banjo player, not her husband, was always edging around the woman. He was a hot musician, so good that lesser musicians got nervous if he was even standing nearby. And when he played, he wasn't aware of people or time. He could play for hours. His eyes became dreamy, his lips parted. When the music finally ended, the other musicians closing away instruments, the banjo player would come startled back to place. When that happened, he far too often moved in one direction—toward the sunshine of a bucked-tooth smile.

"Those two are drawn together. It's as evident as the nose on your face. I wonder her husband doesn't see."

"He sees. He just doesn't have to worry about her. He's got her under his thumb. You wait. I bet he'll start coming without her."

The husband did come alone for a while, and he seemed much darker, even sinister, though perhaps that was due to his new dress style—all black, highlighted with a gold chain and pendant that fell right in the vee of his shirt. "She's feeling tired," he said. "She's been working overtime." "She's changing jobs." Then he shared a confidence with someone who couldn't keep confidences, which perhaps he knew: his wife had hepatitis B and had given it to him. He was heartsick, burning with shame and pain.

But the story took a spin as it passed. No one believed she had given him anything nasty like that. She wasn't that kind of woman. Like it or not, she was wholesome and honest and true. Whatever reared up so ugly hadn't come from her.

Then she appeared one night, after he had already arrived and was harmonizing with the other musicians. She stopped just inside the doorway, looking shy and vulnerable, like a young girl trying to pass for the woman she would be but wasn't yet. She had on jeans, a white shirt, and, incongruously, red shoes with tiny French heels.

Though thinner, and pale, she walked with the same lusty grace as always, smiling, eyes skimming the crowd but resting on no one. Obviously she was being brave, and every heart welled up with her. The scoundrel. He had done something to her, and she was fighting back. She was welcomed warmly, offered a seat at every table. The bachelor banjo player brought her a beer from the bar and stood beside her. They were about the same size and, people suddenly noticed, very similar in shape. An intensity emanated from them that caused quick exchanges of glances and intakes of breath. These two were going to make trouble.

And so they did. The husband put his banjo on a table, walked toward them with a righteous stiffness, said something no one could hear but certainly knew intuitively, and then the husband swung a blow into the other man's abdomen and when he doubled over, clipped him on the back of the head. The woman immediately bent down, her voice frightened and unintelligible, and her hand rested on the stricken man's back. The husband grabbed her elbow, jerked her up, and pulled her to the door, though she couldn't keep up with him and staggered endearingly to everyone who watched.

"The son-of-a-bitch. She wasn't doing anything wrong."

"Not that we could see. Remember that hepatitis? She got it from somewhere."

"She wasn't sick. She was bruised, banged up."

Anger and pain shone from those eyes each time she came to the bar, always after the husband did, always defiantly. The other banjo player didn't approach her, but the draw between the two was like the coming of an electric storm. It underlay every song. People waited. Life was an adventure. Here was a heroine and there was a villain.

When she divorced the husband, rumors were rife, but only one mattered—had she stayed faithful? The group looked to the hot banjo player. The saga was far from over.

That the two became lovers was certain, but when? They were never seen together outside the musicians' gatherings, or at least no one admitted to having seen them. The woman was centered on her family—or they were centered on her. Apparently the husband's rule had been taken over by her relatives, all of whom knew what was best and appropriate for her. She couldn't even go shopping without her mother or sister in tandem. All the poor thing did was work and take care of her kids. But still. Who could doubt that their passion had been consummated, unleashed, and was now shared by everyone who watched the man and woman exchange glances— loving, intense glances, restrained. Painful. People shivered for the two of them.

"Maybe she sneaks out at night, after the kids are asleep."

"She wouldn't do that. Maybe lunch hours."

"They should just get married. They're perfect for each other."

"I don't know. He's a self-centered man. Music means more to him than anything else. He never has any money."

"I doubt anything means more to him than she does. He's tight as a drum when she's near. Makes me a little hungry myself."

The women smiled. Yes.

Finally the couple would arrive together, speak one another's name even when with others. Even the ex-husband was gracious about them, nodding recognition or exchanging a word or two. He and the other banjo player discussed riffs and techniques, and she kept her eyes down or chattered gaily with the women till the ex-husband moved on. She wasn't, they all knew, going to live with her new man until her children no longer lived with her, and that was at least two years away.

He was in a band now and at first made her sit at a front table so when he played, she'd be nearby. If a man talked to her too long, the banjo player would redden and join her fiercely. The men backed off. She had another herder for a companion. They couldn't blame him, though, nosirree. The women wondered if she knew she was giving herself up again, and even to a grand passion such servitude was dangerous. Her lover had told her to dress more sedately. Then she wasn't to come at all, because she distracted him. His music was suffering.

She came anyway, which was a delight to all. And she deliberately spoke to the men as easily as to the women. So the banjo player had to suffer disruptions or lose the woman. She wasn't a total fool, then. Maybe not quite as innocent as everyone had believed. Her appearance was changing, too, the hair more blonde, the eyes shadowed, the lips reddened. Jeans were her common wear to the bars where he played, and her tiny high heels perked her body just so. No woman could keep a shape like that after two children. How old was she anyhow? She was acting like a high school girl, and it wasn't very becoming, was it?

"Who can blame her? She got married when she was sixteen. This is her first chance to shine. Let her be. I wish I could look like that."

"She's wearing old clothes, actually. She doesn't spend much on herself."

"She doesn't make much. And all the child support goes to the kids. Her daughter's getting married and that's expensive. She bought her son a car, too. He wrecked the old one and she got a good used one. She has to make payments."

"I guess her lover buddy doesn't help her out."

"Him? He'd starve to death if it weren't for his friends. When they go out, she pays for herself and sometimes for him, too."

"Bad move. He'll not care for her long if she lowers herself like that."

"He's already cooled down. Everybody knows that but her."

"She knows."

The couple fought. She had hit him with a pan, thrown chili into his face, kicked him the groin, and once had taken his banjo out into the rain. She had laid it in the yard, screaming at the top of her lungs. He threatened to kill her. Neighbors had called the police. Another time he had locked her out of his dingy, rented shack, because he had to practice and he wasn't going to argue anymore. She wouldn't go home. She banged on the door, kicked it, banged on all the windows, broke one, and then got into his car and leaned on the horn till he, himself, called the cops. But if they touched each other, even stood close, they were together. The banjo player and his lady were magic, fire, waves, dreams, an unending longing.

The banjo player left with his band for another state. They were going to make it big and he would send for her. The woman didn't leave, and she didn't go crazy, though there was a madness about her determined cheeriness and her constant presence at all the music events. She couldn't sing, couldn't play, but she sat with the musicians and their wives like she was a regular and had earned the place. Now she was working two jobs, in a doctor's office as receptionist and at a doughnut shop on the weekends. "I'm so tired," she said, "but it's worth it. I've gotta get money ahead for my son and for the move. It'll take me awhile to find a new job when I get there and he's not making much, you know. He's sharing a house with two other musicians."

When he sent a plane ticket for a weekend visit, she explained that this was the first step of the actual move and she wasn't going to waste it. She would apply for jobs while she was there, and if she got one, she'd move right away.

"You better check with him, honey, before you make permanent plans."

"Oh I told him. I tell him everything."

"And what did he say?"

"He said it wouldn't hurt to look for work because he wasn't making much and probably wouldn't for some time. The band has to buy a new sound system."

She was so happy, they left off warning her. She'd never been on a plane before. She'd never traveled anywhere alone. She was even going to charge some new clothes, so he'd be proud of her.

Poor little fool.

When she returned, a light had dimmed, but she came to every musical gathering. The trip had been fine. Really. They hadn't had much privacy, because the other two men were in the house. She paid for a motel the second night. Moving there wasn't such a good idea right now, the band had to concentrate on music and connections. They were moving up rapidly. And he was too thin. He wasn't eating right or sleeping much. He missed her so much it made him ill. He thought he was no good for her, because it'd take him years to establish his career.

"I told him we should get married and let the money take care of itself. I could always work. Actually, things would be easier on him."

"And what did he say?"

"He said I shouldn't sacrifice for him, that he wasn't worth it."

"He's got some sense, anyhow."

"He is worth it, though, you know." She had taken up smoking, though she didn't inhale, and everyone loved her for the tough little gesture.

She began dating. Sometimes she brought a man with her, and he'd be friendly with everyone while she chattered about trying to afford college for her son, her daughter being pregnant. More often, she came alone, and when a banjo sounded, she might suddenly be quiet for a moment, but would rally quickly. Her applause was loud and genuine. She would even whistle, a sharp, high, forceful whistle like a man might make. She had developed a taste for beer and usually drank three in an evening. The beer didn't change her, though—she didn't get sloppy, or slurry, or flirtatious. She'd leave an ashtray full of red-tipped whole cigarettes and a pile of loose change for the waitress.

The banjo player didn't send for her. Instead, he returned, broke but fired up with possibilities, all of which now included her. He moved in with her, though the son was still home, and the boy let him use the car when necessary. She was most happy, most happy. She shared it with everyone. Then everyone waited, because no good could come of this.

A secret became open knowledge, about the lump in her breast, how she had shown up at one woman's house crying that she could handle the cancer if she could just see her son grown up. She had planned her freedom for when her children were all right, and her son was such a baby in many ways. He couldn't manage money or his clothes, and he resented her for the divorce. If she could make it up to him with college, then she could die easier. And besides—sobbing so deeply the listener had sobbed too—now she was truly happy, and why did this have to happen now? Who could love a woman with one breast?

"You're not going to die," the listener reportedly said. "Look at it this way. Even if the breast cancer has spread to the bone, which isn't likely, because it's a small lump, right?"

"Yes."

"Then even if it has spread, it won't kill you for years. At least not for two or three, and your son can be well on his way by then."

The women were appalled by the blunt, almost brutal statement, but the listener insisted it had been the right thing to do. "That's all she needed," she said. "She calmed down, had one of her safe cigarettes, two cups of coffee, and left. That woman can handle the truth."

"I doubt it was the truth. It wasn't her son she was worried about."

"Yes, it was. I could tell."

"Then she's fooling herself."

"Well, if it gives her peace of mind, let her."

The banjo player was with a local band then, and she never missed one of his performances. She announced her radiation treatments and their effects as she had announced her travel plans. "I thought for sure I'd get sick," she said, "but I haven't. At least not yet. I'm burned, though."

Everyone knew she was burned. She wore sleeveless dresses and propped one elbow out to the side, and the deep, cracking red of her skin was obvious to all. But she was ever merry. "I'm so happy," she said once. "Even if I had to die now, and I probably won't, the doctors said it was early, you know, just a small lump, but even if I did die now, I'd die happy. I love him."

Of course she did. He didn't warrant a lady like that, one who could give and give and hurt smiling and have hope everlasting. Jesus. She was a gutsy woman.

"He's staying with her, though. A lot of men would disappear at the mere mention of cancer."

The banjo player left six months later, to join a promising band in a resort city. She sold her furniture and cashed in a couple savings bonds to give her son his first year in college without having to work at all. She was ready to follow her musician.

He never sent for her. Gradually, people realized they knew more about the banjo player now than she did, so they never spoke his name in her presence. One night when his name slipped into the conversation and everyone fell quiet, she said, "You don't have to protect me. I'm not a child. I'd like to know what you were going to say." So they talked about the success of his band, of the album that was being cut, of the fact that he still hadn't been seeing another woman.

"You're the best he'll ever find," one man ventured, and his wife didn't get angry.

"I know that," she said. "And my biggest hope is that he knows it, too." She stayed with the group for a half hour or so, though she didn't speak at all, and everyone felt the lump in her throat and filled the silences for her. When she did leave, she strode between the tables and out the door like a big, strong, woman. Her blonde curls reflected the neon lights, and someone thought "tarnished angel," but he didn't say it aloud.

The banjo player came through on tour and people wondered. Would she come? The banjo player asked about her, so everyone knew he wasn't privy to her life anymore. During the last set of the performance, she came in, alone, and waved away the offers to join friends at their tables. Instead, she sat at the bar, turning her stool to face the band and holding a beer in one hand and a cigarette in the other. She was again in jeans, white shirt, and the little red shoes that by now should have been worn old and tossed away. She crossed her legs and her right foot kept time with the music. When she finished that beer, she got another.

"They're going to get together again."

"She wouldn't be so stupid."

"Look at them. They can't take their eyes off each other."

No one left. After the last encore and the last applause, the banjo player propped his instrument on a stand, stepped down from the stage, and walked directly to the woman at the bar. She wasn't smiling. She held the beer with both hands on her knee. He seemed slightly curled toward her, intense, as if he would scoop her to him, but he didn't touch her. He was so close that when she raised the bottle to her lips, he had to lean back. Words were being exchanged but they weren't affecting her. She had never before been somber. She put the bottle on the counter, stood, and he took her arm. They walked out the door together.

"My God. She'd ruin her life for him."

"Maybe it's worth it. Must be."

They each wondered how it felt to love like that. What coursed through the body, heart, and brain? Was it bearable?

"Maybe they'll stay together this time. Maybe he's learned his lesson."

The band left town and she stayed. Occasionally she came to a gathering and was much her old self, but not enough to feed the love they'd felt for her. She was, after all, an older woman, who most likely bleached her hair, and was, in fact, a grandmother. Now she drank only soft drinks and didn't light her cigarettes, just held them. "My kids think I'm an alcoholic," she said. "They want me to get in therapy."

"You're no alcoholic."

"I know. But if I don't get in therapy, I can't see my grandchildren. My daughter and son have agreed that somebody has to step in and change my lifestyle. I'm self-destructive. I love my grandchildren, you know." She put the unused cigarette back in the box. "And maybe they're right about my needing help. I haven't made the best choices I guess."

When she came out of therapy, which people knew only by word-of-mouth, she got a different job and no longer followed the music circle. She was dating a skinny man who made knives and other items from ironwood and silver. She moved into his small trailer for a few months, and then he sent her on her way. For a while, she lived with her sister.

"Maybe she needed that therapy after all. Has to have a man in her life."

"Maybe men need her. You could have it twisted. They won't leave her alone."

"Looks like she'd just get a job and hold on to it. Maybe get ahead in life."

"How? Doing what? She's done the best she can."

"No she hasn't."

"Like hell."

Someone encountered her in a mall and reported that the lovely woman was no more. Cancer had struck again, and this time chemotherapy had stripped her of that gorgeous hair and those firm, uplifting curves. She was bony now and slouched as if curving into pain. "Still got bright eyes," he said, "and still talking up a storm." She had even brought up the banjo player, asking how he was doing and saying she'd rather he didn't see her now.

That hurt. It hurt everyone who heard it.

The banjo player's band came to town. As the performance neared, people wondered if she knew. What was the end of this grand passion? They wanted to see some final scene, or at least to know it occurred. Their greatest fear was that she wouldn't show, and they would never know.

She didn't disappoint them. She arrived during the second set, in the midst of the banjo player's lead spotlight, as if she had been outside the door waiting on the right cue, and her entrance collapsed time. There she was, jeans, white shirt, red shoes. The blonde hair, rich and full again, shone from the soft bar lights, and her smile was sweet and shy, like a young girl's. With her was an older, slender man, who held her hand by the fingertips. Though she waved at former friends, she and her companion sat at a table alone. People dropped by her table, unable to resist a closer look. And they reported to one another throughout the evening. A wedding ring was on her left hand. The new husband was an accountant, of all things, not an artist or musician at all. He met her when she was in chemotherapy, when she was bald. Imagine that. How could he have fallen in love with her then? And knowing she had cancer. They turned often to peer at the happy blonde. When the banjo and fiddle blended in a sad song, a waltz they'd all heard many times, a lost love melody, they felt a pain at what she had been and what she was now. At the end of the song, above the applause, they heard a sharp, healthy whistle. She could still whistle, by god. They watched and sighed and ached and wanted to applaud themselves when the banjo player put down his instrument at the end of the night and sauntered sloppily and surely toward the table where the woman sat with her new man.

"She'll tell him where to go."

"Nah. Why do you think she's here?"

"Something will happen."

"Doesn't really matter."

That, they knew, was the truth. Across the room, the musician was shaking the hand of the new man, was pulling out a chair, twirling it so he could straddle the seat and rest his elbows on the back. The sheer grace and masculinity of the movement brought new appreciation to the onlookers.

"Here's to him," one said, and raised his mug. Another joined in, "And to the new guy. I'll bet you he can hold his own."

"What about her?"

"Okay, then. To the whole damned show."

They raised glasses, clinked them, sipped, gulped, laughed, winked at one another. The toast went beyond their table and her table, and maybe even beyond their lives. The outcome didn't matter at all. This was a story they all knew and held dear in their hearts.

R. M. KINDER

is the author of three prizewinning collections of short fiction,
including *A Near-Perfect Gift*, winner of the University of
Michigan Press Literary Fiction Award, and *Sweet Angel Band
and Other Stories*, winner of Helicon Nine Editions's
Willa Cather Fiction Prize. She has also published two novels,
An Absolute Gentleman and *The Universe Playing Strings*.
Her prose has appeared in *Passages North*, *Other Voices*,
North American Review, the *New York Times*, and elsewhere.

CPSIA information can be obtained
at www.ICGtesting.com
Printed in the USA
FSHW022210200621
82537FS